The Ulti...

The Chairman's words had been startlingly clear.

"...You are the final hope of our race. We send you forth with our love and blessings in hopes that you will succeed where we have failed; that you will win where we have lost; that you will achieve where we have been negligent. You are the finest mankind can offer and we know it is no small task to say farewell. The only consolation we can offer is that you will know we send you out into the uncharted stars to carry on for us..."

As she looked around her, the sun disappeared leaving a vague, green glow in the sky. Suddenly she felt the world fall oppressively down upon her shoulders. She realized that she was possibly the final naturally born one of the line. A blind fear paralyzed her and sent the blood rushing through her veins. It sounded as if all the souls of man were screaming together, protesting the final state of the race.

She had never felt so utterly alone!

■ ■ ■

EVE'S RIB

BRYN CHANDLER

PAGEANT BOOKS

Publisher's Note: This is a work of fiction. The characters, incidents, and dialogues are products of the author's imagination and are not to be construed as real. Any resemblance to actual events or persons, living or dead, is entirely coincidental.

P

PAGEANT BOOKS
225 Park Avenue South
New York, New York 10003

PAGEANT and colophon are trademarks of the publisher

Printed in the U.S.A.

Cover artwork by Romas

First Pageant Books printing: January, 1989

10 9 8 7 6 5 4 3 2 1

For Bache

PART I

Chapter One

———◆———

THE EERIE WIND which rose every day at sunset made a
swirling dust devil in the sand encroaching the door space
of Evelyn Conner's shelter, which was nestled into the long
vertical crack in the mountain foothills.

She stood in the doorway, almost motionless, watching
and listening to the fall of night. The wind invaded the crevasse over her roof, singing its dusky song, whispering and
sighing, then increasing to a howl that made the primal
nerves stir in Eve's spine and the hair rise at the nape of her
neck.

She had grown used to the wind in a year of residence,
but recalled with a shiver her first encounter with it. She
had been working very hard to finish assembling the plasteel sections of the shelter so that she could move out of the
cramped dometent she had erected on her arrival. She had
chosen the crack because it would provide insulation and
protection as well as a channel for the rain to fill her
water-holding tanks. The cliff above her curved outward so

there would not be a flood of water, even if there were a heavy rain, but the natural condensation of the rock, as well as the rain which would collect in the crack during a shower, managed to keep her supplied with water, even during the dry season.

At the time of building the shelter, its position had been an educated guess; now she knew she had been right and the victory pleased her, as did all the small victories over this place. But that first evening in her newly finished shelter had made her doubt her choice.

She had been completing the installation of the food processor and the atomic battery units to power it when a particularly brisk wind had invaded the mountains and begun its lament in the crack above her. She had leapt from her task and turned to the door, expecting to see some manifestation of childhood nightmares charging into reality. She practiced the control learned from her earliest training, returning her heartbeat and breathing to a normal level, then warily moved to the door, peeking out into the advancing night, suddenly very much alone in this alien place.

Another howl erupted over her head, but this time she felt the wind and realized the source of her terror. She had tried to laugh, but the sound that came out was a dry, almost inhuman squawk.

While there was still some light, she walked down the steep stairs she had cut into the rock with the laser gun and went over to the dometent. By reflexive compulsion, she checked the door on the supply shuttle to be sure it was still locked, then tested the biolock to be sure that the door would open when she wished. She slid her hand around the grip and tightened. As the on-board computer read her biological imprint and compared it to the programmed record, the door slid silently to the side, revealing everything she, and nine crewmates, would need to live for a year, unsupported from the outside. Or, she had thought for the thousandth time since her landing, enough to keep her alive for ten years. She had forced herself to gather the supplies she needed, in addition to her sleeping mat, from the dometent, then, closing the shuttle, returned up the stairs to her new home.

As she had climbed, the sun had disappeared, leaving a vague, green glow in the sky. She had been out of breath in the thin atmosphere and from the exertion, even though the reduced gravity made it much easier to carry large loads, and was just setting down the bundles when an almost human shriek paralyzed her and sent the blood rushing through her veins. It had sounded as if all the souls of man were screaming together, protesting the final state of the race. It started as a low moan and rapidly rose, sounding like one prolonged word: "No!"

Now leaning in the doorway, listening to the breeze testing weaknesses in the crevasse, she recalled that scream, reflecting on it as a symbol. Perhaps it was as it had seemed, a protest registered by her accumulated ancestry that she could very possibly be the final, naturally born one of the line. By now Earth had perhaps finished its prolonged death throes and had become a deserted hulk drifting silently around the sun, its pollution-clogged atmosphere preventing sea and land from healing. That wind scream haunted her because it never happened again after that first night, but its memory in her senses made it very real, a constant reminder of her lonely and alone state.

Well, not alone, she conceded, looking out across the plain at her feet, watching the soft green of the sky as it turned to deep green over the distant mountains. Far across the valley, fire lights twinkled and several columns of smoke rose from the small village nestled there. It was deceptive in the thin atmosphere of this place, for the village was more than one hundred kilometers distant. Eve had gone there once in the small hovercraft and had greatly frightened the villagers: vaguely humanoid creatures with bodies larger than the average human's; long arms reaching almost to the ground; and short, stubby legs contrasting with grotesquely small heads which came to a point at the forehead area. Their eyes were on a level with their nostrils and the stalks on which they grew swiveled instead of the head turning. They had large, toothless mouths that gaped open when at rest. They were apparently insect-eaters, for their mouths contained long, curled tongues that darted out at passing bugs.

She had watched, hidden among the rocks, for most of a day as they went about their lives, eating, playing, and tending to the small ones. They apparently had little verbal communication and seemed to rely on gesture for broad concepts and a clicking noise combined with gesture for specifics.

It had been like a living textape to watch them going about their business with no knowledge that she was hidden there in the rocks, and she had learned enough to feel that they could be of little use to her. There seemed to be little organization to what they did, and, because they had seemed only to be insect-eaters in addition to being a different species, she could not gather from them clues about which of the plants growing on this planet could be safely eaten.

She had kept an eye on her chron, not wanting to take a chance crossing the valley in the dark, and, as she had begun to slip away, loose stones rolled down the hill, attracting the attention of the creatures. They turned their strange, dark, slightly bulging eyes in her direction, then began a frantic, clicking, gesturing conference. She fled down the hill while they continued to discuss her appearance.

When she reached the hovercraft, she looked over her shoulder, but no one was visible. Obviously, their head size reflected their mental capacities and her sudden unexpected appearance had overtaxed their limited abilities, both mental and communicatory. She had not made the journey again, but did enjoy seeing the lights from their fires at evening. It gave her a sense of being somewhat less alone.

The sky had become a deep forest green at the western horizon with the last light fading and the bright stars beginning to appear. Evelyn loved the night here because the thin, unpolluted atmosphere didn't dim the brilliant sparkle of the stars. Or the brilliance in the day of the nearest star. To remember Earth, she'd named it "Sun" and the largest of the night-appearing sky objects "Moon."

But the constellations were new and she had begun to name them, charting them as astronomer and astrologer. There was Adam, the first to appear in full, then Cupid, petite and second to show in the night sky. They surrounded the center star that Evelyn had named Home. Its brilliance and steady light reminded her of the lighthouse beacon along the shore where they had spent holidays in the summers of her childhood. Home, too, had become a beacon, its steadiness a point of reassurance in the alien night.

Opposite Adam, but less bright, was the horse's head constellation, Equus, with its mane of small stars flowing behind it. Between Equus and Cupid was the other major constellation that she had not yet named. Sometimes it looked like a flower to her, other times like a tree, and still other times like a butterfly. None of those seemed dignified enough to be a constellation.

Evelyn stared up at the nameless shape, watching it brighten as the last light left the sky. Tonight it was a tree, boughs flowing to the ground like the willow on the antique plate her mother had treasured.

"And this, Eve, belonged to your grandmother's grandmother. It's called a Blue Willow Plate and I don't think many of them survived the wars. Do you see the tree in the center? That was called a willow."

"Was it blue?"

"I don't think so, but I'm not sure. It could have been. I never saw a real one."

Standing outside her new home in the alien wilderness, Eve could almost hear her mother's voice, and she was overcome by her exile.

She raised her arms, opening them wide, and became an ancient priestess, inflicting small humanity on the vast universe. "I, Evelyn Conner, the last and the first, proclaim that the constellation located between Equus and Cupid shall be known as the Blue Willow, the Tree of Life."

Had anyone been watching from the plain below they would have been struck by the primitive forces flowing from the mountainside. As Evelyn lowered her arms, she felt as though she had made another inroad, another effort at pushing back the alien hostility of her new home. Her victories were small, but each one was, to her, a great triumph.

"Well, now what?" Evelyn had conquered the terrors of the night within her first two months, for the animals she feared might have a taste for her tender flesh had never materialized. In her hovercraft sorties into the surrounding wilderness, she had observed nothing larger than a doglike creature that fled at her approach. There seemed to be no large, predatory creatures in her area, so she had relaxed some of her security measures, feeling more free to leave the doorway open after dark and setting aside her shield belt, which created an electrical defense field but also hampered her movement. Any close contact with metal objects would set off an unpleasant tingling, and the weight of the belt was most uncomfortable. She had felt very vulnerable without it at first, but now rarely thought of picking it up, even to venture out across the land to some unexplored spot.

Without the terrors to occupy her mind, she had been free to explore the computapes thoughtfully supplied by the Project Directors. The on-board computer, now safely ensconced in its own room in her house, carried in its mechanical mind literally millions of amusements. There were video programs: movies, old television, old stereovision, holographs, and image realities of plays and concerts.

It was the latter two she had to avoid after experimenting with them once. Their projections of people into her living space were so real that it had thrown her to the brink of screaming hysteria, emphatically reminding her of her prolonged lack of human contact. She couldn't stand the projections of others of her own kind, walking and talking around her in fleshy detail but as remote as the people who made the tapes.

Also included in the tapes were millions of books on every conceivable topic from philosophy to self-defense. Evelyn thought it ironic that she could intelligently converse on such a huge variety of subjects and hadn't a living soul with whom to converse. The one thing they had left out of the computer was perhaps the most important: She could talk, but there was no one to talk back. The mechanical whining voice of the computer informed her of immediacies: "Notice! Notice! Battery levels function normal. Food process functions normal. Electrical output normal. Defense systems operate with no change. Biolab functions continue normal . . . ," it would drone every twelve hours for about fifteen minutes, cataloging the normalcy of her abnormal life, as if trying to convince her that everything was supposed to be this way.

At first she had looked forward to the mechanical voice enumerating the details, but now she resented it, at the same time fearing to cut the volume in the event of the exception. So, she endured it, sometimes patiently, other times with anger and resentment, standing before the console, screaming in mimic of the nasal voice.

Pushing herself away from the door where she had been leaning, she said aloud to the desolation of the night, "And now the ultimate question: When there is no foundation for comparison, how does one determine madness? Am I mad? A woman completely alone, thousands or even millions of light years away from anything familiar, who screams at her computer and names stars and terrorizes the local populace. Is she mad? She sometimes talks aloud to herself and to the entertainments, reciting the familiar lines so she can feel as though she's having a conversation with someone. Is she mad, Dr. Freud? Or is that a moot question, considering madness is defined by comparison to the norm of the population? Get back to me on that, will you?"

Evelyn turned from her nightwatch post and reentered the softly lit interior of her home. "Why, computer, you think of everything. How nice of you to adjust to the night. I wish, just once, you'd let me turn on the lights myself. At least I can choose what I want for dinner. And don't you dare start doing that. It's the only free choice you allow me in here."

The infinite variety available in the food processor was amazing, considering the lack of imagination shown in some other areas by the manufacturer of her life. Each meal could be a gourmet feast, created from a few basic raw hydrocarbons, but supposedly indistinguishable from the real thing. She didn't know for sure, never having tasted real food, even on Earth.

If she could find comparable hydrocarbons here, the processor would continue infinitely, producing as much as was demanded: meals for a person or a population. It even manufactured containers for the meals, which could then be recycled. A giant step above roots and berries, she thought as she read the menu tapes, seeking something unexplored. She finally settled on New Zealand mutton stew, punched in the appropriate coordinates, noted the preparation time, and went to read the dials on the monitors of the computer console.

Everything was humming as it was supposed to, the dials and gauges reading stability. Her attention was particularly drawn to the biolab, in which grew the source of her greatest hopes and fears: the first four.

The constantly turning, incubating, growing, exo-conceived children who would, by the time they were ready to be decanted in another six months, be crammed full of prenatal education and conditioning, as well as drugs that would double their growth rate so that they would be adult, physically, emotionally, and intellectually, by the time they were ten years old chronologically.

Evelyn feared these children for what they might be. The time warp had killed ninety-nine exo- and endo-conceived people as they slept in suspended animation. What damage had that time warp done to the genetic structures of the gametes in the biolab? What would she do if they turned out to be mutants: monsters...unhuman. Could she kill them?

And the other side of that coin, even more fearful to her: the gift of almost indefinite life she carried, courtesy of the technology that had brought her here to carry on the life that it had killed on Earth. Unless she could muster the courage to take her own life, another moot question, she would live here, alone, for hundreds of years if these children weren't successful. The fear of it permeated her days and infused her dreams, even though she controlled it as best she could, using the chants of yoga rituals intended to restore peace to troubled souls. There is a vast difference between a troubled soul and one in abject panic, she had observed, and Eve knew that what she suffered was akin to panic.

Equally terrifying was the other option she had. The biolab facility contained a complete medical unit to cover any emergency and the mechanical hands to carry out the necessary ministration. Also included was a gamete reserve with which she could become impregnated and bear an endo-conceived child. She intended to do that, but only after the first group of exo-conceiveds were grown and she could have help from others for the delivery.

With all the medical miracles the human race had accomplished, they had never discovered anything to shorten the birth process. She would, like the thousands of generations of women that stretched behind her, bring a new life into the world with pain and pressure. She feared doing that alone, even with the mechanical aid of the medical unit, so had avoided making any decisions in that direction. After all, time was hardly a problem.

Since the biolab's reproduction unit was sealed until the children were ready to be decanted, she had no way of observing their growth other than through the dials and meters that registered their lives. Each showed normal bodily functions. She activated the monitor and listened to the four hearts beating, a hypnotic reassurance that she would not be alone forever.

The sound seemed to release some of her tensions, for she knew that, should the computer's monitoring devices detect any abnormalities, it would coldly and mechanically cease to nurture that child and would quietly recycle the accumulated hydrocarbons. Heartlessly efficient, but highly practical.

Evelyn had known many exo-conceived people and all of them were highly intelligent, amiable, well-adjusted personalities, but she had, particularly since her recent infusion of philosophy, wondered what provision had been made for their souls, that essential spark of humanity which carried the race forward from a point in the infinite past with a stream of consciousness marking the difference of man from the other animals of the Earth. None of the philosophers from Plato of the ancient Greeks to Yuk San of the modern doomsmen, seemed to have an answer to that question. Did the exos have a soul, and, if so, from whence did it come? From whence did any soul come? Had she left God behind? The debates of the Clone Trials in the early twenty-first had covered much the same territory, with equally unsatisfactory results.

Now that she would have to spend the rest of her life among exos, it had become a great concern, which led to a peripheral concern: if they could be human without a soul, was anyone, exo or endo, in possession of that illusive quality, or had it been a rationalization throughout the centuries to explain an only imagined difference, making man more than an animal in his own eyes.

The philosophers all dealt with the soul as a part of the humanity of man, either reinforcing it or denying it, but none was totally convincing. It would be her responsibility now to imbue these four creatures, and the many that would follow them, with a sense of their own humanity, especially here where she was the only living example of the race. Certainly a deep investiture of charge to the one remaining of a species egomaniacal enough to believe that it was important to perpetuate itself, to the extent of exiling a thousand of its finest to ten unknown planets in ships capable of making the necessary time jumps.

Had all their triumphs failed so miserably? She was the only one of her group of a hundred that had survived the terrible physical torture of the time jump. The nagging question that would never be answered: Had others survived or was she truly the only one left of her species? And, if they had survived, where were they among the vast stars?

The Project Directors had been most secretive about the possible directions each group would take, feeling that no one should know how they got where they were going so they would never be tempted to return. Even the navigating tapes in the on-board computers had been destroyed at the end of the voyage so that there could never be any return attempt.

Evelyn had no way of knowing how far she had traveled or in which direction to look when the pull of home became strong. Perhaps, with the time warp, all that was left of Earth was a silent cinder, or perhaps she had traveled backward in time and her most remote ancestors were just now teetering those first few erect steps with a club in their hands.

At least she had been lucky enough to be deposited in a reasonably welcoming environment: gravity about seventy-five percent of Earth; atmosphere about the same proportions, but thinner; hydrocarbon composition and balance approximately the same; reasonably familiar life forms and some that seemed almost identical; even a day that spanned almost the same amount of time as at home, registering twenty-three hours, ten minutes on the computer before she had adjusted the computer chronometer to register the local time.

There even seemed to be slight seasonal changes, and the computer had informed her a couple of months before that they had now completed one local year according to astro observances, just two weeks short of an Earth year.

She had shouted "Happy Anniversary" to the computer and to her house, but nothing had changed. It could have been worse, though. Since the on-board computers were programmed to seek a similar environment and to keep looking until they found one, perhaps some of her compatriot colonists were still streaking across the uncharted stars, looking for a new home while others may have been colonizing for a hundred years. That was one of the disadvantages of not knowing how long she had been in transit; speculation had no foundation.

She had tried to extract the travel time from the computer with a bit of mathematical trickery one day, but it promptly informed her that the requested information was not available in its memory banks. No matter what format she had used for the question, the answer had always been the same: no answer. She had finally given up in disgust, realizing that the Project Directors had prepared for everything, even unwittingly leaving room for fantasy.

The buzz of the food processor finally penetrated her reverie, and she snapped off the heartbeat monitor and returned to her living area to find that the processor had presented her with dinner and appropriate utensils.

"The only things you've forgotten, as usual, are the wine, the candles, and a charming dinner companion." As she sat down, the video screen sprang to life with a film she had selected from the library. A primitive period-piece that had been popular two centuries before her birth, but that fascinated her with its stilted formality and complex characters. The stereo speakers filled the room with the haunting theme and she surrendered herself to the romance of the Old South of her homeworld.

Chapter Two

———◆———

EVELYN SAT DOWN on the stool with disgust. The machinery of the biolab hummed in anticipation of her next request, but she couldn't determine what was missing from the chemical tests she was conducting.

The hydrocarbon content had proven to be close enough to Earth's to supply the necessary materials for the food processor and other fabrication machinery which provided clothing, shelter, and necessary supplies for her and the society she would build. But somehow the tests she had run on the sample hydrocarbons had come out slightly wrong in textures and colors, tensile strengths and sizes; and she had exhausted her somewhat limited mechanical and chemical abilities trying to correct the adjustments.

In irritation, she ran the program for adjustment again, hoping to find the missing key to her problem, but the computer hadn't changed anything in its programs and she had tried all of what it had to offer. According to the records, there were only five manual adjustments to be made, and the computer would handle the rest.

"All right, we're starting over from the very first test. Maybe you've lost touch with one set of results."

She scooped up some of the hydrocarbon mixture she had made from the recipe in the computer, combining soil, plant life, and water and dumped it into the hopper. She programmed the biolab for the carbon content test and set the machinery to motion, then watched the printout on the screen and made her own notes, just to check the results the computer would later feed. It checked exactly with the first set of results.

The second test determined hydrogen content and she repeated her procedure. Again, it checked.

The third test computed fiber content, and that also checked with her first results.

The fourth test was for silica content, and the results were somewhat more complex than the others. As she wrote, she discovered her previous error just as the computer halted the process to announce in its mechanical self-satisfaction that there was a variance from the first test.

"I know it, you horrid creature. And I found it when you did, this time."

She selected a new sample and ran that test for a third time. Again the results varied from the first test, but matched the second. She punched in the reprogramming signal, then tried the synthesizer to produce the flannel-like cloth.

The dim lights and mechanical whirring of the machinery as it carried out her instructions were soothing, and Evelyn felt her accumulated stresses beginning to subside. This was crucial for her to continue living and, more important, for the life support of the four children who were only a month from being decanted and the four more who had been started automatically by the biolab computer about two months earlier.

She was going to be overrun very soon with four additional mouths to feed and four additional bodies to clothe and care for.

She had also needed to solve this problem in order to manufacture additional living space for the new arrivals. Fortunately, the crack and ledge would support a substantial housing complex and she could expand right here for a long time to come. She hoped this would solve her problems so that there would be no further difficulties in her synthesizing program.

She had used a lot of the transported hydrocarbons in the past eighteen months and wanted to be sure there would continue to be food and supplies before she decanted the new children, especially since the biolab was not beginning its full reproductive cycle and there would be four new individuals every six months.

"Being the sole mother of an entire civilization is no bed of roses, you know," she said aloud to the humming machinery. "You can't possibly appreciate what I have to go through." It sounded like something one of the stereovision actors would say and she laughed at her own pretenses. Mother of a civilization, indeed. Pusher of buttons, perhaps.

Listening to the machine, she wondered if the biolab would suffer birth pangs at the decanting.

"Evelyn Conner, you are quite definitely mad. Just think, you will spawn an entire race of madmen who will all think they're sane because the only norm for comparison they will have is other madmen. Well, at least they won't be alone."

The synthesizer buzzed its readiness and she nervously pulled the fabric out of the hopper.

"Victory!" she yelled, for it matched the quality of the fabric made from transported materials.

Suddenly she stopped, realizing that now she was truly a citizen of this place. A permanent resident. She could now live from the resources around her, no longer dependent on the invisible umbilical cord leading across the void to Earth. She had been irrevocably cut loose by the act of producing a square meter of cloth.

Tears welled in her eyes and she felt the emotional wrench as never before. Now she was truly on her own and the choices and changes which would occur here were now hers alone. She sank to the floor of the biolab, feeling the cool plasteel lending reality to her waking nightmare.

"When you have established a colony, a most important facet of your function will be the continuance of a governmental function by those among you who have been designated, through the testing program, as natural leaders. We, of course, discourage you from the establishment of deviant forms of government which have proven in our history to be ineffective, inefficient, or debilitating to the good of all the people."

Evelyn stirred in her seat in the vast auditorium that contained the hopes of humanity. One thousand people of varying backgrounds and skills, chosen from the entire population of the Earth for their genetic, intellectual, physical, and emotional attributes, preparing to search through the far galaxies with the most advanced machinery that science could devise, for a place where mankind could continue. To her left, Morris Watson, an astrophysicist from United Europe, moved slightly in response to her action, then comically concealed an exaggerated yawn.

"The lectures alone are enough to drive you into space," he whispered before returning his attention to the professor.

Evelyn smiled, then tried to focus her attention on the content of the presentation. She had not been chosen as one of the "natural leaders," but was required, as were all the candidates, to attend all preparatory classes. She was certain that the natural leaders were equally disinterested in planetoid ecology, her field.

"... sociological engineers and economists. Therefore, governmental and bureaucratic functions have been programmed into the on-board computers and they will establish the initial patterns of sociological interaction in the new colonies. After an appropriate period of orientation and establishment, more and more functions of government will be released by the on-boards to the designated leaders who will carry out courses for the benefit of the colony."

Evelyn tapped out "government controlled by on-board" on the keys of her stenocorder and stifled a yawn. As long as they didn't interfere with her research, she didn't care who became the bureaucrats or what they did.

"...afford them your consideration and cooperation. Of
course, as the colonies expand, both through exo- and endo-
conceived births, more government will be needed to continue
the smooth operation of the colonies. As this becomes necessary, further leaders must be selected from among the trans-
portees and the native-born members of the colony."

Morris leaned over and whispered to her: "Not to mention
the little green men who already live there. I'm sure one of
them will want to grow up to be chairman."

Evelyn suppressed a giggle, imagining a mythical space
creature wearing the draped white robe and ceremonial chain
of the Chairman.

"...cooperation with locally existing societies. Of course,
the on-board navigational and location selectors are programmed to eliminate densely populated planets from among
the alternatives available in the zones to which you will travel,
but in the event that there is a small but sophisticated local
populace, it is our expectation that you will make the appropriate adjustments to integrate your colonies into the mainstream of their civilization. Need I mention that this is to be
accomplished without violence of any kind if it is possible to
avoid?"

"Do you think he means that we're not carrying neutron
eliminators on each colony ship? How dull." Morris was certainly enjoying his role as commentator, and Evelyn was glad
for the distraction. That was the frustration of so many of
these prep courses. The lecturers giving them knew nothing of
what they would be facing, but could only speculate, which
was no more than the colonists themselves could do. She became irritated with the lectures because, having chosen the
thousand best in the world, the project directors were now
treating them like adolescents.

Evelyn knew the others in her colonial group and had great
respect for each of them, feeling that there was a valuable
mixture of personalities and that each would be able to make
a working contribution to the function of the colony. It was
most unlikely that they would feel compelled to make war on

the existing civilization, should there be one, or on each other over the running of the colony. It wasted valuable preparation time to listen to pompous fools who hadn't been able to offer salvation to the Earth, but felt qualified to direct, in advance, the running of a colony they would never see nor understand.

She tapped "Don't make war" into the stenocorder balanced on her knees, which drew a snicker from Morris.

"Back in the mid-twentieth century, before the big wars, they had an expression," he whispered, "that sums it all up. They used to say, 'Make love, not war.'"

Evelyn obediently tapped out, "Make love, not war," into the stenocomp, then tripped the "erase" key, not wishing to have her monitor see such insolence.

"Cowardice or conformity?" Morris hissed.

"Both." It was an honest answer. Even though she was ter-rified of the impending journey, the fear of staying to die a lingering death with the planet was greater. If conformity would buy freedom and cowardice guarantee passage, then the answer was most definitely both.

"... our expectation for you: to carry forward the human race, building on the good foundations we and our ancestors have constructed on this planet. You are our only hope, and it is a blind hope, for no one living here will ever know whether you succeed or fail at your tasks. We can only pray that you succeed. Blessings to the Chairman of Earth and to each of the Chairmen of the United Governments. I thank you."

The audience stood in respect, tapping polite applause with their feet. The speaker bowed, then left the stage to an accom-paniment of the murmuring of beginning conversations.

Morris took Evelyn's arm to steer her out of the assembly hall and into the cool corridors of the project building. "Got time for some tea?"

"Yes, thank you."

They walked in silent companionship through the halls to-ward the commissary. Neither of them spoke until they were settled in a far corner of the room, away from the buzzing groups of other colonists.

Morris sipped at the citrus tea, then said, "I wonder what real oranges tasted like. Perhaps we shall find out when we reach Utopia. Did you know that's what they used to call a paradise? Utopia: the ultimate. And now, my dear Evelyn, the real question: What do we face out there? Utopia or Hell?"

"Morris, you ask the most convoluted questions. One minute you're talking about oranges and the next about Hell. I'm certain there is some touch point in between, logically. And I don't know the answer to your real question any better than you, or any of the others, do. Also, you're ignoring the third possibility: eternity. It is possible we may drift in suspended animation forever."

"Ah, and that poses another philosophical query: What, then, happens to our immortal souls? For we are then neither dead nor alive, but achieving the point ultimate in scientific advancement: eternal life. Hardly, I'm sure, what the doctors were hoping for in their life extension experiments."

"Another convolution! Could we please go back to the oranges?"

"As you will, Colonist Conner. Do you think there will be oranges and apples and corn and fish where we're going? Or will we have to depend on the synthesizers just as we do here?"

"I hope, Colonist Watson, that we will have all of that and more. We will have clean air to breathe and clean water to drink and trees and grass and...well...everything we used to have here." Evelyn paused, distressed by the emotions that Morris could arouse in her normally logical and emotionless intelligence. All this talk of oranges and Hell had nothing to do with their purpose in colonizing, but he had suddenly made it important to her to taste a real orange. Impulsively, she took his hand. "Morris, I wish we were going to the same colony."

"Why?" he asked, not removing his hand from her grasp to ease the impact of the moment on her. "Are you afraid that no one will play with you and run in the grass and drink the water and eat the oranges?"

"Yes, and I'm afraid that no one will laugh." She looked

*over her shoulder at the groups of colonists sprinkled around
the room. There was much buzzing conversation, but no
laughter, as though confirming her fears. "I want someone
else to think that oranges are important."*

*"You won't know until the first one you find. Then I think
you'll be surprised at just how important they become. And
laughing, too, will be important. You like and respect your
group. The rest will come later." He patted her hand, smiling
into her eyes. "It sounds like a line from one of the old stereos,
but it's true: We just need to take advantage of whatever time
we have now, and then go our separate ways. Unfortunately,
our separate ways are going to be quite separate, but we have
about a year. That's a nice amount of time not to bore each
other."*

*"With the turns your mind takes, it's hard to imagine ever
being bored with you."*

*"It is also hard to imagine the Chairman of Earth taking a
sonar cleansing, but we know that he does. And now, another
puzzle to tease your fertile mind. What would you do if you
were to be designated one of the natural leaders? Would you
become queen of your new world? A galactic Cleopatra, perhaps, riding on your hovercraft barge over the terrain of some
far-off world, picking those elusive oranges? Or perhaps another Elizabeth I, encouraging the arts and living in sinful
adventure with every man who strikes your fancy? Or perhaps
serene and dignified like Madame President Ferguson who
fearlessly led the United States through the interwar period in
the early twenty-first? Or would you be sinister and vile like
Catherine the Great of Old Russia? Tell me, what would you
do if you could be queen of a world?"*

*Evelyn sighed and leaned back into her chair. "Do you want
to take up the whole year with one question? I don't know
what I'd do . . . and I hope I'm never confronted with having to
answer it—not for you and, certainly, not for reality."*

Now, alone in her biolab, ages away from that conversation and from the warmth and security of the Project com-

pound, it haunted her. Morris had been prophetic in his joking and she wished he could be here now to help her answer the question he had posed rhetorically. He had never asked her again, and now she wished he had pursued it and forced her to articulate her concepts of building a society. It might have helped to share her ideas with a fellow Earthling. As it stood now, she had only the compu-tapes of the Earth's past to help her; and little of that had seemed to work. Now that she would be in charge of starting and educating and governing an entire civilization, she needed as much help in practicalities as she could get.

So much of the information on the computapes was sketchy, a distillation of myriad processes that led up to the making of the final decision which was recorded. She longed for time to question some of the figures in the histories, to find out how they felt and thought and reacted and then to base her governing on the best they had to offer.

She twisted the square of fabric in her hands: the first product of the industry of her new world. Her new, governmentless, populationless, nameless world. All it possessed was a tribe of primitives, an intergalactic wanderer, and an industry.

"Aha, Computer Dr. Watson, a clue. If there is a tribe, why not many tribes? Why haven't we thought of that before? Perhaps we've landed in the middle of a primitive reservation, and right over that next hill there is a bustling city filled with people. Or perhaps right under that next hill."

Evelyn left the biolab, the cloth forgotten but still clasped in her hand, and went to the main computer room. She snapped on the viewing screen and settled into the console chair, unconsciously spreading the cloth over her lap with one hand as she searched the library. Finally, after punching in the arrival date, the screen showed: "Records: shuttlecraft landing. Visual and bio.,geo.,geog., bot., life-study survey reports. 122-657-0999."

Evelyn pushed "hold," then "seek and play" on the console. She settled back into the chair, waiting.

After a short pause, the screen silently lit up. She saw her world from a distance, a green balloon lightly frosted on either end, accented with puffs of drifting cloud. It became larger and more defined as the cameras zoomed in. She watched carefully, looking for signs of cities or roads or other indications of habitation but could find nothing other than natural formations: kilometers of mountain ranges that interlaced with valleys filled with trees and grass. Lakes and rivers abounded, several of them very large.

The land masses alternated with four ocean-sized bodies of deep green water, sparkling in the sunlight and capped with wave tips moving in orderly rows. There were deserts in the center of each of the three land masses, surrounded by the inevitable mountains. But, nowhere was there any sign of a city or population center of any kind.

As the shuttlecraft moved closer, seeking out an ideal spot for habitation with its sensors, she could see several villages like the one she had gone to investigate. At least her neighbors had others like them sprinkled across the land masses. They had relatives they could visit, but it didn't look like there was anyone she could visit. So much for the population center theory.

She was interested to see how close she lived to the ocean. As nearly as she could guess, the shuttle had landed only about thirty kilometers inland. Behind her, over the mountains, the slopes became gentler, edging toward the golden sand of the shore and the green water. She stopped the tape and looked at the mountains in which she lived.

Down the range, she guessed about ten kilos, there seemed to be a valley passage through the mountains. She was thrilled by the discovery. To be so close to a body of water, just like the seashore of her childhood vacations! It was better than finding a city.

"A holiday! I'm going to take a holiday at the shore, just

like when I was a kid. I'll take a dometent and some food and my new cloth and I'll go on a holiday. I can swim and build castles in the sand and play on the shore and find shells. And Mom will let me..."

The sounds of her hysterical crying echoed through the empty rooms.

Chapter Three

THE SEABIRD RAN along the shore, its waddling gait incompatible with its sleek lines. It squawked its disapproval of the alien invader, stretched out naked at the water's edge, reveling in the warmth of the sunshine and the chill of the water.

"There's enough beach for both of us. It pays to come early in the season before the crowds take over and you can't find any clean sand."

The bird stopped, cocked its head and eyed her suspiciously. It assumed a defensive posture, wings cocked to flee if she seemed threatening, but Evelyn stayed still, returning its stare. The bird, thoroughly puzzled by her lack of aggressive behavior, stood its ground.

"You're the first inhabitant of this godforsaken planet to take any interest in anything I have to say. And certainly the first to try any kind of communication. So please don't leave. I'll share a meal with you." She moved very slowly, reaching for the packet of crackers beside her. The bird backed away, but didn't try to leave. His beady black eyes watched her movements carefully. She removed a cracker from the package and set it on the sand an arm's length from her body.

"Come here, little friend. Have a taste of what it would be like to have been born somewhere else and have other skies to fly. You know, I've flown farther than you could ever imagine, and, you'll notice, I have no wings. Now, you not only have a meal but also a riddle. I try to entertain my guests as best I can."

Evelyn lay very still and the bird watched her, waiting. Finally, he waddled forward, his eyes fixed on her but aiming his body toward the cracker. Keeping one eye still on this strange creature, the bird bent to the cracker, then pecked at it experimentally. He took several tastes, then with a squawk, extended his wings and flew off along the shoreline. His wings were very large for his body, adjusted to the thin atmosphere, and he was extremely graceful in the air, swooping down to skim the water, then rising high into the sky.

Evelyn rolled over and sat up. "Ingrate!" she yelled after his retreating form. "What were you expecting, after all?"

She rose, stretched, and walked into the chilly water, feeling it tingling against her skin. She sank into the sensuality of the moment, slowly immersing herself up to her shoulders, dipping her head and tasting the slightly alkaline water. As she stood and walked out of the ocean, she was again intensely aware of missing Morris far beyond his teasing and his mind.

"Project Director Lamson spoke to me today about our relationship." Morris's fingers tickled the skin of her stomach, lazily moving in a circle, ruffling the tiny hairs.

"He doesn't approve?" Evelyn's voice was husky with sensuality, but a knot began to grow in her stomach. The time she shared with Morris was little enough, considering that there were only five months until isolation, and she wasn't ready to give it up yet.

"He doesn't approve. He said that I should be spending more time with my own colonial group, as should you, getting to know the members and deciding on potential future relationships."

The huskiness was gone from her voice, replaced by a thin line of tension. "So are we going to be forbidden to see each other?"

"He didn't go that far. I didn't give him the chance. I asked to be transferred to your group or for you to be transferred to mine."

Evelyn was caught off-guard, not expecting his revelation, as she grinned into the dark. "And?"

"Well, he didn't flatly say no, but he certainly didn't say yes. He spent about fifteen minutes explaining the genetic cross-matching within each group, the low mutant or recessive probabilities and the necessary interpersonal typing within each colony, then said he'd take it under advisement." He paused reflectively. "I think I'd rather he'd have been more definite. The additional pressure is not making it easy for me to concentrate on other things."

Evelyn let the silence build between them. From the intercom speaker, soft music gentled the sudden tension.

Finally she sighed, then said, "I don't want to hope and I almost wish that you'd not told me. Too many things are indefinite now. I've grown used to the idea that we only have five months left. Now I can't even count on that." She turned away from him, holding tightly to the edge of the sleeping mat, practicing the calming yoga.

"Hey," Morris said, putting his hand on her shoulder and gently pulling her toward him, "that was supposed to bring hope, not despair. Remember? Whatever time we have . . . you know, the old stereo lines?" Through his hand on her shoulder, he felt her trembling. "Eve, we've told each other many times that we would take what we could get and have it for later."

"You're right, and I know it, but I wasn't ready to give up quite yet." She forced herself to relax, controlling her emotions. "And you know I care deeply for you. It's just the surprise that he would interfere."

"No it's not, if you think about it without emotion. They're trying to find the best possible balance within each colony, and we're not helping by out intergalactic mingling."

"When will he let you know?"

"He didn't say. Let's both try not to let his impending decision influence our time together. After all, he could decide that we do belong in the same colony. Maybe it's the wrong time to bring it up, but there's something I want you to know. I do love you and if we lived in the past, or if we continued to be here, I would want to marry you."

Evelyn felt the tears running from the corners of her eyes and across her temples into her hair. She tried to stop them and control her breathing, but she knew that he expected an answer. All she could manage was, "I feel the same way," which didn't carry what she truly felt.

She put her arms around him, feeling the smoothness of his skin and the subtle flow of muscles underneath, missing him long before he was gone. She held him tightly, her body saying what she couldn't.

Morris's breath was warm on her neck and his voice filled her world, "Being the last hope of mankind isn't easy." He shifted slightly and she responded, finding security in their familiar love ritual. Their joining drove the fears from her mind and she gave herself up completely to the mindless pleasures.

The squawk of the bird, returning to the cracker he had abandoned, broke through her reverie and she was embarrassed to find her body now responding to the memory of her body then. She hurried to the cloth on which she had been lying and busied herself shaking the sand from it.

"Eve Conner, that is the very last thing you should be thinking about. It will be many years before you can revisit that part of your life, so dismiss it from your thoughts once and for all. Add that to the rest of the pressures of this place and you will surely be mad."

She folded the cloth carefully and walked along the sand to the dometent, deliberately. Her mind could dismiss and suppress the thoughts, but the demands her body made were very real. She had discovered long ago that self-release brought no release. It was an insoluble problem, for, until there was someone to hold her, to perform those little rituals as had Morris and the other men she had made love with, to share the effort and the joy of reaching a climactic moment together, the climactic moment meant nothing.

The inside of the dometent was dim and warmer than the outside air. She opened the foodpack and considered the various packets containing her picnic, but nothing was appealing.

"There is little to be gained by feeling sorry for yourself, you know. So it's a problem you can't solve right now. You just have to function around it."

She found her light coverall and slid into it, carefully brushing the sand from her feet and body. Even so, there was some scratchiness, vastly different from the sterile cleanliness of the complex on Earth and even from the smooth plasteel of her house on this planet. She felt the mixed blessing of communing with nature which so many of the philosophers on the tapes espoused.

"I think I prefer communing with nature on a more distant level. Sand in coveralls is just plain uncomfortable. Now I have two itches to contend with." Her laugh sounded hollow inside the dometent.

She threw back the doorflap of the dometent and was surprised to see the thunderclouds building over the ocean. The wind was freshening and the waves were capped with foam as they rolled into the shore.

"If there's going to be a storm, I'd just as soon be back in my house than be here with the tent." Her bird friend had disappeared and the beach was totally deserted. She removed the supplies from the tent and packed them into the carrier of the hovercraft, then dismantled the dometent, all the while aware of the threatening rumbles out over the ocean. A flash of lightning punctuated the rolling of the clouds and she hurried at her tasks.

It was at least ten kilos along the sand to the pass through the mountains, then another thirty-four kilos through the pass, and still another twelve to her complex.

Even though the hovercraft had a clear cover to protect her, she dreaded having to navigate through the mountains in a driving rainstorm, which would make visibility diminish and increase the possibility of an accident.

She finished packing the dometent into the carrier and climbed into the hovercraft, closing the cover over her. The sounds of the approaching storm lessened, but the sun had completely disappeared and she switched on the navigating lights. As she touched the controls, she felt the slight instability of the lifting cushion of air under her, then a side-slipping from the force of the wind.

Staying close to the dunes and as far from the water as she could, she sped along the coast, fear growing as the intensity of the thunder and lightning increased. The winds buffeted the small craft, making navigation difficult, and clouds of sand prickled against the cover. The speed indicators showed that she was only able to maintain thirty kilos per hour against the forces of the shifting winds, and she cursed, trying to produce more speed from the small machine.

The first drops of rain plopped against the cover, leaving wide splatters for a moment before the wind spread them into a sheet of rain. She switched on the clearing blades, but they were of little effect against the force of the rain, so she was forced to navigate almost by memory, using the brief clearing of the cover to check her progress.

With her foot, she sought the sonar warning system switch, hoping it would prevent crashing into some unremembered rock or outcropping. The muscles in her shoulders ached from the battle with the control wand and the cords in her neck stood out as she peered forward.

To her right, on the lee side of the force of the storm, she could vaguely see the landscape, and she divided her attention between forward progress and watching for the entrance to the pass through the mountains. It would not have been hard to see in clear weather since she had left a pile of marker stones, but she wasn't sure she wouldn't miss it in the fury of the storm.

While she was peering to the side, seeking the marker stones, the craft was hit by a vicious gust of wind and bounced jarringly into the dune. She was able to stabilize during the brief lull that followed, but there was now a clattering noise coming from the bottom of the craft and her speed was slowed. The jolt had also made control more difficult, and she had to use both hands on the wand to maintain her course.

Her search for the mountain pass had now become frantic, for landmarks were almost invisible in the driving rain. She was torn between wanting to flee the surrounding violence, which terrified her, and wanting to stop and wait until the storm spent its fury. To control her terror she focused on the serenity of her shelter complex, nestled into its mountain crack.

The clattering noise from the hovercraft seemed to increase whenever the wind slowed slightly, and she cursed the fragility of machinery. She realized that she should have taken the time to remove one of the larger hovercrafts from the shuttle. After all, she had a fleet of transportation suited to the ten who should have been with her. Several vehicles of that fleet could carry many more than the two-person craft she now occupied.

The clearing blades swept a brief path through the rivers of water coursing down the cover and she spotted her marker stones through the storm. She slowed the craft and turned into the notch in the dunes leading to the gentle valley through the mountains.

"I've won! I've won!" She yelled her victory into the noise of the storm, almost dizzy with relief as the wind she had been fighting now helped her to lift over the obstruction of the moving mountains of sand butting up against the foot of the mountain cliffs. "I'll beat this place yet. This is my planet and I will be the ruler. No one can deny my power here. I am the mother of a new world and I will control it."

Her fears gushed with her words, the relief bringing a
headiness. Her attention wandered slightly from the lash-
ing storm outside the cover of the hovercraft as she tried to
relax her shoulders and arms.

Suddenly, as she navigated through the cliffs leading into
the valley, the storm exacted its revenge. A particularly violent burst of wind thrust the hovercraft solidly against the
rocks, dealing the deathblow to the mechanism and throwing Eve against the cover, knocking her unconscious. The
unconsciousness was a blessing: she didn't feel the bone in
her arm snap with the force of the blow.

Her head throbbed and her return to consciousness
moved the broken arm. She was jolted awake with a nau-
seating rush of pain. Through her confusion, she fought to
control the pain, the fear, and the nausea as she tried to
remember where she was and what had happened. Slowly,
trying not to move her arm, she raised her head slightly
and was instantly dizzy. She fought the black edges that
threatened to return her to unconsciousness.

Her head cleared, and she remembered the storm and the
accident. That explained the odd angle at which she lay, the
headache, and the pain in her arm. Reason told her that
her arm was probably broken, for, as she became more
awake, the pain was intense and constant.

She shifted her eyes to the chron on the dial panel of the
hovercraft. In the dark, its luminous dial faintly showed
3:10. She was distressed to realize that she had been unconscious for almost nine hours. With her uninjured arm, she
explored her scalp and found, without surprise, a large
lump on the left side of her head. She couldn't feel any cuts,
so at least she hadn't lost a lot of blood, but she knew that
any prolonged period of unconsciousness could be an indication of skull fracture or concussion. Slowly, she took in-
ventory of her working parts, wiggling one foot, then the
other, and sending out sensory checks to be sure there was

feeling if she didn't want to try movement. Nothing seemed to be numb or paralyzed, to her vast relief.

Gingerly, she explored her left arm. Between the shoulder and the elbow, the arm was badly swollen and extremely painful to even the gentlest touch. The situation was worsened by pressure of her body leaning on that side, due to the angle at which the hovercraft lay.

With her foot, she tried snapping the starter switch for the craft's engine. The vehicle shuddered after several tries, a grinding noise emerging from the bowels. The shuddering accomplished one thing: The craft slid sideways to a more manageable angle. The movement brought the black edges and dizziness back, but Evelyn was determined to stay conscious and fought to drive away the fog.

"No! Not again. Now come on, machine, we've got to get home to the biolab." She snapped the switch again. The shuddering resumed, but the machine refused to move. The headlamps were still bright, showing the territory in front of the machine to be approaching the crest of the pass through the cliffs and into the narrow valley. From here it was about forty-five kilos to her home.

"Please, damn you, do something. I can't walk forty-five kilos." In fury, she shoved the control wand forward to its fullest extent. The craft wobbled slowly forward, dragging its right side along the ground. The wobbling motion was producing jolts of pain in her left arm, but she was afraid to stop in case the machine wouldn't respond again.

She braced her knee against the control wand and reached for the piece of cloth on the other seat. Holding one corner in her teeth, she wrapped the cloth under her right arm and around her back, while fighting to maintain her balance against the lurching hovercraft. Continuing to bite hard on the cloth, she put her left hand against her shoulder and wrapped the cloth over the left side, then tied it as firmly as she could to her chest. At least that would hold her arm somewhat immobile during the jolting journey. As long as it lasted.

Through experimentation, she found the point at which the craft moved forward as rapidly as possible with the least amount of wobbling. The speed indicator showed 10 KPH, little faster than walking, but she was glad for any motion at all.

The machine slowed as she reached the crest of the pass through the cliffs, then, in an agonizing lurch, breasted the hill and began the descent. The machine picked up speed slightly, increasing the jostling, as she descended into the narrow valley through the mountains. Fortunately, there were few rocks or bends in the valley, so she didn't have to do much steering with the control wand, which was almost completely unresponsive to turn controls.

The eeriness of the empty valley in the dark was oppressive. Evelyn would have been glad to see some sign of life within the light of the headlamps, but nothing was visible. The pain was her only companion, constant and overbearing, and, at times, almost a physical presence within the tight confines of the craft. She wished that she had brought a music program for the on-board computer. Bach, perhaps, or Strauss, celebrating the grandeur of man in a golden age.

By dawn, Evelyn had bumped her way almost the entire length of the valley in the damaged hovercraft. Her shoulders felt hot with fatigue and her head ached from the flow and the strain, but she had covered almost thirty kilos in the three hours since she had discovered that the craft would move.

The first light of dawn had begun to bring detail to the mountains around her and the headlamps seemed to pale in the increasing light. She could clearly see the notch in the mountains at the end of the valley ahead of her and knew it would present a challenge to the machine, which was becoming increasingly clamorous in its protests against moving. Obviously, the dragging of the right side was further increasing the damage to the hovercraft.

"Please, keep going. Please," she encouraged it. "You've

done so well up to now. You just have to get through that narrow passage ahead, and we're on our way. You can make it."

As though in answer, the machine groaned and shuddered, slowing slightly. She again experimented with the control wand, coaxing as much forward progress as she could from the hovercraft. But now, the maximum speed she could produce was 8 KPH. The ascent into the mountain pass had begun and the crippled machine was unable to maintain progress against the increasing incline.

As she came nearer to the pass, her progress slowed again and again, until, as she entered the shadow of the pass, she was moving at only 1 KPH.

"Come on, please, only a few more meters, and then you're over the top. Come on." She switched off the headlamps, hoping to channel all the power to the rotors, and the machine inched forward, jarring her painfully with its progress. "Come on. You've almost done it." The clattering was deafening as the machine strained over the last centimeters of the crest, then lurched as they came to the top of the pass.

"See, you didn't give up and we've made it." But ahead was a kilo of mountain pass strewn with rocks and requiring careful navigation. She hadn't remembered how many twists and turns she had made on the way over, but now it was quite clear.

The hovercraft began to pick up its speed with the flat terrain. She tried several methods of steering, finding that violent jerks of the control wand were the most effective means of navigation, though personally the most painful. She approached the first of the boulders littering the pathway, jerked the control wand to the left, and the hovercraft moved around the rock. The next boulder required an equally violent jerk to the right, and again the machine missed the rock.

She skirted a few more obstacles but, during a particularly difficult series of turns, heard a screeching, grinding noise and felt a violent lurch. The contact threw her against the cover of the hovercraft and sent thundering waves of pain crashing over her. She fought back the black unconsciousness threatening to overcome her. The machine had stalled and she flipped the starter switch several times. The only response was a thudding, grinding screech. In disgust, she snapped the switch off.

"Now what?" But she knew that the noise and the stall represented the final efforts of the machine and that she would have to walk from here. "At least it's only twelve kilos instead of forty-five."

She reached across her body and released the cover catch. It sprang open a few centimeters, then stuck. By turning in the seat, she was able to get enough leverage to push on the cover with her good arm, but had to struggle to keep consciousness against the pain from her injured arm. She pushed, rested, and pushed again until the cover finally opened.

The fresh air felt good after the confinement of the hovercraft, and she sat, relaxing, trying to return the pain in her arm and head to a manageable level before getting out of the craft. She rested her head against the backrest, looking up at the cover standing open over her head.

Suddenly she was totally alert, the pain and dull aches forgotten. Along the back left side of the cover, the undamaged side, running from the center to the edge, were four deep, parallel scratches, repeated several times. They hadn't been there before her accident. She tried to think of how they might have been caused by the accident, but that side had remained undamaged.

Cold chills ran along her spine and primitive fears enclosed her. The scratches were too long and too symmetrical to have been caused by rocks while she had been moving, and she realized that they looked like marks left by claws.

The thought that, while she had been unconscious, something large and frightening had been trying to remove her from her plasteel casing brought a fresh wave of nausea and terror, and her stomach heaved. Her heart pounded as she carefully extracted herself from the seat and slowly stood, and climbed out of the craft. There were still vestiges of dizziness, but she ignored them as she turned to the side of the craft. There, below the edge where the cover rested, were more of the scratches, deeper into the opaque plasteel. Parallel declarations of a violent visitor in the night.

She looked in the rocks around and above her for something large enough to have made those marks. Nothing moved in the light or shadows except a bird which drifted lazily over her head against the bright sky. She heard the scurrying of small animals going about their business, but nothing large could be seen or heard lurking in the area.

She struggled to calm herself, but the adrenaline continued to pump into her body, racing her heart and echoing with thudding in her head.

"It must have been something that comes out at night in that area, which doesn't mean that it would be here during the daylight."

With another flood of terror, she realized that, had she not been able to start the hovercraft moving, she might have walked through the night which contained the creature.

She slid her fingers over the deep grooves in the plasteel. It took a great deal of force to scratch plasteel, and these were deep scratches. She walked around the craft, driven by the fascination of the escaped horror. Whatever the creature was, it had been determined, for the scratches appeared all around the craft. Particular attention had been paid to the carrier which contained her food packs and to the area right beside where she had lain unconscious.

"That storm may have saved me from something far worse," she said with a shudder, envisioning the thin fabric of the dometent, which would not have prevented the entry of something as large and dedicated as whatever had made these scratches.

Again she looked around her, searching for movement, but the quiet remained. She released the catch on the carrier, removing the food pack, and tried to eat something to give her strength for the walk ahead, but the presence of the creature in the night haunted her.

She took several packets of high-energy food and water from the food pack and set them aside. Everything else she dumped into the carrier and closed it again. The food pack was now light enough to carry without effort, and she put the packets inside it. She then pulled the emergency kit out of the hovercraft and took from it the things she thought she might need.

She debated for a while, then popped one of the energy intensifiers into her mouth and swallowed it with a sip of water. It would help her body rally its forces for the long walk she faced. She put two more into the food pack and added two painkillers to the collection. She didn't think she'd need the bandages and was reluctant to unbind her arm to try to place one of the quick-splints over the break, even though it would give her use of her arm.

Finally, after debating for a few minutes, during which she found herself checking the landscape again and again for movement, she decided that it might be important to have the use of her left arm and gingerly untied the binding.

The release of pressure was excruciating, and she vomited violently, swaying dizzily. As the pain subsided, she found a secure seat on a nearby rock and, grinding her teeth against the pain, slowly slid the quick-splint over her arm, positioning it over the ugly blue-red bruises and swelling. The sensors in the splint were adjusted to reposition the break so that it met properly, then the splint would harden, holding the break in place until she could return to the biolab.

Bracing herself for the pain she knew was coming, she activated the splint. There was a grinding pressure in her upper arm as the splint positioned the bones to an exact match, then increased pressure as it hardened. Suddenly, there was no pain at all, and she remembered, almost too late, that the splint contained nerve blocks that cut off pain impulses issuing from her arm. They also blocked most of the feeling in her left hand, but the respite from the pain was so welcome she regretted she had not thought of applying the splint before she began her nightmare ride through the valley.

The increased mobility made her feel more secure and she returned to the hovercraft. She took another energy intensifier to replace the one she had vomited, ate another protein cracker, and then gathered up her belongings. She rummaged through the emergency kit, looking for anything else that might be necessary, and was about to abandon it when she remembered what else it contained.

Lifting everything out, she released the catch on the bottom container and removed the laser gun and its power pack. It was not intended to be a weapon, but would afford protection against anything that might exhibit too much interest in her. She snapped the power pack into place and aimed the gun at a rock about thirty meters away.

The rock exploded, sending a clattering cloud of pebbles skittering down the hill. She sighed with relief, again feeling confident at being able to control her environment before it controlled her. She closed the dome on the hovercraft, shouldered her pack, and began threading her way through the rocks of the mountain pass.

The energy intensifier had taken effect and she walked at a brisk pace, soon emerging into her own valley. In the distance, to the north, she could see the huge shuttle shining in the sunlight, a beacon bringing her home.

The dismissal of her fears about the creature in the night and the euphoria of the energy intensifier made her optimistic, and, with a final glance over her shoulder, she began the descent into her valley. She covered the distance to her shelter in about two and a half hours, exploring her valley more intimately than she ever had.

As she climbed the steps to her shelter, a bunch of flowers clutched in her hand, she looked out across the valley. A reassuring column of smoke rose from the village and everything seemed at peace.

Through the medical research that had enabled science to arrest aging on Earth, the art of healing had also been highly developed, and its zenith was reached in the biolab, designed especially for the ten colonies. The biolab was a condensed version of a major hospital, offering all the healing facilities in a concentrated space.

One capability was cellular reorganization, which had eliminated the need for surgery. Any breakdown in cellular function or bone break could be repaired by cellular reorganization without the need for supportive splints.

Evelyn stretched out on the cool plasteel table and centered the machine over the break in her arm. The machine would perform the repairs through the splint, which she could then remove after the healing had been completed. She touched the control dial and the biolab hummed to life. The only sensation was a slight tingling above the splint and across her shoulder, but there was no pain or discomfort. The healing cycle for a broken bone took about an hour and she dozed as it progressed. She was exhausted, but the energy intensifier was still at work and she couldn't release herself to sleep.

The biolab, its work completed, fell silent and Evelyn turned to her right side, repositioning the cellular reorganizer over the lump on her scalp. If there were a concussion or fracture, the machine would identify it and repair it without damaging her brain.

When the reorganizer had first been developed, the side effects had been horrible, producing physical and mental monsters in the research labs of Earth. Most of the reports of this had been suppressed by the controlling agency, but rumors had circulated among the scientific community and had leaked out to the general population with the usual attendant governmental cries for control of the "monster machines." The research had been outwardly abandoned, while secretly continuing until the second of the great wars when it came into common usage to heal the massive radiation burns so many people had suffered. With such vast sources of experimental bodies, the difficulties had been corrected, solving problems for the vast masses of humanity who had been unable to afford medical attention from expensive private hospitals where the true health care was concentrated.

The machine whirred and hummed, printing out an analysis on the screen as it made the corrections. The information it relayed would be filed permanently in Evelyn's medical records and instantly available for future reference.

As she lay, listening to the machine and feeling the tingling of its healing process, she was again grateful to the Project Directors who, in their blind wisdom, had attempted to provide for every possibility. Without the biolab facilities, she would never have been able to survive, much less maintain other lives that would be coming.

The machine ceased its humming, the short period of time indicating that there had been no serious damage from the blow to her head, even though she had been unconscious for so long. If there had been any tissue damage, the biolab would have corrected it.

Just to be sure, she sat up quickly, but there was no dizziness and she felt clearheaded. She removed the splint from her left arm and flexed it, astonished that there was no pain or stiffness.

She walked over to the console and pushed the control for the monitor on the four lives only a month from decanting and the four lives who were four months from humanity. The steady thudding of heartbeats was a chorus of life and Evelyn felt renewed and refreshed. She realized that she was looking forward to having the company these children would afford. They would fill up her days with activity and her nights with companionship.

Chapter Four

———◆———

"... decanting process can be traumatic for the exo-conceived child just as birth is traumatic for the endo-conceived. The additional threat of trauma comes from the advanced growth stages of the exo-conceived child. Bear in mind when dealing with exobabies that they are far more advanced at birth than their endo counterparts.

"The exo-conceived child has received extensive prenatal education on a subconscious level and you will discover immediately that they have a much higher information absorption level.

"Their physical growth will also be astonishing to the uninitiated, for they mature in about half the time of an endo child. Consequently, remember that motor skills, training, language, and education will be more advanced and far more rapidly developed.

"I cannot stress enough the differences in the first ten years between exo- and endo-conceived children and the need for keeping them separated from each other as much as possible. Once they have reached the maturation level, you will find that peer interrelationships are normal and there is absolutely no difference discernable between the adequately raised endo and the usual exo.

"Naturally, there are exceptions on both sides of the case,

but the norm has proven us out, and that is on the basis of eight generations of exo-conceived children. Questions?"

One of the women from her colonial group, an earnest person with an intense and serious manner, stood, raising her hand. "Professor, separation of exo and endo children is possible in our society where the population is large. In the colonial situation, however, where the initial population is only one hundred, in communities of ten, how will it be possible for exo-conceived children to be kept separate from those endo children who will be born at the same time?"

The professor looked down his long nose with the hairs that protruded so noticeably from the end like an old broom, staring her down. "Madame, it seems to me that the colonists will have to make adjustments appropriate to their own situations for just such emergencies. Perhaps you should consider painting one group blue if you are concerned about confusing the two."

The professor was famous for his acid tongue and equally famous for his hatred of anything or anyone female.

The woman who had asked the question sat down in anguished confusion.

"Addressing ourselves to the question of separation, you will find that the exo children tend to seek out their peers in development as opposed to chronological age. Also bear in mind that their growth rate physically will almost keep abreast of their growth rate mentally. Voluntary intermingling would be rare. Educational requirements will be vastly different and you will certainly be able to recognize these differences immediately. Questions?"

This time no one gathered the courage to voice a question, even if he or she had one.

"The exo-conceived children will reach puberty at a chronological age of about six. Please be certain that you are not deceived by chronological age in this case and make provision for the sexual education this life-period demands. Naturally, the usual sex education courses will be included in the tapes provided for the education of all children. Questions?"

Again there was silence in the lecture hall. The professor leaned forward across his lectern, draping his hairy arms, which protruded from the white coat, across the stand, then dropping his head and staring at the group over his old-fashioned eyeglasses.

Evelyn thought: He espouses all the ideas of modern science, but will not take advantage of it to heal his precious eyes. That makes me doubt everything he says. She longed to say something to Morris but knew that the wrath of the professor would fall on whomever made the mistake of speaking aloud in his lectures, so she made a mental note to question Morris about his feelings later.

"Exo-conceived children, because they are special and unusual, demand more of our attention than the endo-conceived child. They afford us less time to correct our errors in parenting and are more likely to grow out of control without more supervision than generally given to endo children. You must never lose sight of that concept, no matter what other mistakes you may make in your colonial structures."

He stood, a gesture of dismissal, then leaned forward again, adding, "And I am more than certain that you will make many mistakes. The nature of mankind is many things, all of which are difficult to define. The one thing upon which we may rely, without question, is that the most true nature of mankind is imperfection. That will be all."

Morris leaned over to her as they stood and said, slightly mystified, "It's rumored that he refused the age arresting treatments when he was young. Can you imagine anyone doing that?"

Evelyn had a backache from reading the microtexts while sitting at the console. She touched the "hold" button, stood up, and stretched, flexing her neck in a circular motion and slowly raising her arms over her head, then lowering them. The motion provided some relief from the pressure.

"Maybe I'm having prenatal pains. I'm certainly the foremost authority on decanting in this corner of the universe!"

She left the biolab and walked across the expanse of living area to the door to her shelter. Almost twenty months separated her from the confines of the intergalactic transport that still circled the planet. Another four months would pass, then the huge space structure would leave its orbit, proceeding under the direction of the small on-board computer guiding its actions into deep, unoccupied space, and then it would explode, scattering pieces of technology through the void.

Why the Directors had programmed it to stay for two years was a mystery, since, once the descent shuttle had left it behind, there was no way to return to it. Furthermore, the intergalactic transport was only a shell containing the empty suspended animation capsules in which the colonists had traveled.

In this case, she thought, not empty. Filled with ninety-nine former colonists who were now as much shells as the transport itself, floating through weightless silence, locked in the grip of perpetual preservation by the machine that would soon destroy itself, and them.

And yet, in a bizarre turn of events, they would live on, not only through their gametes stored in the biolab, which would eventually become exo children, but also in the computer, their biological imprints stored in mindlessness by a machine that never forgot.

"Wherever you are up there, my fellow travelers," she whispered to the bright sky, "you have a part in what happens now and for all time on this planet. I hope I can live up to all of our dreams."

She watched a predatory bird circling the plain, hunting. Across the valley, the smoke from the village rose in a column in the still air. She could hear vague animal noises from parts of the valley that she couldn't identify, none of them more than rustlings or barks, until the bird found something to his taste and swooped, coming up with a screaming creature clutched in his claws.

Evelyn felt a slight wrench of nausea as the death scream

suddenly stopped and the bird flew off to its hidden nest in the mountains. "Better you than me."

As she turned to go back to her studies, she was caught by a thought. Tomorrow she would decant four new lives into a world without a name. It was fine for one person to operate without formal designations of location, but not a whole community.

Evelyn returned to the doorway and sat, braced across the frame, surveying her world in a whole new light. "It has to be something symbolic and new." She laughed aloud as she had a mental picture of a committee sitting down to arrive at a name for her new world.

"Aha, Project Directors! I've finally found something big you neglected. Or were you expecting us to make such an important decision on our own? That's hardly your way of doing things. Could it actually be that you'd overlook something?"

She jumped up from her position and hurried to the main computer room. She plopped down in the console chair, activated the library tapes, and tapped in **"Location names."** The computer flashed: **"Library references available: Geography, Earth, Moon, Mars. Colonies; Astronomical names; Historic names, no longer in common use; Oceanographic names; Family names associated with locations; Mythical locations;"** She stopped it before it could continue.

Next she tried, **"Names for new colonies."** Again the computer printed: **"Colonial names: Historical, Religious, Archaic, Fictional, Committee selected."**

"You didn't forget, you old interveners. Let's see what you decided would be appropriate." Evelyn tapped in **"Colonial names, committee selected."**

The viewing screen displayed the library tape reference numbers for her selection, then began printing out the stored information, matching its printing speed with her recorded reading speed. The message spewed out of the library, so typical of everything written by the committee.

"WE ARE PLEASED, DEAR COLONISTS, THAT YOU WOULD SEEK OUR ADVICE IN SOMETHING SO IMPORTANT AS THE SELECTION OF A NAME FOR YOUR NEW PLANET, FINDING A TOUCH WITH THE MOTHER PLANET WHILE YOU ARE SO DISTANT FROM US IN TIME AND SPACE.

AFTER EXTENSIVE STUDY, ANALYSIS, AND DELIBERATION ON YOUR BEHALF, WE HAVE THE FOLLOWING RECOMMENDATIONS:

ONE: SELECT A NAME WHICH IS ACCEPTABLE TO THE ORIGINAL COLONISTS.

TWO: SELECT A NAME WHICH IS COMFORTABLE FOR ALL TO USE.

THREE: PERHAPS THE MOST EFFECTIVE SELECTION PROCESS WOULD BE BY POPULAR VOTE ON A SERIES OF NAMES RECOMMENDED BY YOUR LOCAL GOVERNMENTAL COMMITTEE.

FOUR: WE RECOMMEND THAT YOU DO NOT USE ANY OF THE NAMES IN OUR SOLAR SYSTEM SINCE YOU HAVE NOW ESTABLISHED YOURSELVES IN A NEW AREA AND SHOULD HAVE A NAME APPROPRIATE TO THAT NEWNESS.

FIVE: NAMING A NEW PLANET AFTER A COLONIST MIGHT CAUSE DIFFICULTY IN SOCIAL INTERACTION WITH THAT COLONIST. THEREFORE, IF YOU CHOOSE A PERSONAL NAME, PERHAPS ONE OF THE INFLUENTIAL MEMBERS OF SOCIETY IN EARTH'S HISTORY MIGHT BE MORE APPROPRIATE, SUCH AS LINCOLN, LUTHER, STALIN, OR MANFIELD.

WE WISH YOU SUCCESS IN YOUR ENDEAVORS."

"Well, thank you, gentlemen, for your enlightening instructions." She shook her head, perplexed. "Thank goodness you weren't so vague on the scientific parts of this operation, or I would have been dead months ago. When you fail, you fail!"

She snapped off the viewing screen and returned to the living area of the shelter. She had been busy in the past

month since her discovery of the conversion of local hydrocarbons to necessities, enabling her to produce things she
needed to expand.

Evelyn had added four rooms to the shelter. In one room
she had created her own suite of private living quarters.
She felt the need to have a place where she could be alone,
a recluse from her charges. She had spent too much time
alone in the past twenty months and had come to realize
the value of solitude. It was on that premise that the dormi-
tories had been divided into individual rooms. Her colony
would value aloneness as well as togetherness.

The others were large, dormitory rooms, divided by par-
tition into eight sleeping cubicles each. Each cubicle measured two and a half meters by three meters, which would
be more than adequate for her charges who, by design of
the biolab, would multiply rapidly. She would acquire
eight new members of her society every year for the first
twenty years of colonization, and that could be continued
indefinitely if she, and the others, so desired. There was no
way to prevent biolab from exo-conceiving these children,
so she had to make provision for their presence. The only
saving factor was the doubled rate of maturation and
learning. Without that increased growth, she would be
completely swamped with impossible tasks.

Part of the prenatal learning program was basic education: language and social behavior. As a result of the language and social behavior training, they would be talking
and interacting socially within the first two months.

Another part of the program was what the life science
technicians referred to as precantal movement training.
Before they were decanted, the babies were imprinted with
movement conditioning so that they would be walking by
the time they were about four months old. They were also
preconditioned to toilet training, and all would be independent of diapers by the time they would walk.

Also included in the prenatal program were nutrition
provisions so that the exo-conceived babies would be

healthy. In the nutrients they received, they were also given all the necessary immunizations.

Evelyn walked into the dormitory, now silent and waiting. "By this time tomorrow, I won't be totally alone anymore," she said to the empty cubicles.

Up to that moment, she had held her excitement about the coming event under control. There were so many things that could have gone wrong, but now many of them were past, and the only potential trauma left was the decanting itself.

The excitement swept over her in an avalanche of emotion and she threw back her head and let out a whoop of joy, throwing her arms wide and turning a pirouette, still yelling.

"Human voices! Human bodies! I've done it! Now this is truly my planet and another stronghold for the human race. It's a whole new Eden, but instead of coming from Adam, it's come from me." She paused, suddenly stilled by an idea.

She walked briskly to the door of the shelter. The sun had passed its peak in the sky and was traveling toward the distant hills. The birds circled the plain and life bustled about her. A soft breeze had come up, and the grasses on the plain flowed with the tides of air.

"Pay attention, all of you, because this is important. I hereby claim this world in the name of the human race, and I choose to call it Genesis, the beginning."

With a glow of satisfaction, she returned to the computer and sat at the console. On the keyboard, she entered, "History: Planet Genesis. Perpetual entry, verbatim. Please indicate library catalog reference."

The computer responded, "Library reference: 010-000001."

Evelyn then entered: "Include in 010-000001 all data collected concerning present location and planet in appropriate subcategories."

She waited while the machine searched its library for

everything relating to this planet, then printed it out on the screen as it changed the classifications. She was surprised to note that the machine substituted *Genesis* for the word *Planet* as it transferred the information.

When the computer had finished, she settled into the console chair, bending over the keyboard, her studies about the new babies forgotten as she recorded the history of her new home from the day she had arrived.

Chapter Five

IT WAS RAINING. Evelyn awoke in her living quarters, hearing the gentle tapping of the rain on the roof surface of the shelter and the gurgling as the water flowed into the storage tanks under and behind the shelter.

She was waking slowly, languishing between dream and real worlds when the realization of the decanting jolted her awake with a rush of excitement, and she hurried from the sleeping mat and into her light coverall, stopping only for a brief moment in the sonar cleanser. She brushed her long hair, then caught it into a knot at the back of her head to keep it out of her way.

The food processor's presence in the main room reminded her that she had skipped eating the day before and she selected a hearty breakfast.

While the machine set about fulfilling her requests, she went to the dormitory she had prepared for the four new colonists and retrieved the four wheeled cribs she had made, placing them side by side in the biolab. The design of the cribs was plain and utilitarian, but she had given in to a whim and had painted cartoon animals on each of them. She had also made soft animal-shaped toys for the new babies from the fabric her processing machine produced.

The idea for the decorations and toys had come from an old reference text in the library tapes. It had apparently been used extensively in the middle twentieth as a guide for raising children. The author had some good ideas and some that seemed even radical to Evelyn's experiences. She had found, to her surprise, that she referred more and more to the wisdom of the late Dr. Spock in her ideas about raising these children.

Her breakfast was accompanied by one more review of the decanting procedure. It was deceptively simple: receive the child from the growth capsule, check the child's physical structure and function with the biolab, cleanse him and use the antibiotic ointment to protect his skin, then place him in a warm, relatively enclosed space.

Deceptively simple, but with much room for error. She had only held a baby once before, long ago on Earth, and was worried about the slipperiness of the child's body coming from the liquid environment of the capsule. She was also concerned about being correct in interpreting the tests for normalcy. There were so many variables to assess in such a short period of time, for she had only ten minutes between decantings.

As she ate, she used calming yoga to clean her mind of all but the immediate problem. The blockage worked and she felt the details of the decanting come together in her mind, restoring her confidence in her ability to perform the necessary tasks.

The monotone voice of the computer interrupted her meditation. "Attention, please. Biolab reproductive function warning. Please prepare for conclusion of cycle. Attention, please. Biolab reproductive function warning. Please prepare for conclusion of cycle...."

The voice accompanied her as she walked across the room and into the biolab, continuing its insistent warning until she reached the console and entered: "Prepared for cycle conclusion."

The computer stopped in midsentence, leaving a momentary silence in the room. Then, to Evelyn's surprise, music filled the room, calming gentle music from the mideighteenth century. The lights in the biolab dimmed, red filters sliding silently into place. Evelyn felt a strange, calming security flow over her as she settled into the console chair at the exit port of the growth capsules.

The panel covering the exit port slid aside and the first capsule appeared. Mechanical grippers inside the biolab turned the capsule, matching the opening in the container with the exit port.

Evelyn felt her heart thudding as though at a distance, as the child began to emerge from the capsule, a fuzz of blonde hair covering its head. The mechanical grippers assisted the baby's emergence from the capsule, sliding it gently onto the receiving platform.

Evelyn was hypnotized with fascination at the process. The baby was fully emerged and the first member of her new colony was a boy, now waving his arms and kicking in protest at the change in his environment. He drew his first breath and his cry of aggravation galvanized her to action. The mechanical grippers ignored his wiggling, neatly severing the umbilical connection to the biolab, tying it off, then retreating into the biolab.

Evelyn picked up the slippery, screaming child, her instincts taking over, and moved to the examination table. She set him down in the middle of the soft cloth covering the table, keeping a restraining hand in the middle of his stomach while she reached for the examination recorder. Slowly she moved the rod over his body, watching the printout on the screen.

He was perfect, according to the medical report, and she spoke soft reassurance to him as she cleaned the tiny body with warm water containing antibiotics and moisturizers.

He was still yelling protests at the unfamiliar activity,

and she was puzzled at how to get him to stop. She checked the elapsed time monitor which showed that she had five minutes until the next emergence.

She was reaching for a diaper when she felt a warm wetness spreading down her arm. "Well, little one, now we know that part of you is working, too."

She diapered him, wrapped him in a new blanket, and held him for a moment, looking down at his wrinkled face.

"Welcome to Genesis," she said softly to the baby. He stopped crying as she held him, rocking slightly back and forth. One small hand, balled into a fist, emerged from the blanket and waved aimlessly.

Evelyn walked slowly to the line of cribs, cooing to the baby, then set him into the first one in line. His face screwed up and he began to cry again.

"You'll just have to cry for a while, friend. I've got work to do. I have to go get your next compatriot."

She rubbed his stomach gently, and his crying slowed down. "That's a good boy."

He stirred in the blanket, then began to cry again when the warning buzzer sounded that the next baby was ready for decanting.

Evelyn, ignoring his insistent howl, returned to the exit port where the grippers had already begun the second decanting. This time it wasn't so overwhelming to her and she knew when to assist.

The second baby was a girl, dark curls covering her head. Her cry was much softer and stopped sooner than the boy's. She, too, checked out as physically perfect and Evelyn had more time to spend with her because her skills were improving in cleansing and diapering.

Evelyn placed her into the second crib, then stood between the two cribs, patting both babies. The boy watched her, sucking his tiny fist, and the girl began to fall asleep.

"I know who's going to be easier already."

The warning buzzer sounded again, and she returned to the exit port, assisting confidently with the decanting. The third baby was another boy, dark haired and the most vocal of the three. He continued to yell all during the physical check, cleansing, and diapering. She picked him up, rocking back and forth, but even that didn't stop his animated vocalizing. His noisiness started the other two and the chorus accompanied her back to receive the fourth baby.

The baby had partly emerged by the time she returned and she reached to help the grippers, almost without looking at the child. The machine seemed to be having difficulty producing the final child, and Eve directed her attention to the baby, realizing the source of the problem as she focused on it.

The child was mutant, its head and upper body badly deformed, grotesque and monstrous. Evelyn felt a rush of nausea, but fought it back, knowing that she had to be in control, but also knowing the decision that would be made. Entwined with that fear was the worry of what had gone wrong with the computer. It should never have allowed the child to grow at all. Eve felt terror rising. What if the computer produced mutants in every decanting?

The baby, fully decanted, was a girl. It took a breath and began to cry, as had the others, but even its cry was inhuman. The grippers severed the umbilical cord, then retreated into the biolab, the exit port closing behind them, leaving Eve alone with her decision.

She picked up the howling monster and moved it to the examination table. Knowing the outcome, she moved the examination rod over the tiny, deformed body, watching the printout, her eyes avoiding the child. The printout indicated a myriad of physical malfunctions, finalizing the inevitable decision.

"Stand clear. Stand clear." The mechanical voice of the biolab injected reality into Evelyn. She backed away from the table, watching in horror as an opaque hood emerged from under the table and covered the child. Her last view of the baby was obliterated by the hood. Its cry stopped

abruptly, and the printout stated coldly, "Hydrocarbon recycle," a mechanical euphemism for murder.

The hood retreated, revealing the empty examination
table. Evelyn was weak and shaking. She knew that the
machine was programmed to eliminate mutants, a programming which had been added because so many exo and
endo mutants had emerged after the nuclear wars on
Earth. It was a clear, standing order, but seeing it happen
removed it from the abstract in an abrupt and horrible
way.

She slid into the chair at the console, still staring at the
table, fighting to reassume control.

"... And if you don't watch out, the mutants will get you
and take you to their caves in the mountains." Billy's voice
carried the implied threat that he knew how to encourage the
mutants to do just that, and seven-year-old Evelyn cowered in
fear.

Billy was the twelve-year-old son of the family who lived
next door. He was large for his age, especially for an endo, and
had all the children in the complex terrorized into doing his
bidding. Evelyn had defied him, refusing to give up her treasured seashell, recovered from the very edge of the ocean in
direct defiance of her mother's orders to stay away from the
polluted water that was so poisonous. It was a small shell,
swirling in on itself. The inside held all the colors of the rain-
bow trapped in its pearly luminescence, and she adored it,
carrying it everywhere. Now Billy had demanded it as a token
of subservience.

"No they won't." Evelyn clutched the tiny shell in her hand,
protecting it from Billy and steeling herself against the expected violence.

He came closer to her, menacing her into the corner of the
hallway. She looked beyond him, seeking some sort of aid, but
the hallway was deserted. She put the hand holding the shell
behind her, covering her head and face with the other arm.

"Give it to me, or I'll beat you up." Billy loomed large over *her and she shrank farther into the corner, crouching down and ducking her head.*

"No. It's mine and I love it. You won't hit me because I'll tell your mother." Her position belied the bravado in her voice.

Billy's advance stopped as he weighed the threat. He was well aware that his mother would not take kindly to violence toward this smaller child, but he really wanted the shell, if for no other reason than a symbol of his personal power in the complex.

"The mutants will get you if you don't do what I want. Now give me the shell." He used his ultimate threat again.

Evelyn lifted her head, looking into his face with the fiercest expression she could muster. "What makes you think the mutants won't get you for hurting me?"

Billy looked shocked, then fearful. He didn't retreat, but she had obviously found a weak spot in his bravado and she pressed her advantage.

"They're looking for you now, Billy, because you're so mean, and pretty soon they'll be here to get you and take you to their caves." She studied him carefully, seeing the fear rising in him. "They'll make you do all their work and beat you and you'll never hurt me again."

She could feel her victory approaching and delivered the final blow, looking directly into his eyes.

"They're coming down the hallway right now, so you'd better run."

Billy turned in panic, and she used the diversion to bound from the corner and run toward her apartment. Billy's surprise put him off-balance and gave her the few extra seconds she needed to reach the door.

As she frantically pushed her palm against the lock, she could hear him approaching, and she bounced up and down with fear and urgency, waiting for the door to slide open. As soon as the crack was wide enough, she slid through to the safety of her home, knowing that Billy wouldn't come into the apartment.

He reached the threshold and stood there, glaring at her.

Through his gasping breath, he hissed, "You'll be sorry you did that. I'll get you and your lousy shell, too. Just you wait."

Hurling his final threat, he stomped off in search of easier prey.

"Eve, what was all that about?" Her mother stood behind her, a concerned expression on her face.

"Nothing. I just told Billy that the mutants were after him and he got mad at me." She kept the forbidden shell hidden as she touched the switch close to the door.

"That boy! He's going to hurt one of you children someday. Please stay away from him, Evelyn, or I'll have to punish you. You mustn't provoke him that way when you know what kind of a boy he is. What about your schoolwork? Is it done?"

"Yes, it's done. Can I help you do something?" Evelyn was relieved to have the subject concluded. Any mention of Billy's behavior to his parents would simply provoke further threats and attacks, and she knew that her use of the mutants could only work once.

"Come on, you can help me with dinner." Evelyn's mother disappeared into the food processing center and Evelyn followed, putting her shell into a fold of her tunic. She wasn't absolutely sure of what a mutant was, but she was secure that she could control them if they ever came around. After all, they'd just proven themselves to be friends.

Now she was no longer secure about that control. The mutant that had emerged from the biolab had begun life as a human being, but the genetic message had gone wrong and it had grown into a monster. It had been a simple matter for the biolab to simply dispose of the offending organism, and she knew the reasons that it was necessary. Still, it was a human creature with a mind and she was badly shaken by the experience.

The crying of the babies reminded her that she had responsibilities to the other three lives and she was glad for the diversion from her thoughts. She was grateful that the mutant had been the last to be decanted, for had it been the

first, she might not have been able to care for the three
normal children.

The two boys were crying lustily, but the little girl lay
between them, sucking her tiny fist and watching Eve bend
over her. One by one, she wheeled the cribs into the waiting
dormitory and hooked up the feeding tubes. The food processor would give each child a measured amount of nourish-
ment concentrate at each feeding, enriching their bodies
for the rapid growth that would occur.

The two boys ate eagerly, sucking at the nipple on the
tube. The little girl sucked quietly, cooing contentedly. Evelyn watched each as they ate, amazed at the differences
showing in their personalities already.

"It really shouldn't surprise me, I guess. You're all from
completely different genetic matches, but I didn't really expect to see personalities so soon."

The first boy finished eating and fell asleep with the nipple still in his mouth. Dr. Spock had said that a baby
should always be burped after eating, so she picked him up,
holding him against her shoulder and patting his back
gently. She was rewarded with a small burp. Dr. Spock also
cautioned that a baby should be encouraged to sleep on his
stomach, so she returned him to his crib, then rolled him
over. He was asleep instantly.

She repeated the process with the other two and left
them sleeping as she returned to the computer room, trying
not to think about the fourth child. She was personally offended by its mutancy but felt some responsibility for its
death, and was distressed by the emotional conflict.

She sat at the console, yanking her mind away from the
mutant child. An old saying, "Don't brood on what's done,"
popped into her mind, and seemed somehow to settle some
of the distress she felt.

She was curious about the background of her new
charges and requested information from the computer library.

She had ignored this aspect before their decanting, but

now it could be entered into the permanent records of Genesis, and she waited impatiently for the records to emerge.

The computer began its response to her requests: **"Genetic history: first child decanted, male. Female gamete source: Marilyn Kay Ferguson, 339-12-4590, United Europe, northern sector. Intelligence rated at 162; no genetic aberrations indicated; height, one meter, sixty-five centimeters; physiology, normal; hair, blonde; eyes, blue; complexion, fair. Chosen career: genophysicist. Male gamete source: Harold Kenneth Clarkton, 541-07-8009, United North America, southern sector. Intelligence rated at 159; no genetic aberrations indicated; height, one meter, ninety-six centimeters; physiology, normal; hair, blonde; eyes, brown; complexion, fair. Chosen career: nuclear fusion technician."**

Evelyn pushed the hold button on the computer, trying to visualize what her first colonist would look like on the foundation of his genetic background. It was fairly certain that he would be rather tall and blonde, probably quite intelligent, and perhaps the first scientist of the colony, but could determine nothing else from the sterile information.

She released the hold button, allowing the printout to continue.

"Record information as requested: Date decanted."

Evelyn entered the date, according to her local calendar.

"Name designation:"

Evelyn hesitated. She had vaguely thought about naming the children, but hadn't made any decisions. Now she was confronted with making them quickly. The computer hummed patiently, waiting for her. Finally, she reached her decision, leaned forward, and tapped in: **"Kenneth Ferguson Clarkton."** She felt it was important to continue the chain of humanity begun so far away.

"Numerical designation:"

Evelyn thought for a moment, then tapped in: **"001-111-0002."** She decided she would give herself a new number, different from her Earth designation, so, logically, she should be number 0001 and the designations would increase from that point.

The computer seemed satisfied with her answers, so she tapped in: **"Enter in permanent records, planet Genesis, under number designation, colonist information."**

The computer whirred as it transferred the information adding the medical records from the decanting, then presented the genetic history of the second child.

"Genetic history: second child decanted, female. Female gamete source: Elizabeth Ellen Waters, 492-90-6092, United West Asia, northern sector. Intelligence rated at 154; no genetic aberrations indicated; height, one meter, fifty-five centimeters; physiology, normal; hair, black; eyes, brown; complexion, dark. Chosen career: ecobalance technician. Male gamete source: Alexander James Ashanti, 227-301-9547, United African States, central sector. Intelligence rated at 171; no genetic aberrations indicated; height, two meters, three centimeters; physiology, normal; hair, black; eyes, brown; complexion, dark. Chosen career, educator.

Record information requested: date decanted."

Evelyn entered the date, then pushed the "hold" button, deciding on a name for her only girl. Decided, she released the button, tapping in the name.

"Name designation: Ellen Waters Ashanti
Numerical designation: 001-111-0003."

Evelyn added, **"Enter in permanent records,"** and the computer continued with the record of the third child.

"Genetic history: third child decanted, male. Female gamete source: Ann Louise Marks, 380-051-0568, United South America, southern sector. Intelligence rated at 165; no genetic aberrations indicated; height, one meter, seventy-two centimeters; physiology, normal; hair, brown; eyes, brown; complexion, fair. Chosen career: medicosurgical technician. Male gamete source: Morris Edward Watson, 243-346-5543, United Europe, northern sector—"

Evelyn lunged for the "hold" button, staring at the printout. Could it possibly be an accident or had the Directors really shown some compassion for their forced separation?

Evelyn nestled into Morris's shoulder, seeking a more comfortable resting place in her half-sleeping state. He stirred in response to her movement, curling his arm around her.

They had made love with great intensity, almost violently trying to absorb each other. Both knew the time for parting was rapidly approaching, so both studiously avoided the subject.

"Evelyn, there's something we have to talk about."

She stirred against his arm, resisting the wakefulness, but knowing she had to face it. "I don't want to."

He moved her hair to expose her ear. "Ever?"

She shook her head slightly. "Ever. I just have one thing to say. I love you."

He kissed her exposed ear. "I love you too, and I'm sorry they couldn't make the change in the crews. I really tried, Eve, but they…"

"I thought we weren't going to talk about it. We're a month from isolation, so let's just take advantage of that time. But, please, let's not talk about it."

Eve stared at the records, sifting through the project people in her head, trying to remember Ann Louise Marks, but the name didn't sound familiar. She wouldn't have had to be, for gametes were taken from nonproject sources as well, from the finalists who weren't chosen as well as from some of the leaders and scientists who hadn't taken the age arresting treatments.

She released the "hold" button and the computer continued its printout: **"Intelligence rated at 187; no genetic aberrations indicated; height, two meters, three centimeters; physiology, normal; hair, black; eyes, brown; complexion, dark. Chosen career: Project Group IV, astrophysicist."**

Eve watched the printout screen as the information disappeared to be replaced with **"Record information requested: date decanted."**

She tapped in the date, then knowing what the machine would next request, added, **"Morris Mark Watson, 001-111-0004. Enter in permanent records."**

She leaned back in the console chair, absorbing the idea of another Morris entering her world and almost regretted naming him after his father, even though that had been her decision with the others. She would have to be careful not to ingrain any of Morris's characteristics on his child and allow him to grow into his own person.

"So now," she said to the computer, "the population of Genesis is four." The statement brought back the memory of the mutant child and she leaned to the console, unable to control her curiosity, tapping in **"Fourth child decanted—information requested."**

The computer hummed with what Evelyn would have sworn was disapproval, then printed out: **"Fourth child decanted: Mutant. Hydrocarbon recycled. Information removed from records."**

"Computer, it makes me furious when you do things like that. I'm the Chairman here, not you, and there are certain things I want to know. Don't tell me it's none of my business."

She pushed away from the console and wandered into the nursery. She checked each crib, noticing that the viewing screen in each had been activated and was filled with ever-changing shapes in bright colors. Soft music accompanied the video, but all three babies were oblivious, each sleeping peacefully.

Ellen's little fist was in her mouth, but she wasn't sucking and Eve was afraid to move it in case she'd wake up. Besides, Eve remembered reading that the sucking impulse would be natural in babies, so it was all right to let them suck if they wanted to.

She went out of the door to survey her valley. In the distance, the smoke rose, trailing away like a banner over the far village.

"You all might be interested to know that there are three

new additions to the population of Genesis today. Ellen, Kenneth, and Morris arrived early this morning and are resting now, but you'll have a chance to meet them later."

One of the wide-winged birds circled lazily over the valley and the transport ship gleamed in the sunlight, but there was no visible reaction to her announcement.

"You'll begin to care," she said, sitting down in the doorway. "When we overrun this place. Then you'll wish you'd paid attention to me now."

She felt a letdown after the decanting as if there should be something more. The babies were all sleeping peacefully, named, recorded, and here she was, sitting in the sun. "Nothing to this mothering business," she thought.

Of course, she would have help from the computer. It had already begun presenting learning experiences to the babies. Shapes, colors, written words, and numbers would flow across the screen accompanied by words and music to condition the children to life in the world.

With a start she realized that the education they would receive was the same as all humans on Earth had received for a long time, and she wondered if, in that education, there was a built-in tendency to make the same mistakes that had driven her and the others out into space in one last desperate lunge at salvation.

It couldn't be the numbers and basic science because those were just tools necessary to the daily mode of living. The same was true of shapes, colors, and words.

She stood up, fists clenched in concentration. Language. There was the culprit, or at least the beginning of the problem, for language could communicate aggression, anger, and hatred, all of which had been part of the problem on Earth.

If she could modify the language training in the computer, as well as the history tapes which recorded all of man's mistakes and wars, she could perhaps eliminate aggression in her own society. After all, the rules were hers to

make in this world and she didn't want to see another
Earth.

*Evelyn had always loved school, but history classes had
never been her favorites. While she had lived at home, her
father's vivid interest in anything scholastic had kept her interested in the history courses. He could make her see the total
picture of how history flowed, beyond the wars and documents and people involved. Now she was in community
school and found herself getting lost in dry detail, unable to
re-create his enthusiasm.*

"*In the wars of the nineteen-nineties, we experienced the
first use of nuclear weapons on a general level, although you
will remember that nuclear weapons had been used in what
was referred to as World War Two, occurring in the early for-
ties of that same century. During the period between those two
major wars, there were several local instances of fighting: in
the southeast region of United Asia, which was then called
Vietnam; in the Middle East Region was a religious war between two long-standing opposing philosophies; outbreaks on
the borders between the old countries of China and Russia,
caused by a vague ideological difference between the two com-
munist countries; and, of course, the great African struggle,
which some scholars still refer to as the Third World War.*" *The
professor looked around the lecture hall, then leaned forward,
eyeing them all.*

"*I am well aware that history is not the highest interest in
this science-oriented school, but I would expect the necessary
respect from all of you for the past of your race. Hopefully, you
will learn from the mistakes of others.*" *There was a rustling in
the lecture hall of embarrassed students. The school was
science-oriented, as was most of the world, seeking relief from
the damages which had been done.*

"*Now, with respect to the nuclear wars of the nineteen-
nineties, the entry of nuclear weapons in the war theaters
were, at first, restricted to small-yield bombs in relatively deserted areas, primarily considered to be threats more than vehicles of destruction. Documents of that period indicate the*

*world leaders on both sides of the conflict were well aware of
the implications of the use of nuclear weapons not only to the
population of the world, but also to its ecological and energy
resources."*

Evelyn moved the recorder to her other knee, shifting in her
seat. What offended her about history was the repetition of it.
Every history course she had ever taken had talked about the
same wars, the same destruction, the same catastrophes and
the same regrets and recriminations on the part of the leaders
once it was over. Each professor would tell them that war was
wrong, and each would give them every gory detail with the
same relish. They seemed to enjoy man's failings as if they
were more right than their predecessors because they could
identify the problems and therefore were better people.

She knew where the course was going as she'd heard it all
before: nuclear wars in the nineteen-nineties; laser wars of the
twenty-thirties; biological wars of the twenty-seventies; hydrocarbon wars of the twenty-one-teens; and finally the orbi-
tal wars of the twenty-one-eighties after everyone claimed they
had finally eradicated war forever.

After the last wars, government had been turned over to the
United Governments with one Chairman. But, by then it was
too late; there was no Earth left to save. While the militaries
had fought over the ever-diminishing habitable lands, the in-
dustries had gone on sucking up the last resources to build the
machinery of war, the diplomats had created the facade of
peace while planning their next assaults, and the scientists
had labored to undo the ravages on the people and the planet.

Her father claimed that was the biggest mistake of all, for,
in an effort to save lives, they had found the key to arresting
the aging process. The people of Earth, tired of being surrounded by death and destruction, had heaped awards and
praise upon those men. They had been called the Murderers of
Death and had been almost canonized.

Her own grandfather had been one of them, but he had refused to use the treatment himself. She remembered seeing a
tape of him pleading with world leaders to ban the use of the

treatments. He had been ignored, even ridiculed, and had died, hating himself and the world he helped to create.

Her parents had both had the treatments for their own reasons, in their thirtieth chronological year, and had celebrated their decision. Her grandfather, she had heard from an aunt, had tried to prevent them from doing it, claiming that the Earth would never be able to support the population that would explode. They had called him foolish, citing the Zero Law of Propagation that would prevent just that. Over time, however, her father had come to see her grandfather's wisdom, regretting the choice he had made and becoming an activist against the procedure.

Her aunt, an unlicensed breeder, had been bitter about that law and claimed it was unfair. She had shown a genetic weakness in the testing for license and hadn't been allowed to breed. The man with whom she was in love was an available breeder, so they were not allowed to marry and she had remained single.

Eve, sitting in the pale sunlight of Genesis, thought how much she'd like to have Aunt Rosemary here now. She had directed her energies, frustrated in one area, into philosophy and psychosciences and she was fascinating to be around. She had, through her studies, eventually come to realize exactly what it was her father had objected to.

The population of the Earth, under the strict rules of the Zero Law, had maintained its level of about four billion, but two other things occurred.

First, each year fewer and fewer people died. The first fifty years, there were many deaths. People who had been unable to take the treatments for reasons of age, illness, or deformity had let their lives take the natural course. Many children were born to maintain the balance. After those deaths began to diminish, the government allowed fewer and fewer breeders. Only one couple in ten thousand, matching the annual death rate, was allowed to produce a child.

This led to great resentment on the part of the disallowed

until living complexes were built for those who had children, isolating them for twelve years from the rest of the population. As their child reached the age of twelve, the parents were transferred to work locations where their skills were needed and the children to community schools for ten years of intensive education.

The rest of the population, with some notable holdouts, were all locked at age thirty. Chronologically, there were differences, but they were not apparent to the eye, and the children didn't enter the mainstream of society until after they were twenty-two. The adjustments were difficult for all concerned.

Secondly, even though the population remained at one size, the resources of the Earth began to diminish. Hydrocarbons dwindled, and even with the extensive recycling of used materials, shortages were a way of life. Schools and other information sources stressed the need to conserve, but an irreversible natural loss of hydrocarbons occurred in usage of a synthesized product. Scientists began predicting the end of the world.

It wasn't a difficult prediction. The nuclear wars had contaminated vast areas of land, wiping out the vegetation and earth-stored hydrocarbons and forcing the population into small, relatively clean living areas where enormous complexes of buildings rose hundreds of feet into the dirty skies, each inch used efficiently. They were all sealed, the outside air too contaminated to breathe over long periods of time. The areas on Earth where one could be outside almost without damage were held as public preserves, and vacations were scheduled carefully to allow each member of the population to take advantage of them at least once every five years.

But each year those relatively untainted areas became smaller, less desirable, more polluted. They had been able to reopen some of the really old contaminated areas, but people were afraid to live there, fearful of the lingering radiation and incurable sickness it produced.

The biological wars shared the blame. They had wasted the land, preventing the growth of vegetation and introducing man-made viruses the scientists were unable to kill.

But the worst had been the hydrocarbon wars. At the beginning of the twenty-first century, only three sources of oil, the most concentrated and therefore the most desirable hydrocarbons, still remained: the Middle Eastern Region, the Arctic Region, and the Asian Region, and those areas were jealously guarded by the countries which owned them.

The Arctic hydrocarbons finally ran out and the Asian were rapidly following. The countries of the world, desperate for hydrocarbons for synthesis, had paid terrible prices for the remaining Middle Eastern oil, while those countries grew in wealth and power until finally they united and it became the Middle East against the rest of the world in open hostility.

The other countries surrounded the oil powers with troops, lasers, and nuclear weapons and demanded the oil be released to everyone to share equally. The oil powers laughed in their faces, setting up their own defenses, determined to hold the world in the grip of an embargo.

But the non-oil powers were beyond threats and embargoes. They set a deadline after which they would attack. Hiding under a cloak of silence, the trapped and angry oil powers opened the valves of their reserve tanks and wells, allowing the oil to spread out over the land and flow into the sea.

When the non-oil powers' intelligence systems reported this, they attacked. During the fifteen weeks of the war, the oil had continued to run out, polluting the land and sea, and depleting the resources even further.

When the non-oil powers finally won, they rushed to turn off the flow, but the damage had been done. The oil slick in the seas continued to spread, killing fish and animals, as well as the oceans themselves.

The final nuclear wars, the Orbit Wars, had dealt the

coup de grace to Earth, contaminating the upper air with
fatal pollution and blocking the healing sunlight which
might have helped Earth to recover. The scientists, seeing
the inevitable, went to the new Chairman of the United
Governments with a scheme to save the race, and the
Project was started.

The transports had been built in space, orbiting between
the Earth and the Moon, equipped with the untried warp
engines, the suspended animation capsules, and the most
advanced computers ever developed. It united the Earth in
the effort to build and create the best for the travelers.

The Project spanned almost fifty years between the moment of its conception and the final departure. The competition for the thousand Project memberships and hundred
alternates had been intense.

Looking out over the green valley, Eve realized how accustomed she had become to the beauty and cleanliness of
it, compared to the filth and pollution of the Earth, and she
was struck again with her luck to be here instead of dying
with her home planet. She looked out across the valley, an
intensity of resolution reflecting in her face. "I won't allow
that here. These children will grow up believing that war
and violence and hatred are wrong and that they must preserve and respect their planet."

The hunting birds continued circling in the sky overhead
and the smoke rose from the village across the valley, lazily
sending its message of life, reminding Evelyn of a further
responsibility to this planet: the protection of those gentle
creatures she had observed so long ago.

PART II

Chapter Six

———◆———

EVELYN STOOD IN the door of the complex listening absently to the din of activity behind and above her. She was glad that she had taken the time and energy to add the two upper floors of room for the children as her population grew. Now she had enough room for the next five years of population growth and, by that time, there would be others who could assist in the construction.

Thirty-nine children, with a four-year age range and an eight-year maturity range, made a tremendous amount of noise simply in pursuit of normal activities. It astounded her that the infants could sleep through it, but they did with a comfortable complacency. Each infant had an older child to attend to its needs for feeding and diapering, so at least she was spared that work, though that had only come about with the maturity of her first seven.

She was daily more grateful for the doubling of maturity in the exo-conceived children. Without it, she would be thoroughly exhausted instead of just tired most of the time.

The Project Directors, she was sure, never imagined that
there would only be one adult to deal with their baby machine or they never would have programmed it for eight a
year. Her latest four infants were now a month old and
would soon begin the learning process which would have
them talking, walking, and out of diapers in another three
months.

As the next four arrived, they would take over the infant
nursery and these four would move into the individual
compartments they would occupy until they were adults.
Each compartment contained a bed, storage space, a desk,
and a viewing screen for learning and amusement. Each
viewing screen had a small computer terminal for program
selection, but Eve could override the selections with the
main board to prevent "hookey playing."

She had been careful to eliminate certain programming
from the lesson tapes, and had added other lessons, stressing love, cooperation, sharing, and caring, to strengthen
the negativity of hatred, violence, aggressiveness, and
thoughtlessness. She was careful in her dealing with each
of the children to demonstrate courtesy and affection, and
to gently chastise the behavior she considered to be antisocial.

So far, she reflected, it was going well. Of course, there
were the typical childhood squabbles over toys and territory, but in each case, she attempted to use them as learning experiences for the children and felt they proved a
successful tool.

She had little with which to compare her children, for
she had not been one of the ones in her group trained in
child-rearing. She regretted now that she hadn't at least
audited some of the classes, but at the time it had seemed
like a waste of energy, for the ten who were designated for
those tasks in her project group were competent and interested. Now they were atoms spread across space and she
was contending with her own personal population explosion.

The valley looked the same, pale grasses flowing in the gentle winds, wide-winged predators floating across the sky, and the plumes of smoke across the valley declaring that they were not alone.

Eve smiled at an outburst of childish giggling behind her, remembering how she had stood in this same place seven years ago, fearing for her life and sanity in the overwhelming silence of her new home. Now it was more familiar than Earth, which had begun to pale in her memory, though she had noticed the other day how much Morris was beginning to look like his father and it had wrenched her heart. She still missed him greatly and had to struggle to keep him in perspective in her memory so that he didn't become faultless and larger-than-life. It was difficult. She thought of him often, particularly when she was trying to make a difficult decision and needed another adult mind to try it out on. She would conjure him up, sitting in the doorway, looking out at the constellations in the night sky, pulling him to her across the vast reaches of space. Sometimes she would almost see him there, sitting beside her in the quiet nights, the only noises coming from sleeping children and humming machinery performing household chores in unobtrusive ways. They would talk, Evelyn aloud and Morris in her mind, and she would try things out on him. He had approved of her plan to spare the children the knowledge of war and hatred, she had sensed it.

Sometimes she wondered if he had died in the space transport and if his spirit had somehow found her. Other times she wondered if she had become schizophrenic. She wasn't sure of the answer. She tried to remember the others in the Project, to use them as a means of comparison, but they were all shadows without form or substance. She couldn't remember much about them, physically or psychologically.

The entertainment tapes were some help, but the people were all in situations so unrelated to her own, she found it difficult to draw comparisons. She had found herself getting lost in the stories and enjoying the films. She remembered with a smile the times when she had turned off the tapes in the middle, unable to watch anymore because it had reminded her too much of her isolation. Now she would sometimes think she'd like to have some of that isolation back again.

"Excuse me, Eve, have you got a minute to spend with me?" Ellen's voice was soft, matching her personality. She had the gentle Oriental eyes of her mother combined with the proud carriage and brown skin of her father's race, and Eve knew she would be a beauty when she grew up.

Evelyn smiled, putting her hand on Ellen's shoulder. "Of course, Ellen. Are the babies all right?"

Ellen nodded seriously. "Oh, yes. They're all sleeping now." She shook her head. "I don't know how you used to take care of all of us before we could help. It must have been very hard."

Eve stooped down and put her arms around Ellen, giving her a hug. "It wasn't easy, dear, but much of what we've been through hasn't been easy. Remember, we're pioneers, just like many people in our history, who have gone to new lands to make a life for themselves. Have you looked at the tapes about the pioneers in Earth's history?"

Ellen nodded. "But we're different from them, Eve, because they were grown up."

"You'll be grown up soon, Ellen, and we'll still be pioneers here for a long time to come. There's so much of this planet that has to be explored and eventually colonized. Someday, we'll have cities all over this world, and transports will run between them. If you're living in one of those cities and I'm living here, you can come to visit me and we'll have a good time talking with each other."

Ellen thought for a moment, her pretty face serious, then said, "I think I'd like to just keep living here and helping with the babies. That way we can see each other all the time."

Eve hugged her again. "We'll leave it open to see what's going to happen. What did you want to talk about?"

"Well, I've been thinking about what career I want and I need some advice."

Eve sat down in the doorway and Ellen joined her. Eve had discovered that when Ellen wanted to discuss something it was usually important, even if only to her, and she would give the child her attention. The children didn't have to focus on career studies until they finished their preliminary learning tapes, at about the chronological age of eight, so Ellen still had four years to make up her mind. Eve knew that Ellen, Morris, Kenneth, Jeremy, Cilia, Janet, and Mark all talked about it among themselves.

They were the first seven and she called them her deputies. Ellen, Cilia, Jeremy, and Kenneth were the best with the new babies, gentle and confident with them, and Morris and Janet were the most interested in the mechanical functions of the various computer operations.

Mark, she knew, would choose one of the medical fields for his work because he spent hours in the biolab helping her monitor the growing lives there, as well as learning to use the medical functions to repair the normal scrapes and injuries of the other children.

They were all good students as well, interested in and dedicated to their studies. The deputies tended to be a bit cliquish toward the other children, and Evelyn had heard Jeremy telling one of the younger ones that they were the first seven, so they were the best. She had intervened to quell his egotism, explaining that they were the eldest, but that no group was the "best" and that everyone was equal on Genesis.

Eve returned her attention to the child beside her.

"What jobs are you thinking about, Ellen?"

"Well," her black eyes surveyed the valley, "I really like the babies and like being around them. That might be a good career, but I also like the valley. I sometimes come out here and just watch the grasses and birds and trees, and I think I might like to do something with that."

Eve smiled. "They're both good areas of interest, Ellen, and both necessary to the colony. You still have plenty of time to make up your mind, you know."

"Yes, but I don't want to wait until all the good jobs are taken by someone else."

Evelyn's father leaned back in his chair and studied her with slight amusement.

"Honey, this list," his gesture indicated a printout sheet on the table, "is not a restriction, it's a treasure map. Knowledge is the treasure of mankind and this list of suggested careers for the people in your group gives you a wealth of choices. I don't understand why you're upset."

Eve was spending the weekend with them in their new apartment in the southwest sector of North America where both her parents had been assigned to work on the Project: her father on the warp drive mechanism, her mother on the bio-lab.

"Because, Daddy, I want to be an ecobiologist and it's not on the list."

"So, you'll have to make another choice. Your grandfather had encouraged me to be a philosopher when I was young, but when my time came to choose a profession, we were just entering the uniform classification system, and 'philosopher' was nowhere to be found. So, I became a part-time philosopher and a full-time space propulsion engineer. I enjoy both equally."

Eve looked at the racks of book tapes ranging along the walls of the apartment, floor to ceiling. They were the working tools of her father's avocation and she knew that he had absorbed all of them, sitting in front of the viewing screen, sometimes far into the night, reading and thinking.

There were times that her Aunt Rosemary would come over to the apartment and the two of them would have great, involved debates, tempting each other with logic puzzles to change one or another's ideas.

Eve was aware that her father was watching her, so she reached again for the list of careers which would be open to her group. She had to choose three, in order of preference, for there were limited openings in each area, and she wanted to be sure that her third choice was as interesting to her as her first.

Once the choices were submitted by the students, they would be given a series of tests to determine interests, intelligence, motivation, and maturity levels, then these results would be matched against their job choice.

In some cases, the student monitors would counsel them to make other choices, based on the tests. Finally, the computer would choose the best person for the job to be filled and their training in that field would begin.

"Daddy, what does a 'Domestic Environment Planner' do?"

"That, my darling girl, is a person who designs these living complexes, plans for future needs, and schedules the construction."

Eve wrinkled her nose. "Sounds boring."

Her father matched his fingertips and looked at her over the peak they made. "Quite to the contrary, actually. It involves a little engineering, a little statistics, a bit of fieldwork, and more than some fortune-telling."

"What about genetic management?"

"Aha. More fortune-telling. Genetics managers deal in several different areas. Some work with food producing plants and animals to see if their yield can be increased through genetic engineering. Others work with human genetics, some in the fields of analysis for such things as mating suitability, and others in the endeavor of bettering man's future through the conquest of genetic diseases and weaknesses. And you know how I feel about that sort of monkey business." He scowled.

Eve squirmed in her chair. She didn't want him to get involved in a conversation about the sins of age arresting treatments. "Daddy, I want to work on the Project."

He looked at her, his irritation with genetic engineering forgotten, then smiled broadly. "Well, now that gives us something to go on." He reached for the list. "Lots of the jobs listed *here will work on the Project. There's astrophysics, space biology, and botany, warp propulsion engineering, colonial development, as well as jobs like shuttle pilot or space construction."*

"I mean that I want to go. As a member of one of the teams."

The decision happened without precognition, but she realized immediately that it was what she wanted. There had been no announcement of the competition for the teams, but there were plenty of rumors in the school about how they would be chosen and she had listened to all of them with great interest. Now she knew why, and she also knew why being an ecobiologist had been so important to her. An ecobiologist would certainly be chosen for each team.

Her father looked at her very seriously. "Eve, honey, are you sure? That's a pretty big job to go after, and they say they're only going to take a thousand people. The odds are against you."

She set her jaw defiantly. "I don't care. I've got to at least try for it, Daddy."

He nodded abruptly. "All right, then. The best choices would be, in line with your goal, space biology or botany, colonial development, or one of the physical sciences. Also, should you not be chosen for the Project, perhaps then one of the Moon colonies or space labs would be open to you."

He held his arms out and she went to sit on his lap. After holding her for a moment, he said, "You know, it's a good thing to want to get off this planet and start over in another world. Maybe you'll have a chance to correct some of our mistakes."

Her first choice had been planetoid ecology and, after a year, the assignment had come through.

Eve looked at Ellen sitting beside her and smiled at the memory of herself. Once she had made the decision about getting into the Project, she had pursued it relentlessly, finding out what the requirements would be and working toward them. She had thrown herself into physical and mental conditioning, preparing like an ancient Greek Olympian athlete.

Now Ellen wanted to begin studying toward her chosen profession. "Ellen, any studying you do to increase your knowledge can't be wrong. Our planet is going to need all the skills and learning we can muster. Go ahead and explore the tapes."

Ellen's smile was animated. "All of us?"

Eve laughed. "So you're the spokesperson for the whole group, are you?" She thought for a moment. "I guess it's all right for all of you, but don't get so far ahead of yourselves that you lose understanding or get confused. You all have a lot of basic learning left and a lot of years in which you can study."

Behind them a disagreement erupted between Donald and Harrison, and Eve hurried to mediate. They were both decanted in the fourth year, so had a maturity level of six and both were quick to disagree in all circumstances.

As Eve approached, she heard Harrison saying, "...and you can't come in my room again. You...take things." His fists were clenched at his side as were Donald's. Both of their faces reflected their anger.

She put a hand on each small, tense shoulder and said soothingly, "Can we talk about it?"

Both of them continued to stare each other down, unwilling to be the first to break away, so she turned them bodily to face her, then knelt so she could look into their eyes.

"What's the problem?"

Harrison scowled, indicating Donald with a toss of his head. "Whenever he comes into my room, he...takes things. This time he took my rock from the valley." He shot a glare in Donald's direction.

Eve, still holding their shoulders, turned to Donald. "Is that true?"

Donald returned Harrison's glare. "Everything here belongs to all of us. That's what you said."

Eve sighed. "You're right and you're wrong. Everything

on this planet belongs to all of us: the land, the resources, the hydrocarbons, and the possessions I brought on my journey like the computer and the biolab are all things we own in common. Do you understand that?"

They both nodded. She noticed that Donald's fists had relaxed, but Harrison was still angry.

"But, what I think you haven't understood is that we must respect each other's privacy. For example, the coverall I am wearing was made from hydrocarbons belonging to all of us by a machine that belongs to all of us. However, I am wearing it so at this moment it belongs to me. If you asked me, I would give it to you, but when I did, I would go to get another one because we all wear them. Then, this one would belong to you and the one I would put on would belong to me.

"Donald, Harrison's rock comes from the valley that belongs to all of us, but he picked it up and carried it up here to his room. Therefore, even though the rock is a possession of everyone here, Harrison is taking care of it and you owe him the respect to ask him for it before taking it. Harrison, you have the right to give it to Donald or to keep on caring for it. Does that make sense to both of you?"

Donald nodded quickly, glad to be so easily dismissed, but Harrison said, "Yes, but he does it all the time to all of us. It's not just my rock, it's James's rope and Tai's cloth and other people's things, too."

"Donald, is that true?"

He hung his head and said in a very quiet little voice, "Yes, I guess so."

"Do you understand now the difference between all of us owning something and some of us taking care of various things that we all own?"

He nodded quickly, then held out his hand toward Harrison, opening it to reveal the rock. Harrison took it, still looking disgusted.

"Donald, will you also please return the other things to their caretakers?"

He nodded.

Eve watched them carefully, seeing the anger dissolving from both their faces. "I don't think it will happen again, do you?"

Both boys shook their heads.

She held her arms out and each of them came to her.

"I love you both equally. That's another thing we all share."

Both little voices responded, dutifully, "I love you," one into each of her ears, then they broke away and went off together, talking.

Eve looked around the room. It was still the same room that had seemed so huge to her when she was alone, but now it was populated with children in various sizes, ages, and skin tones, playing quietly in groups.

She had programmed various simple toys into the fabricator but the most popular were the blocks. Boys and girls alike seemed to enjoy playing with them. The youngest children carried them around, sometimes banging experimentally on their environment or on each other, though Eve did everything she could to prevent that, while the other children used them to build fanciful constructions. The blocks became hovercraft, humming between the blocks that had become buildings or mountains, and the games that they evolved fascinated her.

There were soft toys, too. Dolls and animals that, for the younger children, were objects of affection, and for the older children populations for their invented cities.

She was constantly astounded by the children, and was never certain how much she was raising them as opposed to how much they were raising each other.

She tried hard to spend time with each of them every day, but it wasn't always possible, and she worried about retaining control over the ever-growing population. She was concerned that the youngest weren't receiving the amount of attention she had been able to give the first several groups.

She wanted her world to be right by the standards she had evolved, so that when the children were grown-up they would pass along the ideas of love and sharing to their own children. She had to allow for individual development so she wouldn't have a society of robots, but at the same time, there had to be controls so that wars would never occur.

Over the past five years, in the evenings when she had time to herself, she had restudied the history tapes; the prevailing theme of the wars had always been territorial: one nation fighting another over borders or mineral rights. The other major theme she had been able to find was ideology, either religious or political.

She was determined, in her world, to allow no ownership of land or hydrocarbons or other minerals and to allow no religion or politics to develop. Without those influences, Earth would never have suffered the wars that eventually caused her demise. Eve had no intention of allowing her world to take the same course.

She realized it was easy to control now, when they all lived together and she was the one adult in the community. She was concerned about how to maintain it when the population began to spread out, forming new colonies in other parts of the world, led by other adults who had their own ideas. The best way, she had decided, was control of education. She had made adjustments in the computer tapes, but she had also attempted to use her personal influence with each of the children, reinforcing love and sharing in everything she did.

She heard one of the babies crying and went to the nursery. Cilia was tending to the child, changing a wet diaper and talking animatedly to her charge, Rebecca.

Cilia's enthusiasm was directly in contrast to Ellen's seriousness. Cilia was the clown of the deputies, her face always smiling and her eyes twinkling as she went about her business. She even smiled when she slept, much to Eve's amusement.

Eve stood in the door, watching Cilia with the baby. She

removed the diaper deftly, depositing it in the hydrocarbon recycling tube and reaching for a fresh cloth. As she did, she saw Eve.

Her smile widened. "Hi, Eve. Rebecca is such a good baby. She smiled at me this morning. Let me see if I can get her to do it again. Come on, Rebecca, show Eve that you can smile."

Rebecca gurgled somberly, so Cilia renewed her tickling efforts and smiled at the baby, finally being rewarded with a cooing grin.

Eve hugged Cilia, then picked up Rebecca, who continued to smile and gurgle, drooling.

"Cilia, you do such a nice job with the babies. The ones you care for always seem to smile first." Cilia grinned broadly. "What will you do now that she's awake?"

"I thought I'd turn on the viewing screen and tell her about the colors and shapes. I make up stories for her. I don't think she understands me, but she likes it."

"Will you bring her to Congregation at Evening?"

"Well, she's a month old now. It's time for the babies to start coming."

Eve moved on to the other cubicles with the babies and their deputies to remind them about Congregation. She was interested in watching the children grow and develop, for she remembered some of their parents from other Project groups and wished that she could share these distant progeny with them.

Morris set his tray down next to Evelyn's at one of the corner tables in the dining hall. Watching their fellow Project members in their less guarded moments was one of their favorite diversions. At first, they had guessed at the occupations of the members or at their original homes, but now that they knew almost everyone in the groups, they made comment on personalities and current liaisons within the Project. Eve was glad that the monitors couldn't hear their remarks, since they showed such "social uncooperativeness."

Morris, talking past a mouthful of synthesized meatloaf,

said, "It's becoming obvious that Jessica Van Hooten and Jeremy Wilson are getting very close, which is hard to believe since neither one of them ever says a word that isn't necessary."

Eve smiled. "Just maybe they're all action and don't need to talk."

Morris laughed, then coughed, and Eve pounded him on the back until he stopped coughing.

"You should know better than to make me laugh when I'm eating," he said with mock reprimand. "Jeremy is really very nice when you get to know him. We grew up in the same complex so I've known him for a long time. He's one hell of an ecobiologist. Did you know that he was the one who designed the machine that separates the oil from the salt water to recover the hydrocarbons? That's how he got onto the Project in the first place. That and his genetic purity." He chuckled without humor. "They completely skipped the personality tests with him except to determine he would probably never kill anyone."

"Kill anyone? Jeremy? He even speaks so quietly that you have to lean toward him to hear him."

Morris grinned evilly. "And one of these days, when you're leaning nice and close, he's going to reach out and pinch your tits. Just like this," he said, demonstrating.

Eve shrieked in protest, drawing stares from the rest of the room.

Eve went from the nursery on the first level to the second level to check on the children there. Each of the toddlers had an older child who monitored their activities as well, though not as closely as the supervision given to the babies.

Although each year's two groups of four were a year apart in maturity, they tended to group together socially.

The toddlers were between one and two on maturity levels and tended to amuse each other. The older children rotated duties with the toddlers. Much of their day was consumed with viewing-screen preschool learning activities and they didn't demand the extra attention that the infants did.

The eight toddlers were sitting in a circle singing along with the viewing screen, Janet, and Mark. The songs were old, traditional play songs chosen from Earth's archives of different historical periods. Most of the songs on record in the computer had developmental activities which went with them, either historically or added for Project purposes.

The song that the children were singing had originally come from Eastern Asia. It had long been translated, as had everything, into Uni and involved passing a block in time with the music. She watched them until the song finished, then the children all came to her for a hug and some personal moments, each one anxious to be near her.

When she finally broke away, after they had begun another game song, she stopped in each occupied room to spend a moment with the child there, then returned to the main room of the complex, where Morris was working the food processor, preparing midday meals for the children. They ate in groups at staggered times, according to age. The processor was programmed for correct portions for each age group and added food supplements appropriate to each group's needs.

Eve had been surprised at how tall the children were getting until she realized that the reduced gravity in combination with good nutrition and genetic perfection would probably produce taller children. Morris and Kenneth were almost one and a half meters tall already, and would still continue to grow for at least another four years.

Morris welcomed her help with a smile. Sometimes she wondered if she had thrown too much responsibility on her deputies, depriving them of essential time to be themselves and grow as children. The deputies, however, seemed to be able to take time off in the natural course of events, sometimes coming to her as a group to get permission to go down into the valley and sometimes relieving each other so individuals could enjoy some freedom.

Her decision to appoint deputies had come from two concepts:

First, she realized that without the help of the deputies, she would be unable to function effectively. The children would grow wild, deprived of any quantity of individual guidance, for she would be mired in details.

Second, and of equal importance, she felt the children of Genesis were special, totally unassociated with the children of Earth. Her children were pioneers in a completely unique sense, unlike any of their ancestors, and they had to learn how to take responsibility as a part of the normal course of events.

She had to acknowledge there was a third consideration which entered into every decision she made. Her purpose was to create an orderly, rational society which would remain unsullied by war and conflict. In order to do that, she had to exert her influence strongly over the children. She had to imbue each of them with a sense of being part of the greater organism that was human life on Genesis.

"Eve?" Morris's voice broke through her thoughts. "Are you all right?"

She smiled, putting her arm around his shoulders. "Yes, thank you. I was just lost in thought."

Morris's eyes roved over the children who were eating, but he said, "You think a lot, don't you? What do you think about?"

Eve gave careful consideration to her answer. She tried very hard always to be honest with the children without confusing them. Finally, she said, "What I think about most of the time is us. Our colony. How we will grow and how we are growing now. We're all very special people, you know."

Morris nodded. "I think it's harder for you than for us to be here. You grew up in another place, then came here, so you know what other places are like. This is all we know.

We've seen your home on the learning tapes, but it seems like a story because it's so different from here."

Eve thought how much he sounded like his father with his rational, unemotional approach to life. Genetic researchers had proven beyond a doubt that logic and sensitivity were not inherited, but emotionally she had trouble convincing herself of that when Morris behaved as a mirror of his father.

Congregation at Evening had begun informally when the first group of babies was decanted. She would gather them together in the main room to play with them, tell stories, and, as they grew, teach them her philosophies as they began to evolve. Each session involved practicing yoga techniques.

Congregation had evolved, as the population grew, to be a community meeting complete with almost a quasi-governmental function. It was in Congregation that rules for conduct and safety were developed; goals established; social behavior outlined; and religious concepts presented.

The religious part of their lives had been a trial for Eve at first, for Earth's religions were so diverse and had become intermixed with the world government, the Chairman assuming almost a papal role in addition to his governmental duties. Lines between philosophies had blurred in the face of wars and crises, until religion, like nationality, had become a potpourri of philosophical outlooks.

Eve realized that she had to give the children a sense of a greater power, but didn't want to label it with any kind of religious name for fear of creating groundwork for diversities of belief and thereby a foundation for disagreement. She had read everything stored in the computer on the various religions in Earth's history, then chosen from among them the ideas most suited to what she was trying to accomplish.

What she selected incorporated the loving God of late and early Christianity; the pacifistic notions of Hinduism as espoused by Gandhi in the twentieth and Lenge Maheshi in the twenty-first; the value of the individual from the various scientific religions in the interwar period of the twenty-first; and the notions of cooperation from United Governments with which she was most familiar. She had then frozen the tapes associated with other religions so the children wouldn't stumble onto something which would confuse them.

The first Congregation which a child attended had been established as the anniversary of his first month from decanting and he was formally welcomed into the community by the rest of the children at that time. Eve had decided to make it a celebration, and the children all looked forward to it.

Outside the light had faded to a pale green line at the horizon, outlining the mountains with a halo of green and setting them in vivid relief to the night sky. The computer had mindlessly responded to the growing darkness by softly lighting any occupied rooms. Later it would sense the children settling down to sleep and would slowly douse the lights and play soft music.

The children began filtering into the room, sitting in their decanting groups, faces freshly scrubbed and clean coveralls in evidence. Finally, when all but the eldest and their charges were in place, Eve stepped into the middle of the circle.

"God's blessing to all of us and to Genesis."

"God's blessing to all of us and to Genesis," the children repeated.

"Tonight we welcome the four newest members of our community, joined with us one month ago. Let us extend our hands in love to John Michaelson Adams."

The children in the circle extended their hands, the younger ones just to touch the baby, the older ones to hold him. John gurgled contentedly at the attention as he was passed from child to child around the circle, finally return-

ing to the arms of Kenneth, who joined the circle, holding
John sitting in his lap.

She repeated the process with the other three babies.

Rebecca, much to Cilia's chagrin, howled in protest at
the handling, but settled down as soon as she was seated
with Cilia, closing the circle.

Eve then gave each child a drinking cup filled with juice.
They raised their glasses in a toast to the new members:
"Welcome to Congregation and to our growing family of
man so far from Earth."

Eve then settled into the circle and began to tell a story
about the first Moon colonists and how they had established their community.

She had tried to choose stories for the children that
stressed working together and achievement, sorting out the
stories in the library that spoke of violence or war. When
she told stories about Earth's heroes, she would tell of how
they helped their fellow men, while eliminating the wars
and hatred which had so often motivated their good works.
She wanted the children to achieve the good without the
surrounding violence which had seemed to be a way of life
on Earth.

Eve was a good storyteller, giving vivid details about the
cold and loneliness of the Moon dwellers as well as the
funny parts of their lives. She had told this story often and
it was a favorite of the older children. They drew the obvious parallels between themselves and the people on the
Moon, and sometimes their games would reflect that involvement with children taking the roles of the Moon colonists and building their domed cities out of blocks as they
played.

What she didn't tell them was how the Moon colony had
failed, torn apart by conflicts over leadership and purpose,
and by the divisiveness of the Earth's nations which had
contributed members to the Project. She had frozen that
part of the story in the computer tapes so the myth of love

and peace she had created would never be accidentally destroyed by curious future meddling.

She finished the story with her usual ending: "And the colony grew and grew until they built new cities all over the Moon. And some of your parents came from that Moon colony."

It wasn't true. The Moon colony had been converted to a scientific community under the control of the United Governments, and none of the Moon colonists had contributed genetically to the Project because they were all non-breeders due to the genetic damage suffered from exposure to the direct radiation of the sun.

Two of the babies had fallen asleep during the story and one of the toddlers was snoozing as well. Eve realized that the Moon colony story had grown in length with the embellishments that she added to keep it fresh.

"Good night. I love you."

Thirty-five voices echoed hers, then each child filed past her for a kiss, another tradition she had begun with Congregation.

She and Morris picked up the used cups and put them into the recycler, then she sent him off to bed with a kiss and went to the nursery. The babies were all sucking busily on the nipples of the feeding tubes. Jeremy, leaning against Charles's crib, yawned heartily.

"Go ahead to bed, Jeremy. I'll stay with Charles."

Jeremy smiled gratefully, then kissed her and slipped out the door. She leaned on the rail of the crib, watching Charles who looked back at her, but never stopped eating. Charles's parents were both from Eastern Asia and his dark almond eyes and straight black hair showed his origins.

She waited for him to finish eating, then picked him up and held him against her shoulder. She was immediately rewarded with a burp, but continued to hold him, singing a lullaby with the music coming from the speaker. He cooed in her ear, then settled against her shoulder. Finally she put him in the crib and he fell asleep again immediately. The lights in the room dimmed as she left, leaving only a soft glow.

She went up to the upper levels, stopping in each room to tuck in the child there. Some were already asleep so she tiptoed in, checked them, and left quietly. The ones who were awake each got a moment of special attention before she moved to the next compartment.

The computer would monitor each child as he slept, alert to the movement or sounds in the room, and should something go wrong, the viewing screen in her compartment would wake her with information about the problem.

It had only happened once in five years. Sarah, when a toddler, had rolled over in her sleep and fallen from her bed.

"Alert. Alert. Second level. Child Sarah Abrams injured. Alert. Alert."

Eve had sprinted up the stairs and found Sarah sitting on the floor, crying with terror and pain. She had landed heavily on her arm and it appeared to be broken. Her cries had awakened other children who gathered outside the door of her room. Eve had held Sarah who continued to cry, but sent the others back to bed.

The biolab had healed Sarah's arm while Eve sat with her, holding the other hand and talking soothingly.

Finally, Sarah had fallen asleep as the biolab worked on the break. When it was finished, Eve had taken her back to bed. The next day, she had put plasteel rods along the edges of the toddlers' beds to prevent anything from happening again.

Now it was quiet in the dwelling for the first time since early morning and Eve enjoyed it. She got a drinking cup, filled it with the juice left from Congregation, and went to sit on the ledge outside the door. She cold be alone with her thoughts there, yet not too far from the computer should something happen to one of the children.

She looked out across the valley, her eyes slowly adjusting to the darkness. The moon had slipped above the hori-

zon, but was not yet fully risen so it cast long shadows
beneath the trees in the valley and the mountains left an
outline of deep shadow that would disappear as the moon
came from behind them. She could barely see the wisps of
smoke rising from the alien village so far away, but by now,
after constant observation, she knew where they would be.
Below, on the floor of the valley, the great transport lay in
the shadow of the mountains, but its still-shiny surface
picked up a tiny point of light flowing down from the doorway.

The transport still held many things they would need in
the future: hovercraft for transportation, plasteel rods that
the fabricators could convert to long sheets of the strong
material for buildings, reserve hydrocarbons that she no
longer needed but hated not to use, and three more biolab/
computer units which would eventually be installed in
other cities and tied into each other, providing uniform
communications and fabrication systems for the whole
planet.

The central computer would program the others for local
variances and the frozen information would be instantly
frozen in the other units. As soon as they were linked, the
computer would set about programming the others and the
cities would be linked. Computer fabrication units were
also stored in the transport. Those units would allow other
terminals to be built by the computers themselves so every
community would have its own central computer unit,
complete with every function.

Eve sat motionless, looking up at the constellations she
had named so long ago. Back then it had been an alien sky
and she had sought to impose familiarity on it with famil-
iar-sounding names. Now those stars had acquired their
own familiarity and she felt at home.

Still, when she looked into the sky, sometimes she would
wonder if one of these stars was the sun of her home and
she would long for Earth. Perhaps not so much for the

physicality of Earth, for that was an unpleasant memory of smells and bad air, but for the people she had left behind.

"... are the final hope of our race. We send you forth with our love and blessings in hopes that you will succeed where we have failed; that you will win where we have lost; that you will achieve where we have been negligent. You are the finest mankind can offer and we know it is no small task to say a final farewell to those you have loved here. The only consolation we can offer is that you will know we send you out into the uncharted stars to carry on for us. And we send you with our most fervent prayers."

The Chairman paused, bowing his head. He had taken the treatment and was a handsome, young man despite being well over one hundred in chronological age. He had been one of the first to take the treatment and was living proof that it worked.

Morris held her hand tightly. The isolation would begin the next day and they would soon be thrust into suspended animation and encapsulation for their long journeys. It was their final day together.

The hall was filled with Project members and their families who had come from all over the world. Everyone was forcing gaiety they didn't feel, maintaining a front of optimism and security when everyone privately felt a sense of loss and pessimism.

The warp drives hadn't even been tested. It could happen that these thousand would be put into a suspended state, taken up to the huge ships, then blasted out of the solar system by regular drive only to have the warp drive fail, allowing them to drift forever through space until they either fell into an orbit like a small somnolent planet or were sucked into a sun or a black hole.

What was foremost in their thought, under all the glowing rhetoric about hope and dreams and a future for mankind, was the realization that they would never know the fate of the travelers.

Eve had called her parents on the videophone and asked them not to come. It had been a hard decision for all of them.

She felt now that she was glad she had made it. They would have remembered this false atmosphere rather than her last visit and call, which had been warm, personal, and real.

They had talked honestly—her parents, her aunt, Morris, and Evelyn—about the chances for success of the Project. Privately, without the prying eyes of the monitor, they had agreed the chances were slim for survival and success in the voyages but equally slim on Earth. They had cast aside the false trappings of the "great mission of mankind" and looked at the Project for what it was: the ultimate species ego-extension.

Sitting in the door of her complex, nestled in the mountain cliffs of an alien world, light years away from those people who had hoped so hard, Eve wished that they could somehow know she was establishing a stronghold of mankind in this new place.

Aunt Rosemary would explore the philosophical implications with her father, their debates about potential changes running long into the night. Her mother would smile, knowing she had lived and continued.

Morris? She hoped he would be proud of what she had done, but she wished she knew. She wished she could talk to him, get his counsel, share in his logic. Separately, each of them were strong, intelligent, and independent. Together, there had been a kind of magic that made the two of them stronger, more intelligent, and more independent than the sum of the parts. Together they could create the Utopia they had talked about.

She was suddenly struck with a thought. She had ignored one very important fact in her theorizing about what would have happened if he had been able to transfer to her group. She might still have been the only one to arrive alive. This way she didn't know if he had lived, so could think of him as still alive without fear of contradiction. That way there would be no fantasizing, for she would know for sure. And the knowledge that he was dead would have destroyed a part of her.

She laughed at herself. An old saying that Aunt Rosemary would use when she was a child came back to her and she repeated it aloud: "If wishes were horses, then beggars would ride." She had been able, for two years of solitude, to keep astride her sanity by "wishes." Now Genesis was populated with real people, not with wishes, and she had a life here which didn't connect with the people on Earth except through the legacies contained in her computer.

The moon had appeared from behind the mountains and illuminated the valley with its gentle, familiar light. Even when it was not full, the clarity of the atmosphere allowed its light to come through brilliantly, and when it was full she could see detail in the valley.

It was about half full, so she could see the transport clearly and the outlines of the trees, but the sea of valley grasses was lost in shadow. The grasses interested her. There were no grass-eating animals that she had been able to discover in the valley, yet it stayed at a height of about one meter. Sometimes she wondered if there was new growth or if these grasses were like trees, small and old.

She had cut back a patch of grass near the transport in an endeavor to find out, but it had grown back quickly to the original height and, within a week, it was impossible to tell where it had been cut.

Down on the floor of the valley she could hear the stirrings of small animals. She rarely saw any of the animals here, outside of the birds. None of them had ventured up the steep steps into the complex. She still didn't like to be out in the valley at night. Even with the laser gun and the shield belt, she felt uncomfortable, remembering the parallel gashes in the plasteel of the damaged hovercraft when she had gone to the shore so long ago.

Someday the ecobiologists who now slept inside would study the animal and plant life of Genesis. They would determine if any of the animals would be potential food sources and if any of the plants could be cultivated to reduce the dependencies of the community on the food synthesizer. They would study the life cycles and patterns of

the animals and plants just as the geologists would study
the planet itself.

Looking out over the valley, she smiled at the great adventure that lay ahead of their little community. They were
the first pioneers in the history of the human race that had
the challenge of a totally unexplored, alien environment to
study. The results would be astonishing to the scientists
back on Earth and she wished that they could somehow
share in the discoveries.

Chapter Seven

EVE SAT AT the console in the biolab with Mark at her side,
monitoring the eight new lives. In only a month, they
would again be presented with four new babies, and in
seven months, four more. The heartbeats of the near-
decanting babies were loud and strong compared to the
softer thuddings of the two-month-old fetuses. As each decanting approached, Eve was struck again with concern
that there would be a mutant among the babies, though the
first group had been the only instance. She knew, intellectually, that the laws of probability had simply worked in a
normal way with that first mutant, but she feared it happening again with the children around. She had been able
to protect them from the knowledge of mutants and death
and wanted to keep it that way.

"Mark, after you check the heartbeat of each baby in the
biolab, the next thing you check is the salinity in the capsule. The computer monitors it, of course, but I like to be
sure that the computer and I agree on something that important. Do you remember what the salinity is supposed to
read?"

Mark nodded in his neoprofessional way, reaching for the terminal and requesting "salinity" from the machine. It read 4.989 percent and he nodded with satisfaction. "Right in the correct range, Eve. Just like last time."

"Right. Remember what comes next?"

"Temperature," he said, reaching to the terminal again. "Thirty-six point five degrees. Right again." He patted the biolab terminal as if it sought his approval.

They ran the rest of the tests for nutrition, immunization, and development, all of which came out within normal levels, then left the biolab together.

"Eve, are you an exo?"

"No, I'm an endo."

They got fruit juice from the synthesizer and sat on the comfortable benches in the room. Outside the sun shone brightly and Eve could hear a group of children playing down in the valley.

"Eve, I've been working ahead a bit on the medical study tapes, and I need to know some answers, if you have the time."

"Of course. Just don't exceed your levels of understanding and get into territory where you don't belong yet."

He swung his feet and looked at the floor. "I'm sorry."

"Mark, there's nothing to be sorry about. You haven't done anything wrong by being curious. What were your questions?"

"Well, I know how endos and exos are conceived, but really, what good are endos at all? They take twice as long to mature, are much less predictable, can't be monitored as closely, have no pre-education, and have to be immunized after they're born."

Eve was stunned by his question. She hadn't expected him to take that course, but felt he deserved a carefully considered answer.

"Mark, with life extension treatments, ten years of maturity makes very little difference. As you know, all of us can expect to live at least three hundred years.

"As for predictability, Earth endos were born only to parents who were as carefully genetically matched as the parents of the exos here. No people with any genetic weaknesses were allowed to produce a child, so the outcomes were pretty predictable. Monitoring of a pregnant woman is as careful as monitoring of the exos, except it's not constant. But, when a woman is carrying a child, she does a certain amount of monitoring on her own which is instinctive. And, with respect to pre-education, exos need that to match their minds with their bodies' growth rates. Can you imagine my job having seven of you growing like weeds and not one out of diapers?"

Mark looked at her, then smiled. "I just wondered."

"The time will come here on Genesis, Mark, when we have endos and exos, just like on Earth. Each group has its advantages and every person, endo or exo, deserves respect from every other person. Right?"

He wiggled down from the bench. "Right. Thanks. Can I go down to the valley?"

"Sure. Just keep an eye on the sun and round everyone up when it starts to set. Okay?"

His answer was lost in his hurry to join the children in the valley.

Eve checked on the children still in the complex, then settled down at her screen to study more of the history tapes, editing them carefully to suit her intentions of adjustments. The twentieth was giving her a lot of trouble with most of its historical figures of merit caught up in the wars which ripped the century apart. She found herself caught on the horns of a dilemma, as she had with the American Revolution and the American Civil War. There had been some wars in man's history where one side was clearly right and the other side was clearly wrong. That made it difficult to illustrate that all wars were wrong.

She was determined to prove everything could have been solved by negotiation and concession, but the dictator, Hitler, fouled her logic, for it was clear the man sought

cruel domination of the world and wouldn't have listened
to reason. Her only recourse was to show both sides had
behaved wrongly in that war, committing genocide in different ways, but with the same outcome.

When she had first begun working with the tapes, she
had intended to eliminate all references to war and conflict, but had soon discovered it was impossible. War provided an integral warp in the fabric of history, and there
were people who achieved greatness solely because of their
involvement with those wars.

She had adjusted her direction, focusing on showing the
wrongness of arms conflict and the rightness of discussion
and negotiation. She wanted her children and their children to grow up with an internalized abhorrence of violence, personal or national.

She hadn't looked up from her viewing screen for a long
time, but finally her concentration was broken by the
noises of the children out in the main room and she
checked her chron, then snapped off the screen with a start
of concern. It was late and she hadn't realized how caught
up she'd been in the history tapes.

The main room was full of children, but Morris seemed
to have things under control with the evening meal as he
patiently programmed the food synthesizer while Mark,
Ellen, Cilia, Jeremy, and Janet got the children into groups,
waiting for their meals.

Most of the children who could walk had spent the afternoon in the valley and had returned with various treasures
which they still clutched and were anxious to share with
Eve. Outside the light was fading and she felt surrounded
by a comfortable security in their complex.

She moved from group to group as they waited, examin-
ing the day's bounty of rocks, flowers, and even a couple of
struggling insects imprisoned in juice cups. She patiently
explained the insects would be good study material for the
biolab, but bad treasures.

Most of the insects were common ones with which she

had had contact in the past, but there was one new one with what looked like a vicious sting and she quickly collected all, putting them into containers for biolab study later.

Morris fed the younger children first, as usual, while the others waited. Finally, when he had programmed the last meals, he came to Eve with a look of concern on his face.

"Excuse me, Eve." His insistent voice interrupted her conversation with Harrison and James about how they almost caught one of the valley creatures. She looked up at Morris and felt a twinge of worry at the expression on his face.

She stood up and moved away with Morris. "What's wrong?"

"I had an extra meal for Group Two, so I checked and Richard is missing."

She put her arm around his shoulders, the worry growing but using yoga to calm her features. "I'm sure he's in the complex. Was he outside with everyone today?"

"Yes, we were exploring around the transport. When it started to get near sunset, I got everyone together, I thought, and we came back up. I can't remember if I saw him climbing up. See, the little kids have trouble with the steps so we all have to help them and I didn't . . ."

"I'm sure he's in the sonar or in his room. I'll check while you go eat your dinner."

She tried to appear calm as she left the room, but she was concerned. Richard Alden VanDersant was the second child decanted in the second year, and old enough to have common sense about knowing when to come in. He was almost always first in line for meals in his group and it was unusual for the food to have been served without Richard in visible attendance. As she left the room, she checked the faces, but Richard hadn't appeared.

His cubicle was empty and there was no evidence of new treasures, which added to her concern. Richard was an explorer and a collector and went to the valley frequently, always returning with something new which he would put into a container and study carefully. Everything in his room was already stored, so nothing new had been added.

She checked the sonar cleansing room, hoping against hope that he would be there, but the room was empty. As she hurried down the halls, she glanced into each room, but all were unoccupied. By the time she returned to the main hall, she knew he was still in the valley.

Morris, Kenneth, and Mark had all finished eating and were watching her closely as she came into the room. She called Ellen, Cilia, Jeremy, and Janet to join them, then said, "I guess Richard lost track of the time, so we'll have to go down to the valley and see if we can find him. I'm sure he's fine. Morris, Kenneth, and Mark, why don't you come with me and the rest of you get everyone who hasn't cleansed into the sonars and then ready for Congregation."

She took the three boys with her as she gathered up hand lights, giving one to each of them. Before she left the locker, she paused, then put on a shield belt and tucked a laser gun into it. Outwardly she was calm, but it was only due to the strict discipline of the yoga she practiced.

The valley was large and Richard had been outside for a long time. He might have wandered quite a distance, especially if he was investigating something which had caught his scientific curiosity.

The boys looked at the belt strangely, but she didn't explain it to them. She just smiled and the four of them moved quickly and quietly through the main room. The four deputies left in charge were busy clearing the empty meal containers and keeping the children occupied, so their departure attracted little attention.

They went out onto the ledge and down the first set of steps, before Eve stopped them. "Let's shine our lights together around the area. Maybe Richard is right here and just waiting for us to come with light so he can see to come up the stairs."

She doubted it. There was still an evening glow in the sky and the steps could be seen clearly.

They snapped on the powerful beams of the hand lights and moved them over the surrounding area at the base of the stairs and around the transport, but there was no movement, response, or light-color coveralls sending reflection.

They hurried down the stairs. "Okay, now let's go around the transport. Shine your lights like this." She demonstrated, sweeping the beam of light across the grasses.

Richard was taller than the grasses when he was standing, but if he were hurt or napping, he would be difficult to see.

They moved slowly around the transport, searching the grasses in the area, but there was no sign of the missing child.

"Morris, when you and Richard were exploring today, what were you looking for?"

"Well, there was one of those little animals hiding near the transport, so we were trying to see if it had a nest somewhere around here."

"When the animal ran, which way did it go?" She was trying to stay calm, but even the yoga had only a negligible effect against the rising panic.

"Toward the mountains."

"So you think Richard might have followed it?"

"I don't know, because right after that Harrison and James found one of those bugs, and I was looking at it with them. When I looked up, Richard wasn't there anymore."

Eve thought for a moment. They couldn't possibly search the entire valley, not four of them, not all of them, so she had to listen to her instincts.

"Tell you what we're going to do. Spread out about three meters apart and keep moving your light so it covers all the ground between you and the next person. The two of us on the outside will shine our lights outward. Morris, you go on the outside, since you're the tallest. If anyone sees anything, call out and stop. We'll go in the direction that

Morris says the little animal went. It sounds as though Richard might have followed him."

They spread out in a line, the only sound was their movement through the hissing grasses. The lights played across the ground.

They startled several of the small grass-dwelling animals, who fled before the glare of the lights.

Suddenly Morris said, "Eve, look," and pointed his light at something light-colored in the grasses.

"Stay here," she called, dashing in the direction of the object. It was a torn sleeve from a coverall. She knelt to examine it and was overcome with panic. There was blood on the sleeve.

She fought to control herself, knowing that she had to remain calm, and involuntarily checked the laser gun in her belt. It crossed her mind that she didn't even know if the gun was working. It had been a long time since she had thought of weapons, much less felt the need to check any of them.

She picked up the piece of fabric and returned to the group of boys. "It's a sleeve from a coverall, and there is blood on the sleeve, so Richard might be hurt. We have to hurry."

They went back into their line, moving more quickly toward the mountains. As they approached the foot of the towering mountain, the grasses thinned out and their progress became more difficult with the rocks, some of which were so large they had to be skirted.

Eve was swinging her light across the rocks to her left when she felt the hairs on the back of her neck begin to rise.

"Stop," she said, her voice a harsh whisper. The three boys looked at her curiously, but stopped where they stood. "Be very quiet."

They stood still, listening for something. Eve's fear increased as she listened, her feral instincts taking over as they had when she had first come to Genesis. She realized how suppressed they had been once there were others of her own kind with her. Slowly she moved her light across the rocks around them.

Then she heard with her ears what her instincts had heard before. The low growl came from her right and slightly above them.

She moved her light in the direction of the sound, then gasped as the two red eyes appeared. The animal looked large, its black fur almost disappearing against the rocks.

She grabbed the laser gun from her belt, activating it as she did. "Lie down!" she hissed at the boys as she fired in the direction of the eyes.

Her first shot was high, shattering the rocks over the animal's head. It growled again and moved. In the light she could see what it was guarding: a small boy in a torn coverall.

She fired again as the animal leapt, and this time hit him directly in midair. His chest exploded in a burst of laser light and tissue and she was showered with the creature's blood as it crashed to the ground, still growling.

She aimed again, this time firing at the dying creature's great, black head. The laser was set high and the beam shattered the head, destroying it.

Quickly she dashed to the ledge on which the animal had been sitting. Richard was barely alive, his arm and shoulder torn desperately and claw marks covering his body. He was unconscious.

She swept him into her arms, calling to the boys, "Hurry. Light the way. Take the light and the laser. We have to hurry."

Morris was the first to react, grabbing the light and the gun where she had dropped them, then shining his light for her to see her way down from the ledge with Richard in her arms.

They dashed across the rocky terrain to the edge of the grasses where they could move quickly. They were about half a kilometer from the stairs, but she ran, adrenaline pumping into her body.

Morris ran beside her, holding the light so she could see. Kenneth and Mark ran ahead of them, and she hoped that they would get any remaining children out of the main room.

She couldn't bear to have any of them see Richard so badly hurt. She had no idea what the boys' reaction had been to the animal, the gun, and Richard's injuries, but hoped they were able to cope with it, for her concentration had to be on the child in her arms.

She had never encountered any wild animals on Earth and she had never killed a living creature before. She knew there would be time to explain it all later, but right now she had to hope the boys understood vaguely what had happened.

They dashed up the stairs. Eve's arms ached and her breath was short, but she kept her speed up, knowing how important even a few seconds could be.

As she entered the complex, Kenneth was getting the last of the children out of the main room. Through her fear and concern, she felt a sense of pride that the boys had reacted so well.

Mark was in the biolab, activating the cellular reorganizer and cleaning the plasteel table with liquid antiseptic. He jumped aside as she gently put Richard onto the table. In the bright lights of the biolab, his injuries looked even worse, his shoulder deeply wounded and his left arm chewed to a bloody mass of exposed bone and blood.

Eve grabbed for the diagnostic wand, forcing herself to move it slowly enough so that the machine could analyze the injuries. There were several gashes, deep and parallel, across his body and down his legs. The printout chattered to life, and she heard Mark at the console, tapping in requested information as the machine took charge of the medical functions. Richard was breathing shallowly and his color was ashen, but he was still alive.

Mark, at the console, began calling instructions. "Eve, the biolab says to put the reorganizer over the left shoulder and arm. It also says that you have to move back because you're in the way."

Reluctantly, she moved away from the table. Her conscious mind knew the machine could do far more than she could for the child, but her instincts demanded she be nearby. She moved to the console with Mark. Morris stuck his head in the door. "Is he going to be all right?"

Eve looked at him, unable to control the fears she felt. "I hope so. Please don't say anything about this to the other children. Just get them settled, then you can come back if you want. It's going to take a while for the biolab to do its work."

Morris nodded and left the doorway. She could hear him relaying her message to Kenneth. Their voices faded as they hurried to get the children to bed.

She stood with Mark, watching the machine work over the small body on the table. It carefully rejoined the torn skin of the small shoulder, miraculously eliminating even a trace of scars, then moved down to the arm. While the reorganizer worked, the other arm of the biolab positioned a tube in Richard's uninjured arm and synthesized blood began to flow into his body to replace the blood he had lost. The synthesized blood would not only replace the fluids, but contained powerful antibiotics to fight any infections.

Eve realized she had little or no idea about what microorganisms would be carried by the animals on Genesis and hoped somehow the biolab had been able to analyze at least some of them in the past from local hydrocarbons with which she had experimented.

The machine seemed to know what needed to be done, and she felt rising anger at her own helplessness. The biolab arm placed another tube into Richard's leg and a clear fluid began flowing through it. She knew then the biolab had analyzed what Richard needed most for nutrients and to fight the infections which had entered his body.

Richard's breathing began deepening and some color was returning to his skin. While the cellular reorganizer continued to hum over the badly damaged arm, the other arms of the biolab began to remove the rest of Richard's coveralls, cutting them away and cataloging the other injuries in order of severity. The machine would automatically attend to all of them in the proper sequence, saving the minor scratches for last.

Mark put his arms around Eve. "Richard's going to be all right, Eve. The biolab won't let him die."

She looked down into Mark's eyes and returned his hug. "As soon as the others come in, we'll talk about what happened. Can you keep an eye on the biolab?"

He released her and went to the console. "Sure, though it doesn't really need me."

She smiled at him. "Or me. But it'll give you something to do while we're waiting."

She dropped into one of the chairs at the console next to Mark. The waiting was the worst part. All of Richard's vital signs were stabilizing, to her vast relief, and she began to believe that he would survive.

The tensions were fighting to take over, but she forced them into submission with yoga, knowing her reaction to the tragedy would be as important to the children as the disaster itself.

The machine emitted a quiet warning bell and she turned immediately to the console. Its impersonal screen typed out "Damage to left forearm beyond repair. Recommend amputation above elbow to save patient. Damage beyond repair."

She and Mark looked at each other, then at the biolab and at Richard. She walked over to the table, knowing the machine would wait for her instructions and looked closely at the left forearm.

It was badly mangled, the bone shattered and huge chunks of flesh missing. She felt a wave of nausea and took a deep breath to control it, then turned to the console and tapped in her agreement.

The cellular reorganizer was joined by the surgical arm

of the biolab which used a laser beam to sever the child's arm, then retreated as the reorganizer patched the skin over the end of the stump.

Mark watched in horrified fascination as the machine removed the severed arm and slid it into the recycler. Eve remembered vividly the mutant child and the equally cold reaction of the machine at that time. Again she knew the biolab was correct in its analysis of the situation, but somehow felt it was wrong in its inhumanity.

After repairing the stump, the reorganizer moved to the deep scratches across Richard's body and leg, mending them. Richard still had not stirred to consciousness and Eve worried about it until she remembered that major repairs were always done with an anesthetic, which would be chemically reversed when the biolab had finished.

Morris and Kenneth returned as the reorganizer finished its work on the gashes and moved on to attend to the more minor scratches and bumps. The other deputies joined them.

"Is everyone in bed?" Eve knew that she had to return the situation to as much normalcy as possible.

They nodded dumbly, staring at Richard's missing arm.

"We all will have a lot to talk about once Richard is past the crisis. The reorganizer was unable to repair the damages to his arm, so it had to be amputated. Richard will be fitted with a synthesized arm before he wakes up and it will be hard to tell it from his real one, so let's talk now about how we'll help him adjust. He's had a terrible experience, but he's going to be fine, physically."

As though confirming her words, the biolab began fitting a prosthetic arm to the stump. It would be replaced as he grew and would function as well as his original arm, complete with feeling and natural motion, so the psychological damages would be lessened.

The children watched, fascinated, as the machine worked, and the room was silent. Finally, Morris said, "What was that thing that hurt him?"

All of them turned toward her. Obviously, Morris and Kenneth had told the story to the other deputies and Eve hoped they hadn't fallen prey to the temptation to exaggerate. It was bad enough in reality.

"I don't know what to call it because I've never seen one before, though there was a time when I was alone when one probably very like that attacked a hovercraft I was riding in after I'd had an accident."

"Why did it do that to Richard?" Morris was relentless in his questioning, but she realized it was his way of coping with the fears he felt.

"I don't know why, except that Richard must have looked like food to the animal. Remember, animals don't live by the same rules we do and big animals like that one will hunt smaller animals for food. I don't think there was any evil intent in what it did."

"But if it wasn't evil, why did you kill it? You've told us that killing is wrong."

"Killing is wrong, no matter what the excuse. I should have tried to stun it enough to get Richard away from it, but I reacted in panic and didn't take the time to reset the gun. Then, when it leapt toward me, I killed it to protect all of us."

The children watched the biolab working on Richard's arm, but they were obviously digesting what she had said.

"Why don't you all go out into the main room and get some juice and I'll stay here with Richard until he wakes up. Then we can all talk."

Obediently, they filed out into the main room, leaving her alone with Richard. Finally, after removing the tubes from his arm and leg, the biolab's humming was silenced. Richard struggled to wakefulness. When he saw Eve, he reached for her, crying, and she lifted him into her arms, wrapping him in a blanket and holding him tightly.

"Richard, you're going to be fine. You had a terrible experience, but you're going to be fine. It's okay now."

She continued to reassure him until he stopped crying.

"You had quite an adventure, and the children are anxious to talk to you about it. Do you want to talk to them?" She blotted at his tears with the corner of the blanket.

He sniffled but continued to hold to her tightly. "My arm feels funny."

"I know it does. The animal that attacked you hurt your arm so it couldn't be fixed by the biolab and it had to be replaced. It will feel funny for a few days until you get used to the new one, but then you'll forget which arm you had replaced. I promise."

He pulled his left arm free of the blanket and studied it, flexing the fingers and elbow. "It looks like my arm, but it feels funny. I'm hungry."

"Why don't you put on these coveralls and we'll go out and get something to eat and you can tell everyone your story. We can all learn something from what happened to you."

He took the coveralls off the stack and put them on. No scars showed on his body and Eve could hardly believe this was the same child she had carried away from the animal. The biolab's healing miracles were responsible for Richard's being able to function immediately as if nothing had happened, and she was grateful for that.

Now she had to be able to deal with whatever psychological damage had been done. That was something which would take time, she knew, and she wanted to be sure he wasn't left with permanent emotional scars or unreasonable fears.

He finished dressing, and then, clutching her hand, they went out into the main room. The deputies gathered around him, all talking at once. He continued to hold tightly to Eve's hand, so she caught Morris's eye and said, "Richard says he's really hungry and so am I. Can you work some magic with the synthesizer for both of us?"

Morris rushed to the food processor while the rest of the group moved to the benches. Eve noticed the door to the outside was closed and it made her angry that suddenly fear had become a part of their lives. The animal's attack would change the texture of their community forever, adding caution and fear where there had been confidence and a sense of adventure.

Morris brought trays of food for Richard and Eve and a pitcher of juice for the group. Richard ate heartily, but Eve discovered her appetite was only a function of nerves and she picked at her food. No one spoke.

Richard finished and put his container to one side. Cilia took it to the recycler and then returned quickly to the group.

Finally Eve broke the silence. "Why don't you tell us what happened, Richard?"

He took her hand before he began, then said, "Well, we were near the transport, Morris and I, and we saw one of those furry animals that live in the grass. We looked for a nest of them because we thought there might be babies and it would be fun to have one. Morris was talking to Harrison and James when I saw another one of those animals run into the grass, so I ran after it. It had a hurt foot, so it couldn't run too fast and I caught it near the mountain.

"I was going to bring it back to the biolab and fix it, but it kept wiggling away and trying to bite me, so I was trying to figure out how to carry it back with me.

"It took a long time, I guess, because it was starting to get dark when I finally wrapped it in a sleeve from my coverall to bring it back. It was making a squeaky noise, but I had it all wrapped up and it couldn't get away.

"I was at the edge of the grass near the mountains and coming back here when I heard a noise behind me. It was a big black animal and it had red eyes and it growled really loud."

Eve felt his fear and put her arm around him. "Richard, remember that it's all over now and that you're all right."

The children nodded their agreement. She didn't want the lesson they learned to be one of fear, but of common sense.

"The black animal was behind me, in the rocks. I didn't want him to hurt the little furry one, so I held on to it and kept walking. I could hear the big animal, behind me, growling, and I got really scared.

"The little animal was wiggling and squeaking and I had to put him down because he was trying to get away. He ran into the grass, but the big animal didn't chase him, he kept following me.

"All of a sudden, he jumped on me and dragged me into the rocks, and that's all I remember. The big animal smelled terrible and it growled so loud. I was really scared."

The room was silent, each of them thinking about Richard's story. Eve couldn't let that be the end, so she said, "Well, we found you in time and that's good. And now we know there are dangerous animals on Genesis and that we have to be more careful when we're out in the valley. I'm sure that if these animals were all around, we would have seen them before, so I don't think we have to worry about them, but we do have to pay attention to the fact that they are there and that they are dangerous. Right?"

The children all nodded solemnly. She hoped she was making a positive impression on them, overriding the fears they felt from the encounter with the animal.

"I think, in the morning, we should go and bring the animal back so the biolab can study it. The more we know about it, the less fearsome it will be. We can also give it a name, because things with a name are less frightening."

Morris said, "You mean a name like Morris?"

"No, honey, a name that will cover the whole group of those animals, just like we're all called humans. That's the name of our group of animals."

"Well, was there anything on Earth that looked like that thing?" Kenneth's scientific interest had been stimulated, overriding his fears.

"I remember seeing pictures of an animal called a lion which had lived in Africa, but it was tan and had a mane of hair around its neck. There was also one called a tiger which was striped orange and black, and there was a leopard which was all black, but smaller than this. They're all members of a larger group called the cat family which ranged in size from very small to very large. Some of them, smaller ones, were house pets. From what I could see, the animal Richard encountered was similar to the cats. We'll be able to tell better in the morning, but you can name it now, if you want to."

Cilia said, "I think Richard should name it. It's his animal."

Richard thought about it for a moment, then said, "What did you say they had called the black one that wasn't as big as this?"

"Leopard."

"Then I think we should call it leopard, just like on Earth." His decision seemed to help him to regain some stability.

Richard was basically a resilient child who seemed to be able to cope pretty well with most situations, and Eve hoped it would carry over, turning this into a victory for the colony by his example.

"Leopard it is then. Let's not scare the younger children with stories about the leopard. We'll tell them, of course, that leopards are out there, but let's not make it any worse than it is by making the story more dramatic. Do you all understand?"

They nodded.

"We can learn some valuable lessons from the leopard as well as have the opportunity to closely study an animal from Genesis, since I did kill the animal. The first lesson we can learn is we don't wander away from the group and the second lesson is we must be careful about how we react to the animals on our planet, large and small.

"Maybe, Richard, the squeaking of the small animal attracted the attention of the leopard in the first place.

They've never paid attention to any of us before now, so
there had to be something that brought the leopard to you."

Eve didn't sleep well, wavering between dreams of the
leaping leopard with his red eyes and alert wakefulness,
listening into the night for noises she wasn't sure were
there. Several times she got up to wander through the halls
of the complex, checking on the children. Her tours always
ended at the closed front door.

She wanted very much to open it, defying her planet to
intimidate her, but at the same time fearing what might be
on the other side.

Suddenly the balance was gone, the romance of being
pioneers thrust into the reality of a huge black cat creature
with red eyes that had leapt out of the night, leaving a
bleeding child behind.

Finally, near dawn, she made one more tour of the sleeping children, then returned to the door. Either it could stay
closed, trapping the fear outside and imprisoning them inside or it could be opened as it had been all along and she
could again take charge of Genesis. Slowly she reached toward the touch-control panel. She took a deep breath, then
pressed against the panel. The door slid soundlessly to the
side.

The moon was setting beyond the distant hills and bath-
ing the valley in gentle light. Below her, the transport
gleamed in the light. It was still, the wind waiting for dawn
to appear, and nothing had changed about Genesis. Except
inside her head.

She stood up on the ledge for a while, reconditioning
herself, remembering the first incident with a leopard so
long ago, before it had a name and a form, before the threat
had become action. Now she had to resume control of the
environment in order to lead her group of colonists.

She realized she had been naive about Genesis in assuming she would have seen all the dangers there were in her
first two years, even though she had rarely ventured away

from the complex. Now she stood and looked at herself as an outsider.

Her colony numbered forty and occupied less space than a small village on the face of a planet covered with unexplored lands and seas, and their attendant dangers. She was flooded with the realization of how much work lay ahead of them.

She stayed in the doorway until the sun began to change the color of the sky, then, leaving the door open in defiance, went back to bed, sleeping deeply until one of the children woke her.

"Eve, are we going to get the leopard this morning?" Richard was patting her on the shoulder.

She fought upward out of the sleep that had held her, then remembered that this same child now longing for the adventure of finding the leopard was the one who had almost died as a result of its attack.

As she stepped into the sonar cleanser, then into a fresh coverall, she reflected on how she had probably suffered more psychological damage than any of the children, who were now looking forward to the adventure at hand.

They made an expedition, the deputies, Eve, and Richard, carrying a large piece of strong fabric in which to wrap the animal. Eve carried a laser gun in case they encountered another leopard. They walked along the path she had run the night before, leisurely reaching the area in which they had found Richard.

They started up through the rocks to the plateau, the excitement of the children who hadn't seen the leopard mounting.

Eve could see the plateau from which the leopard had sprung at her and knew she was standing almost exactly where she had stood the night before.

The leopard was gone.

PART III

Chapter Eight

———◆———

"...AND, BY THE signing of this marriage contract, do agree to live as husband and wife for a period of five years, renewable with five-year options. Do you both freely agree to sign the contract, understanding the total implications of a marital agreement?"

Kenneth and Cilia looked at each other, smiling, then said in unison, "I do."

"Further, there is a breeding clause in your contract which licenses you for unlimited endo children, but specifies that you will, should children be produced as a result of this contract, continue to renew your options until they are of age for community school. Do you both freely agree to sign the breeding clause?"

Kenneth and Cilia both chorused "I do" again.

Eve had expected it. They had been begging her for permission to marry and breed for several months, but she had insisted they complete their studies before they married, knowing what a full-time job study was. Reluctantly they had agreed to wait.

Kenneth, fascinated by the animals of Genesis, had chosen ecobiology as his field and had begun an extensive cataloging of the animals in the valley and mountains around the complex. He, too, had ventured across the valley to the camp of the primitives and had returned to the complex with a story that reminded Eve vividly of her trip there fourteen years before.

But Kenneth had returned again and again, each time making himself more visible to the primitive aliens. Soon they had become used to seeing him and were not afraid when he came into their village.

Cilia had chosen genetics, determined to research the genetic structures of the creatures on Genesis and the strains of inherited characteristics. Because of her chosen work, her studies had closely paralleled Kenneth's and they had spent many hours together, working over the lab tables in the additional room which had been added to the biolab.

They had shared their studies with Richard who, following his original interests, had chosen to become an ecobotanist, collecting the plants of Genesis, studying them, cataloging them, and carefully naming each species in Earth's tradition.

Cilia's genetic interests had led her to go with Kenneth to study the primitives. Her fondest hope was to take a skin scraping to study their genes, but neither of them felt the time had been right to be able to communicate why they needed to do the scrapings. Both had learned to express the concepts of peace and friendship to the primitives, using their hand-gesture language, but the clicks and squeaks of verbal communication still evaded their human tongues.

Cilia was a radiant bride, looking up at Kenneth. Her flashing dark eyes and coal black hair contrasted vividly with her pale skin and delicate features. She appeared to be small, petite in stature, but Eve realized she had to look up to talk to her, which meant Cilia was at least one meter, seventy centimeters in height.

Kenneth, too, was tall, but his stocky build and assertive personality matched his size. He was blonde with blue-green eyes and a sprinkling of freckles across his rosy cheeks. They were a handsome couple, standing before her in their youthful excitement.

They were the colony's first marriage contract and the other members of the colony stood behind them, in Congregation, holding flowers gathered from the valley.

The colony numbered over a hundred and filled the main room which had once seemed so large.

"The marriage contract is a legal formality. It can be dissolved according to the provisions. The emotional commitment goes far beyond a contract. We are a small colony of pioneers, grown now from one to a hundred and still growing all the time. The importance of marriage and family life is inestimable to us and we here in Congregation send you out as a couple with our love and blessings."

Kenneth and Cilia turned to face the rest of the colonists, and there was spontaneous applause.

Eve said, "There was a custom on Earth that, after a couple was officially man and wife, they would kiss. Kenneth, you may kiss your wife."

The couple both blushed, but Kenneth took Cilia in his arms and they kissed to the further applause of the assembled Congregation, who then gathered around to wish them well.

Eve watched from the side, studying her colony. They ranged in chronological age from infant to fourteen, but since they were all exos, the visual image was infant to adult.

The first group decanted had matured four years before and were finished with their basic studies, though they would all continue to delve into their various fields for many years to come.

Sometimes Eve felt strange, watching the colonists. They

had grown so fast and she felt as though she had missed pieces of their lives with the pressures of the sheer numbers of children.

Now she had more time to spend with the young ones, and did, but she worried about what she might have left out of the development of the older ones. They all seemed, on the surface, to be intelligent, well adjusted, and mature, but she knew each had problems. Some of the problems were simply a function of the human condition, and those usually came out in personal relationships.

It was difficult for children who had grown up together and seen each other constantly throughout their childhood to suddenly shift their thinking from a vague brother-sister sort of relationship to that of potential mates.

She had always stressed to them that they were individuals and none were related, but the colony did have a familiar aura about it that was undeniable. She had also been careful to downplay the taboos against incest among the children, knowing they would have to be reeducated later as children were born to couples and natural brothers and sisters occurred.

But something more than that was bothering her and she had only recently been able to define it. For a long time she had been the only adult on the planet, the only decision-maker, the final voice of authority. Now there were other adults making their own life decisions, frequently without consulting her. It was a mixed blessing. She wanted them to be independent, but at the same time felt rejected and deserted when they didn't come to her for answers. She had even found herself resentful of good decisions they had made on their own.

She knew it was a flaw in her personality and tried to control it, but sometimes it would affect her relationships with the colonists. There had been times when, needing to share a victory, they had come to tell her of a success and she had needed to control her impulse to criticize, to tear down something which had been built without her approval, supervision, or involvement.

She knew the refusal to grant permission to marry to Kenneth and Cilia had been one of those instances. She could have allowed them to marry before they had finished their studies, knowing their deep involvement with their joint research wouldn't be dimmed by a personal relationship, but something in Eve's personality had made her refuse permission, holding on to her authority protectively, unwilling to admit to herself that by doing a good job raising her charges, she had created her own dilemma.

Logically, she knew that it was imperative for them to develop into a colony of adults, but she hated the loss of overt control. There were still secrets she held and she guarded them ever more zealously. She was the only one on the planet who knew the true reason for the colonizations in the first place. She had told them as they grew that the colonies had been conceived to carry the excellence of man out across the universe. She had not told them of the wars, hatreds, rivalries, and jealousies that had pushed the Earth to the only decision they could make. Only she knew the real history of the race, the rampant wars and inhumanities committed throughout history, and those were secrets she was determined to keep. Genesis would never know the reality of war.

In their studies, they had encountered war as a concept, but carefully slanted to seem a savage and senseless activity engaged in only by primitive societies unable to reason. The colonists had grown up believing war was totally and completely wrong, incompatible with the human condition. More than anything else, she was almost obsessed to preserve that among her colonists.

She watched them milling around the room, groups forming and dissolving as conversations changed. She was satisfied with all of them as people and felt she had lived up to the expectations of the Project Directors. Still seeking their approval, she thought with disgust.

"It's a big step for the colony, isn't it?" Morris's quiet voice startled her and she jumped involuntarily. "I'm sorry. I didn't mean to surprise you. You were certainly lost in your thoughts."

She smiled at him, taking his arm. Morris had become her closest friend among the colonists and they spent many hours together, discussing the future of the colony, the directions it could take and the advantages and disadvantages of each. Morris had, as he grew, begun to show an active interest in the planning for the future of the colony as well as in its past and had finally chosen a dual career.

He was primarily interested in colonial development, following Eve's career direction, but secondarily had become the chief historian of the colony, logging the advances and growth of the group into the computer records.

Sometimes she wondered how much of her affection for him stemmed from her memory of his father and how much of it had grown of itself. Morris had his father's look —tall, handsome, and self-confident. He sometimes surprised her with a sense of humor that paralleled his father's closely. But he was most definitely his own man. Where his father had looked to the stars as an astrophysicist, dismissing the failings and doings of man as inconsequential in the overall picture, the son was vividly interested in his fellow man, the society in which he lived, and the workings of his mind. The younger Morris was also quieter, more serious, and more direct than his father had been.

"I was thinking that we have every reason to be optimistic about our colony and its future. And I was also enjoying the happiness of the moment for Kenneth and Cilia. And our happiness in what their marriage represents to all of us."

He looked at her for a long moment, then said quietly, "Then why did you force them to wait so long?"

She felt a twinge of irritation with his question. He had the freedom to question her, but they had left this topic alone. "I wanted to be sure they finished their studies before beginning a new life together with all the necessary adjustments."

He studied her, making her uncomfortable. "I don't think that's the whole rationale. I don't necessarily want you to tell me about it, but have you examined all the reasons? Are you being honest with yourself?"

She pulled away from him, angry at his presumptive questioning. He followed her across the room, talking softly.

"You have no reason to be angry with me if your only reason was interest in their studies, so obviously there is more."

He took her shoulders, turning her to face him. "I have no intention of hurting you or making you angry, but I know you very well and I've been seeing something lately that I don't think is really you. The permission for Kenneth and Cilia is typical. Just give it some thought."

She still felt the anger, but suppressed it, knowing her reaction would be important to the continuity of their comfortable relationship.

"I guess part of it is that I still have trouble adjusting to the idea that my deputies are adults now. The time passed so quickly."

He took her hand, leading her to the ledge outside the complex. The evening breeze fluttered around them, rustling the fabric of their coveralls. She looked out across the familiar face of the valley, watching the edging of green around the distant mountains and wishing Morris had never started this conversation.

The longer she lived on Genesis, the more lonely she had become, secreting her real self behind a calm leadership facade. She knew the possessiveness she felt for the colonists came from that loneliness and the fear of again being completely alone as she had been at first. She knew marriage for her was unrealistic, not only because of the quasi-maternal way in which she regarded and was regarded by the colonists, but also because of the delicate balance of the society.

While the loneliness was a strong consideration, the other side of the picture was her protectiveness of her solitude, her inability to let anyone into her real emotions for fear of the damage they could do. Morris was treading on very fragile ground.

He gave her a moment with her thoughts, then said, "We were never your children, Eve. We were an accident, as your arrival here alone was an accident. You had a great responsibility thrust upon you and now you can be freed of that responsibility. You can spread it out among all of us just as you would have if the colony had arrived intact.

"You've been here sixteen years and most of that time has been grabbed away from you by the colony, taking your time and personal privacy whether or not you wanted to give it. Now you have the opportunity to go back to your original purpose here, to develop the colony as you were trained to do. I'm not trying to take any importance away from you, for you have given more than anyone has a right to expect. None of us demand it of you, but you seem to demand it of yourself."

"Have you all discussed this?" Her tone was flat.

"No, Eve, we haven't. This is my personal observation and you can accept it or not as you wish. I simply know that I see you drawing into yourself but at the same time unable to let go of us. You must achieve a balance for yourself without constantly thinking of the rest of us. That's all I'm trying to say. I'm worried about you. I'm not your child, I'm your friend. Do you understand?"

She kept her eyes on the horizon, her emotions tangling. His presumptive intrusiveness made her angry, but mixed with the anger was the tempering loneliness and the offer of the confidant she had needed for so long. She said nothing, avoiding his eyes.

He waited, leaning against the complex building, apparently content to stand and wait for her. But, out of the corner of his eye, he watched her. She had once told him about his father and he had filled in the spaces she left, understanding that she and his father had been lovers but had been separated by the Project.

There were a lot of gaps she left in her stories about life on Earth, reasons for the Project, people and history, but in his explorations of the computer record tapes, he could glean no more than she had told them. He felt he had a lifetime to find out what it was she didn't say, so he was, as in all things, patient.

But lately she had been difficult, withdrawn and quick to anger, and he couldn't allow that to happen to any of the colonists, least of all Eve. She was the example, almost held in awe by the other colonists. They knew the sacrifices she had made since coming to Genesis, and, in her first history tapes, Morris could hear the desperate scream of loneliness in her first years before the biolab had begun its mindless propagation.

He had wondered if maybe it was wrong that they had been produced, if it wouldn't have been better for her to be alone or to choose the schedule on which the machine had begun forcing a population of infants on her.

He also wondered if she ever would have made the schedule choice. She was so strong in so many areas, a natural leader, outwardly confident and serene in all situations. He remembered how she had reacted with Richard and the leopard. She had never let her fears show until she thought they were all in bed. He had watched her, sitting out on the ledge in the dawn, and had known how she fought to control her fear.

On the other hand, he knew of her weaknesses. He had watched her in unguarded moments and felt her indecision about so many things. Only he, of all the others, knew how she agonized over her decisions, trying to find the right routes to guide the colony toward peace and growth.

There had been other times he longed to tell her that she could lean on the others, but knew she wouldn't accept their help. Now he had to force her to accept it, before she lost sight of her goals and those of the colony she had designed.

Silence stood between them and Eve let it stay, protecting her against her own thoughts. The noises of the party went on inside the complex and she could hear music and laughter drifting out through the door. Finally she turned toward him.

"I understand what you're trying to tell me, but I think you're being unfair. You make it sound as though I interfere with the lives of the people here. It certainly wasn't my choice or decision to be the only adult, the only survivor of our journey. And, as confident as all of you may be about your abilities to make decisions, you simply haven't as much life experience as I do, so sometimes I can see the broader picture, that's all." She paused, looking at him with a smile.

"And, I will admit there certainly are times when I think of you as my children. It would be hard not to, when I shared in raising all of you. But I do think of you as my friend, Morris, and I appreciate your concern for my well-being. I'll try to take more time, for myself. We all should. Now, let's go back to the party."

She walked past him with a pat on his arm, but he didn't follow her immediately, standing alone in the night, listening to the blending of noises from this world and another.

He had lost the encounter and regretted even bringing it up to her. She was determined, it was obvious, to maintain her solitude and wouldn't welcome any further discussion on the topic from him. He pushed away from the wall with a sigh and rejoined the party.

Eve lay listening to the gentle music coming from the viewing screen, staring up into the darkness, thinking.

Morris was right about her feelings concerning the colonists. They were all very much her children and her responsibility and she was reluctant to let them go. But he was also right in telling her she had to release them to their own destinies. She suddenly realized what she had been missing all along and the realization staggered her. She had spent her first two years getting adjusted to life on Genesis, still tied to Earth through the reserve hydrocarbons, the knowledge, the complex, her very way of life. She had made only three attempts to become part of the planet: her visit to the alien village, her visit to the seashore, and the discovery of the conversion of local hydrocarbons. Otherwise, she had continued to be imposed on the landscape, an alien in her world, clinging to Earth and to the people there. Then, when the children had begun arriving, she had virtually stopped making any attempts to conquer the land, fighting only to provide the children with a home and an education. But even that had been a strong tie to Earth.

She sat up, her mind racing with sudden understanding. She had been so negligent! True, the children in her charge had grown to adulthood with reasonably good educations, but she had unconsciously been resenting that education and maturity for the freedom it represented, fearing aloneness would envelop her again. But she had, to this point, failed, allowing the colony to develop without any particular direction and guidance, losing sight of the long goals in favor of the daily needs.

She got up and slipped into her coverall. The night air was clear and crisp with a few high clouds drifting across the stars. She checked the chron in the main room as she passed through; it was still three hours until first light, but she felt refreshed from her discovery.

She looked out over the valley below her and felt almost ashamed. She had lived in this complex for sixteen years and yet the valley remained virtually unchanged since that night so long ago when she had first stood looking out from the doorway of her new home, fearful of the adventure she faced.

That was the crux of the problem, she decided. She had allowed fear to take the place of her sense of adventure. She had tried to hide her humanity and its evidence rather than trying to dominate the environment. She had clung to Earth almost as though she expected to go back, rather than releasing it and its people from her mind and pushing forward on her own planet.

She rubbed her hands across her face in frustration, realizing the terrible mistake she had made and hoping she wasn't too late to correct it; hoping she hadn't allowed the slow lethargy to destroy the potential of a viable colony.

"...key to colonial development is leadership. Without a dynamic leader who takes charge of the colony, it will fail. Everyone here has read the ancient work Walden I assume."

Professor Lang looked around the room at the students who all nodded, whether or not they had read the textape. Lang had a reputation of being a man-eater, prone to violent rages with students who shirked, and no one in the class wanted to become the object of his wrath.

Eve had read Walden, but had dismissed it as unrealistic. In a world condemned to pollution and technology the idyllic Utopia had little merit in her thinking.

"...suggested that a community could exist with a purely democratic structure, each responsible for his own with no leader for guidance. Unfortunately, that simply does not work in a viable society. Perhaps if we could have an isolated group of slow-moving thinkers, that could change.

"The Marxists based some of their philosophy-of-community on the Utopic philosophers, but soon learned in actuality that pure communism is only a dream; that a strong leader must take charge or the communes will not advance."

Lang leaned forward over his desk, looking at each of them in turn. Eve wasn't as frightened of him as some of the others, but he was awe-inspiring, his demeanor alone demanding respect.

"Some of you will pursue a career in the Project, I am well aware, and feel that expertise in colonial development will buy you a free ride into space. If it does, and if you succeed, you will be faced with an enormous task far beyond the imagina-

*tion of any of us here on Earth, for you will need to evolve a
community unlike anything anyone on Earth has experienced
since the last days of pioneering in the late nineteenth.
Frankly, I wouldn't go on any of the Project ships if they
dragged me, kicking and screaming, for anyone who does has
the opportunity to create Hell."*

She was the natural leader of the colony and she had
allowed herself to avoid that responsibility through benign
neglect, but no longer. Now she had to actively take charge
to develop the potential she had with her colonists before
they grew too numerous and uncontrollable.

They met in the main room.

Morris had come to her after reading the viewing-screen
announcement, but she had laughingly put him off, saying,
"It's a surprise for everyone and I don't want to spoil it. I've
had some time to think after we talked yesterday and I
have an idea which I'll share with everyone at the same
time."

Realizing she wasn't going to reveal any more, he had
gone off to the computer room to continue his studies, his
stride showing his disgust with her secretiveness.

The afternoon sun came through the door, reflecting light
into the room off the plasteel floor, giving a bright optimistic glow to the gathering. Eve stood up on one of the
benches so she could be clearly seen, and everyone began to
quiet down around her.

"You are all familiar with the development of this colony
since I arrived here sixteen years ago from Earth. We have
grown since then, from a single occupant to a population of
one hundred and four. We have laughed together and lived
together, and now we are blessed with not one adult, but
many, and all of diverse skills. We have, together, built the
nucleus of a great population that will someday control
this entire planet.

"Yesterday, we achieved another first: the marriage of
two people born here who never have seen Earth, and that,
to me, is a milestone."

The colonists applauded, looking at Kenneth and Cilia who smiled, holding hands.

Eva continued. "Today we are going to add another milestone to our planet's history. We are going to move forward from this day, no longer tied to Earth as strongly as we have been, for we will never see that planet again nor hear from anyone there, for they do not know where we are or if we even exist."

She looked around the room. This was a new bit of information for the colonists. While she had never told them they could not possibly return to Earth and had never implied the United Governments could find them, she had also never revealed how totally cut off they were from the mother planet. Now they knew.

"What that means to us is that we are essentially alone. Someday we may develop the means to travel in space freely, as did the people on Earth, and maybe some of our descendants will visit that planet in the future, but for us, Genesis is our future.

"However, please do not look on this information as unhappy, for it is our great joy to be true pioneers in a land which is completely fresh and new. We have the opportunity to develop the resources—animal, human, plant, and mineral—to the highest degree; to send out a population to all corners of this world; to make man the dominant animal on Genesis. The Project Directors didn't know what the exploratory ships would find, if anything, but they dreamed of colonies like ours, spread across the stars, carrying the greatness of man throughout the universe."

Eve found herself stirred by her own words and could see the effect they were having on the assembled group. Some of the younger children were listening without truly understanding, but the older colonists were beginning to catch her enthusiasm and she wanted to build a fire of excitement in all of them so they could transmit it to the younger members.

"In order to grow, we must have direction. We must

evolve a Council of Leaders who will guide our growth and expansion and who will help us all to use the resources we have to their fullest potential. Imagine if you will, that a ship would come from Earth to check on our progress, in, say, fifty years. I want to build our colony so if that ship were to arrive, they would look at us and be astounded and proud of the way in which we have fulfilled the dreams of the Project started so long ago in so distant a place. Let us work together to that goal."

There was spontaneous applause from the colonists and she knew she was presenting her ideas so they would be accepted without question. That was the key, as far as she was concerned, for in order for this to work, all of the colonists had to be involved. The applause quieted.

"Each of us has a skill to contribute. The earliest members of the colony, those who are now adults, have chosen their fields of interest and are actively pursuing them. You younger colonists who are just beginning your studies or who are about to choose a field must choose with a care equal to theirs. Explore the areas not yet selected to see what you can best contribute to our great mission. Someday we will have children and they will have children, and we must, together, build a world in which they can live with joy. It is our great responsibility to ourselves and to them, for we are building the foundations of a great home for mankind, far from the planet of his origins."

Again there was applause. She looked around the room at each face. Kenneth and Cilia were, like most of the assembled group, caught up in her excitement and enthusiasm and they visibly glowed with the ideas she was planting.

The only signs of doubt she could see came from Morris and Richard. They had some of the excitement, but she knew they would carefully explore everything she presented to the group in their minds, turning each concept over and over to be sure it was valid. She had anticipated that and knew she could use it to her own advantage in her plan.

"I have evolved a plan of action to present to you to fulfill these dreams for all of us. First, I envision the need for a Council to guide us on our path of growth and expansion. This group will evolve an overall plan by which we can grow. Because I am the eldest and the first resident, I will become temporary Chairman of the Council.

"Everyone here is a member of the government and free to submit ideas and plans to the Council who will then sort among them and make the decision as to which of the plans submitted will be the most effective. Each member of the Council will head a Department of Colonial Growth for which they will be responsible, and each of you will take membership in one of the Departments, according to interest or education.

"As exo children reach the chronological age of ten, they will choose a Department and will begin functioning within that Department.

"All decisions affecting the entire colony will be presented in Council, then offered to everyone for a vote. Majority will rule, as in any democracy. Eventually we will hold elections for Chairman and Council members, so all of these appointments are temporary until we can work the problems out of the government and hold elections."

She noticed the adult colonists were nodding in understanding and agreement and she looked at Morris and Richard.

They were holding a quiet conference, but she couldn't see any signs of what their discussion involved or how it was going.

"I have chosen the members of the original Council from the eldest groups. It is not out of favoritism or prejudice but strictly on the basis of length of life experience and education. They are as follows: Richard VanDersant, our first ecobotanist, will sit on the Council as head of the Botanical Development Department and will be assisted by Tai Tang.

"Incidentally, assistants will not sit on the Council in a

voting capacity, but will help in developing each Department and will have second authority to the Council member in Departmental decisions. Obviously, all ecobotanists will work in this Department.

"The Zoological Development Department will be headed by Kenneth Clarkton and his assistant will be Cilia. This Department will study and project uses for the animals of Genesis.

"Mineral Development Department will be headed by Harrison Weinstein and he will be assisted by Prudence Adams. They will work to discover mineral and hydrocarbon sources and develop their uses to the best advantage of the colony.

"Morris Watson will head the Colonial Development Department assisted by Ellen Ashanti. Their Department will plan for the building of new colonies and the assignment to those colonies of various citizens."

She looked at Morris. His interest in the idea was obvious and she was relieved. He truly was her barometer of the mental weather of the colony and his interest was a strong sign.

She continued, "Transportation will be essential to a growing, expanding colony and Janet Garcia will head the Transportation Department, assisted by Robert Barnes.

"Education of the children will be guided by Barbara Petrovitch and she will be assisted by Olaf Knudson. All questions of career choice, studies, or anything related to the education of any colonist, adult or child, will be handled by their Department."

Barbara looked surprised and pleased. She had always been quiet, but popular with the others, possessing a determination and calmness everyone respected and admired.

"Exploration will obviously be extremely important to all of us. We have seen so little of the face of our world and have only rough maps gleaned from the study of the computer tapes of the transport landing so long ago. We must become familiar with our world, its geography and climate. That Department will be headed by Jeremy Wilson, our first geographer, and he will be assisted by Donald O'Meara, James McCarthy, and Sarah Bell. We will expect them to organize explorations.

"The Medical Department, responsible for the health and well-being of the colony, will be headed by Mark Johnson, and assisted by Elizabeth Crawford, our only two medical specialists.

"The Fabrication Department will be in charge of setting up and assembling all new buildings, manufactured goods, and anything else the colony needs of a physical plant nature. Chen Ngu will head the Department and he will be assisted by Ngiba Sumata.

"Finally, to coordinate the efforts of the Colonial Development Department with the Exploration Department, I propose for us to have an Expansion Department which will make the decisions about locations for new colonies as well as for mines and fabrication centers. That Department will be headed by Joan Crane and she will be assisted by Francis Longman. Obviously, they will work closely with all other Department heads.

"The others who have not been assigned to specific duties, I expect will associate themselves with an appropriate Department according to their skills. Are there any questions?"

The room buzzed with discussions and conversations for a few moments while all of the information she had given was digested. There was a high level of excitement in the air and Eve felt triumphant.

She waited, then again asked for questions. No one stood or moved, so she said, "Obviously what has begun today is an enormous task involving each of us actively and on a lifetime course. We are the founders of the civilization of Genesis and have a big job to do. Let us start now, together, and continue the greatness of man."

The colonists stood, applauding, then broke into groups, the older members discussing their assignments or preferences and the children either listening or dashing off to play.

Morris came over to her. "Brilliant," he said, putting his arm around her. "Absolutely brilliant, Madame Chairman. Isn't that what they called them on Earth? Madame Chairman?"

She smiled. "It is, but I don't think that's necessary here. You don't approve of my being Chairman?"

"Of course I do. I'm sure if you'd thrown it to a vote, you would have been elected. You always have been the Chairman anyway, and all of us recognize that and respect it. The brilliance is in the total concept I can only assume you assembled while you were wandering around here last night."

She looked at him, surprised. "How did you know I was 'wandering around here last night'? I didn't see anyone else."

"I know." He smiled sardonically. "You were much too wrapped up in what you were doing."

"Well, what were you doing wandering around?" She was distressed she hadn't seen him.

"I couldn't sleep because I was afraid I'd spoken too harshly to you, and I wanted to think about it, so I went for a walk in the valley. I saw you come out onto the ledge, then, when I came back up, you were busy in the computer room and I didn't want to disturb you. I wasn't intending to spy on you, if that's what you were just thinking."

It was what she had been thinking, but she wasn't going to admit it to him.

"We'll have to have a Council meeting this evening, after everyone has had a chance to think about what I've said. I guess it must have shocked some people, my suddenly changing direction as I did."

Morris laughed. "You are the mistress of understatement. I know for a fact you shocked everyone, but in a pleasant way. What I was trying to tell you last night after the wedding is that we need dynamic leadership as you have just outlined rather than the passive, intervening leadership you had been giving."

"You planted the seeds, certainly. The interesting thing is I had known all along what was needed, but had become so involved with the day-to-day necessities I'd lost sight of the overall picture. You helped me regain it."

Morris looked at her for a long moment, then said, "Yesterday I told you I was not your child, but your friend. I wanted to add one more thing to that, but you weren't ready until now to hear it. I'm also not my father."

He turned away from her, leaving her with uneasy chills.

Chapter Nine

CILIA AND EVE stood on the ledge, watching the loading of the large hovercraft at the foot of the cliff, near the new addition to the complex. The sky was overcast and rain had been spitting from the clouds most of the morning, but no one paid any attention to it in the excitement of the loading for the expedition.

The breeze pulled at the long robe Cilia wore, outlining her full belly. Her baby was due at any time, but she had almost ignored the effects of the pregnancy, continuing to expand her research with the aliens. The departure of the explorers had been the only thing that had kept her from making the journey across the valley and she was anxious to return to the alien camp.

Jeremy emerged from the hull of the transport carrying a coil of rope over his shoulder and a container of spare parts for the hovercraft. He caught sight of them on the ledge and called out, "Sure you don't want to come with us? We're going to have a fine time."

Cilia laughed, putting her hand on her bulging stomach. "With me you'd get two for the price of one, and I don't think you're enough of a pioneer to handle it. Nor am I."

Jeremy's laugh bounced lightly off the cliff wall, ringing around them, and he stowed the rope and box, then came up the stairs.

"I think we've got everything aboard. There's certainly enough room for the six of us in that hovercraft, plus all the equipment and supplies."

Eve smiled. "There should be. It was designed to carry a hundred people. They were used on Earth to carry people from one location to another on the ground, but there they moved on roads. Here, you'll have to be careful."

"We took your advice and took three of the smaller craft. We'll use the big one for long distances and the smaller ones for local areas. We have a fabricator in the on-board computer to replace food and other basics, and that last box was spare parts we can't manufacture."

Eve listened, nodding. They had planned extensively for this journey, for it would take the explorers away from the colony for two years in a short exploration of the various lands and seas.

Jeremy and Donald had spent hours with the computer tapes, planning their routes and making rough maps they would detail as they explored. Their on-board computer would feed constant data to the main computer, so the colonists would know what they were finding and how they were faring.

The six explorers possessed the diverse skills needed to detail Genesis. Jeremy's abilities in geography were coupled with Donald's expertise in botany; James's in oceanography had already taken him to the seashore nearby for a six-month study; Sarah was adding her geological knowledge; Audrey her education in climatology; and Ronald was the team's zoologist.

They could pull information from the central computer through their on-board terminal, and they could also communicate with the complex. Since they would be gone for such a long time, this communication would keep them in touch with the complex and the colony, something which everyone considered essential.

There had been a heated debate in Council about the expedition's use of laser weapons in case of an emergency. Eve had stayed out of the discussion, allowing them to debate the issues as they felt.

Finally she had intervened when it became obvious no resolution was in sight, suggesting they keep the weapons with them, but use them only on a stun setting unless they were confronted with a life and death situation. There was grudging agreement to that from both camps, and the weapons were added to the list of essentials.

There had been a hum of activity in the complex which had culminated in the loading and it seemed everyone was down in the valley to see them off on their expedition, including the newest infants.

Jeremy interrupted Eve's thinking, saying, "I came up to tell you we're ready to go now and to ask you to come down and see us off. For good luck," he added with a smile.

"Of course, I was planning to come down. I wish I could go with you, but we'll see your tapes and share in your discoveries. It's very exciting, Jeremy, and we all send you off with our best wishes."

He took Cilia's arm protectively. As the first endo mother, she had been treated to special privileges since her pregnancy had first been announced in Congregation, much to her embarrassment. She submitted to Jeremy's ministrations without protest, knowing he would insist anyway, and Eve followed them down the stairs.

The crowd around the hovercraft parted to allow them to pass, and the six explorers stood self-consciously beside the door, as if expecting some sort of fanfare. Eve sensed their anticipation and held up her arms for quiet.

"Today we send forth the first explorers of our world who

will come back after giving us much more of a picture of the world on which we live." Everyone applauded.

Eve turned to the explorers, creating a dramatic moment as much for herself as for the colonists. "You have all our blessings and good wishes for your journey." She stepped to each of them, giving them a hug and a kiss, then to the cheers of the crowd, they boarded the hovercraft and the engines hummed to life. The crowd, still cheering, parted and the explorers started north toward the plains and the first segment of their journey.

Eve watched as the craft sped away and was soon out of sight. The crowd of colonists began to go back to their various tasks, and she watched as Barbara herded her children up to the complex buildings in the cliff. Barbara had not only assumed responsibility for the education of the children, but also for their general care and supervision, and she had a number of younger colonists who helped her.

Olaf took a less active role with the children but a more active role in the planning of their education and career selections. He was a serious man, physically smaller than most of the others, vibrantly alive and very persuasive when he wanted to make a point. He was well respected and had been chosen to fill in on the Council during Jeremy's absence. It had been the first change in the Council since its inception a year before.

Eve started back toward the complex stairs, passing the new plasteel buildings which housed the eight married couples. Their building had been suggested by Joan, since none of the rooms in the complex would be comfortable for two, and the Council had approved right away. The rooms were spacious and comfortable, but there was no common room for gathering which meant they would come up to the main complex for meals and meetings.

Joan had recently suggested the construction of an elevator to link the two sets of buildings, primarily, Eve thought, because of Cilia's pregnancy. It was under construction by Chen, Ngiba, and two of their helpers, and would soon be completed, as would another eight sections for families. The complex was growing rapidly.

As she walked, she heard someone coming behind her and turned to see who was in such a hurry. Kenneth looked agitated.

"What's wrong?" she asked, concerned.

"It's Cilia. She just had a pain, and she said she thinks the baby is coming. She's resting in our room. What do we do now?"

Eve took his arm. "The first thing you do is calm down. Babies don't hurry from endo mothers the way they do from the biolab. We have plenty of time and she's doing the right thing just to rest. We'll find Mark and he'll take over."

Kenneth hesitated, so she said, "Why don't you go sit with Cilia and I'll get Mark. Believe me, there's nothing to worry about, Kenneth. Women have been doing exactly what Cilia's doing for all of history. She's probably much calmer than you are."

Kenneth smiled tentatively. "She is. She told me to go to the alien village and get some work done." He seemed astounded by her suggestion.

"You haven't done your homework, have you? You could probably put in a full day's work over there, have dinner, watch a movie, and still be in time for the baby. Just calm down, Kenneth. I'll go get Mark."

Kenneth dashed off in the direction of the married couple's complex and Eve climbed the stairs to find Mark. His first patient would probably be the father, she suspected.

Mark was in the biolab, studying the console. He jumped when she spoke.

"Mark? Sorry, I didn't mean to startle you. Kenneth says Cilia has had a pain."

"I know. She called me on the viewing screen to tell me. I was reviewing the textapes about delivery of an endo. I think I'll bring her up here just so we have all the facilities of the biolab at hand. The last examination I gave her showed the baby to be well positioned and completely normal, so I don't anticipate any problems, but I'd rather be safe."

She felt his nervousness and longed to reassure him, but knew it would seem like a condescension to him, so instead said, "Shall I go down and help her up here?"

He shook his head, regaining some of his calm demeanor. "No, not yet. She still has the pains quite far apart. I don't want to have her being uncomfortable up here when she can be in her own place. We'll bring her up when the pains get to be about five minutes apart. Can you arrange for a room for her here? I want to keep her out of the biolab until she's really ready to deliver the baby, but I don't want her to try those stairs when she's that close. I wish the elevator were finished."

He tapped in the codes for Cilia and Kenneth's room on the viewing screen, then waited until she answered the call. Her face was glowing with excitement. "Yes?"

"Hi, Cilia. How are the pains now?"

"They're still random, but the little devil is kicking like mad. He's obviously in a hurry to get out here and get started." She smiled. Eve could see Kenneth's face in the background, still looking nervous.

"You don't need to come up yet, but when they get about five minutes apart, give me a call and we'll send an escort down to help you come up to the lab. How's the father doing?"

She laughed and stepped aside. Kenneth smiled without much confidence and waved at the screen. "Fine. I'm helping her stay calm."

Mark and Eve laughed as they rang off.

He leaned back in the console chair. "I think everything will be just fine, particularly if you can manage to keep Kenneth calm while the baby is being delivered. I know he wants to be in here."

"I don't know if he'll be a help or a hindrance. What's new in your research?"

"The interesting thing I'm discovering is how much

knowledge and research the doctors on Earth were able to accomplish before modern technology. Do you know that they used to operate with a knife, and that, in order to cure some disorders, they would actually use that knife to open the flesh of the patient, then dig around with their hands? I couldn't believe it. They lost a lot of patients that way. Incidentally, I wanted to ask you, because I haven't been able to find the answer anywhere in the tapes. In my studies, I've found a particular period where extensive work was done with radiation burns. What caused so many?"

Eve caught her breath. She had forgotten that aspect of concealing the effects of the wars, and wasn't prepared for his question.

"Well, I guess it might have been during the time when they were first developing nuclear power on a large scale. They didn't know what we do now about its safe usage."

She knew her answer was lame, and Mark studied her for a moment, then said, "Let's not play that game anymore. We both know those radiation burns affecting huge quantities of people didn't come from research on nuclear power. Eve, we're not children anymore. The tapes show wars in man's history. I've figured out that the Project Directors must have wanted to keep the colonies from making the same mistakes, so they've slanted all the tapes to pretend war was the exception in history on Earth instead of the rule. It doesn't mean we will make the same mistakes, but we must know about them. For example, I think the radiation burns came from nuclear wars of some kind. That was, like all wars, wrong, but look at the miracles it generated: laser surgery, skin and tissue regeneration, and the groundwork for the biolab. Did the Project Directors change the history they included from what you were taught on Earth?" His eyes held hers.

Finally, she said, "Yes, they did, and you're right about the reasons. We were taught the full history on Earth, but they wanted to spare the colonies from the knowledge of such atrocities in the hope they wouldn't be repeated. We all had to take an oath to abide by the history as recorded in the tapes." She cringed inwardly at compounding the lie.

She returned his intense look, then continued. "Mark, think of how frightened they must have been, and how desperate to ensure the survival of mankind, no matter what the cost in lives or money. The Project forced the economy of the entire Earth into bankruptcy, which led to the completely non-monetary system we now have here. Money simply ceased to exist and people were given what they needed. They cared a great deal about the survival of all of us, and so they did some things which may now seem irrational, here, but at the time seemed the only logical solution."

Mark's intensity had softened to reflection. "It must have been a time of great unity and excitement."

She smiled, almost sadly. "It was exciting to be a part of the Project. The ten years of training after selection seemed to go so fast. Everyone wanted to meet us, to touch our hands, as if we would then take a part of them with us."

She shook her head reflectively. "We were all scared to death, if the truth were known. Though no one ever talked about anything but success, in each of us there was a big doubt that we'd ever go anywhere but off into space to become another piece of floating debris rushing to nowhere at the speed of light or leaping around in time and never ending up anywhere. Sometimes I wish I knew about the other ships—where they are and if they survived and if they are succeeding. The problem with time warp travel is that it adds infinity to infinity and the probability of ever knowing the fate of the others is infinitely remote. I can only guess and hope."

Mark studied her. "What do you guess happened to them?"

"I don't know. Based on my own experience, I hold little hope for total survival. Time warp travel is obviously very dangerous and there must be some special combination of physical and mental conditions along with a myriad of other factors which allow some people to survive while others die. I just don't know. Maybe it wasn't the time warp at all but the failure of the suspended animation capsules. The on-board computer which controlled the ship wasn't tied in to this computer and all the records of the journey were destroyed when the ship warped out of orbit. I'll never know."

"You knew them all, didn't you?"

"It would have been impossible not to have known all of them. We were relatively isolated, particularly in the last few years, so the thousand who had been chosen, plus the backup replacements, were together constantly. Everyone who went out to those ships was my friend. You know, I think the strongest bond we have, still, is the fact that all of us who survived, and I'm sure there must have been others, are commonly wondering about the fate of the rest."

They were quiet together, the only sound in the biolab the humming of the computer and the muted heartbeats of the babies in the machine.

"Do you ever wish you hadn't joined the Project?"

She smiled ironically. "In the first two years here, when I was completely alone, listening to the heartbeats in this room and wondering what in hell I was doing here, yes. Now, no regrets at all."

They were interrupted by the bell on the viewing screen. Mark reached forward and activated it, Cilia's face filling the screen as it came to life.

"Cilia. How are you doing?" His tone was both personal and professional.

"I'm fine. I just wanted you to know that the pains are about five minutes apart and stabilizing. I think I'd like to come up the stairs now rather than trying later when someone might have to carry me." She smiled.

Eve sat with Kenneth and Cilia and Mark in the sitting room of her quarters, playing backgammon. Kenneth and Mark were of about equal skill at the ancient game and their contests were heated, but Cilia's ability was greater than Eve's and, even with the distraction of the pains, she won almost every game. They were all trying to be relaxed for the benefit of the others, but the nervous tension crackled in the air around them, increasing when someone would stop by to see how Cilia was doing.

Several of the younger colonists had just departed when Cilia said, "I wish everyone wouldn't make such a fuss over me. It makes me feel as though I'm doing something extraordinary. Now, if they'd take the same interest in our research with the aliens, that would be gratifying."

Kenneth looked up from his game. "Honey, you are doing something extraordinary. The first human, endo mother in this corner of the galaxy is quite an accomplishment. If they make you nervous, we can ask them to go away."

Cilia grimaced as a pain started. Through clenched teeth she said, "No, they have a right to share in this too, just as they did in our wedding." She inhaled sharply through her teeth as the pain increased.

Mark looked at her and said, "Breathe normally, please. It'll help control the pain."

She struggled for a moment, then relaxed her jaw and took a slow breath as Mark checked his watch. "Three minutes now. We're getting there, Cilia. Why don't you lie down for a while."

He stood, reaching his hands toward her to help her lower herself onto her back on the wide bench. "Sorry to spoil your game, but I think you'll be more comfortable."

She smiled up at him. "Mark, you've obviously never been pregnant because if you had you'd know there is no such thing as comfortable when you're shaped like this." She shifted her position slightly. "And, nothing in this complex is made to accommodate a pregnant woman. Do you have any idea what it's like to get into a hovercraft when you can't see your feet?" She chuckled. "The aliens have been very interested in my enlarged shape. I've tried to explain it by indicating one of their children, then pointing to my belly, but I think they think I'm about to produce one of their babies. As soon as I can go back to work and the baby can travel, I'll take it with me to their camp and show them what was making me so fat."

She grimaced with pain as another contraction started, but kept breathing normally. When the pain had passed, she continued. "Mark, we'd like to have you go with us sometime soon. They've gotten used to humans and don't seem to care how many of us are around. We haven't been able to discern how their babies are produced. The only thing we know is that they somehow appear when we're not around. It might be an interesting research project for you or one of your students."

Mark sensed that she was talking to keep her mind off the pains, so he said, "Have you been able to get any skin scrapings yet?"

She and Kenneth both shook their heads. "They keep their distance and get very upset if we try to touch them. We have learned how to communicate in rough gestures, but they seem to forget things quickly and the progress is slow. The first part of every visit there is involved with re-establishing familiarity. They've gotten used to seeing us, but can't seem to remember why."

Kenneth nodded, saying, "I've thought of taking something to them as a gift of friendship or a display of trading, but can't imagine what they'd want of ours. Fabricated goods mean nothing to them and they eat the local plants, so food isn't a good medium."

Cilia added, "They don't use tools of any kind, and I scared one of them half to death with a mirror. He hasn't been near me since I showed him what he looks like."

When the pains became more frequent, Cilia moved to the biolab, carried by Mark and Kenneth, who insisted on staying. Eve had intended to return to her quarters to accomplish some Council business, but Cilia grabbed her hand.

"Eve, please stay. I want you to share in this with us.

Besides"—she smiled past her fears—"I think I'd like a whole lot of people around me."

The birth was an event. Mark and Elizabeth, the two doctors, attended Cilia while the students who were studying medicine stood in a corner of the biolab with Eve, watching the birth with fascination.

The biolab did most of the work, it's mechanical voice instructing Cilia as well as the doctors with step-by-step instructions. Eve sensed that Mark almost resented the biolab's assistance because often he would have begun a step before the biolab's instructions started. Several times she saw him glare at the terminal.

Cilia repeatedly refused anesthetic blocks which would have lessened the pain without interfering with her consciousness.

"No!" she yelled at one point, "I'm a scientist and I must have this experience."

Kenneth held her hand and mopped the perspiration from her forehead, talking to her all the time, but looking as though he were about to pass out at any moment. Eve noticed that Elizabeth watched him carefully.

Finally, after what seemed an interminable process, the baby's head emerged and Mark, holding the child gently, said, "Come on now, Cilia, push hard. I want to see this baby of yours."

She bore down and the baby slid slowly into Mark's hands. "Cilia, you have a son," Mark said, gently putting the baby onto her stomach while he held the umbilical cord for the machine to tie off and sever.

Elizabeth cleared the child's nose and mouth and was rewarded with a lusty howl. Eve had witnessed the process often with the biolab but felt completely different about this baby. The cry was the same, but the baby was special and she found she was crying along with everyone else in the room.

Gently, Mark checked the baby visually, then with the diagnostic wand. "Perfection, Cilia. Absolute perfection."

Kenneth, still holding Cilia's hand, reached toward the baby, touching him hesitantly, a look of awe on his face. "Look at him, Cilia. He's perfect. Just look at him. I can't believe it."

Tiredly, she smiled and said, "You expected anything less?"

Chapter Ten

———◆———

"...finishing our research here and moving on across the land bridge. We have become more accustomed to the cold, though sometimes the temperature after dark becomes quite frigid and ice crystallizes on the outside of the hull. Climatology studies indicate the cold is persistent in this area and there are indications of heavier precipitation in other seasons. The trees are sparse and botanical studies, summarized, show much more seasonal weather and growth patterns than are indicated in the complex area. Computer will transmit complete studies from all areas of research and we hope they will broaden your picture of this far northern continental area."

Eve smiled with great satisfaction. The explorers' reports had been as extremely thorough scientifically as she had expected, but she had been consistently surprised and delighted at the humanistic insights in the daily summaries.

"Suffice it to say, for the moment, we are looking forward to traveling to a milder climate again. The one advantage of the colder weather is that all of us are getting very good at backgammon and chess, though no one is able to win against the computer as yet. We may have to reprogram it.

"We continue to be thankful we loaded the extra hydrocarbons for synthesis. Because of the reduced number of trees and plant matter available, the hydrocarbon resources on the surface are limited. Also, the cellulose content of the plant matter is extremely high, which gives a strange taste to the food synthesized from those hydrocarbons. Sarah's geological research indicates structures which have, historically, produced oil reserves, but without extensive drilling, we don't know if they are productive areas. Sarah would like us to stay here to continue her research and perhaps to drill experimentally with the laser drill rods, but the consensus is that such drilling should be consigned to a later party of researchers. Her reports are being compiled now and will be fed to the central computer at the earliest moment. I know Harrison will be anxiously awaiting them. Sarah sends her love and best wishes to everyone.

"Geographically, the area we are in is extremely difficult. The terrain undergoes extreme variations within small spaces and the aerial function of the small hovercraft is being taxed. I would like to send special thanks to Janet and Chen for those modifications, because they have made it possible to map this area. Without it, we could be here for years and never cover it all. Sarah and I concur there is extensive evidence to support possible glaciation in the past, though no glaciers in the form we know of them exist in the area now, and we assume they would be recognizable, based on Earth's records. There are many lakes in the area and the water is fresh and very cold. James says the fish and water-dwelling animals are abundant and he has captured a number of specimens for study, all of which will be included in his report. He has chosen to use the classic Earth means of species designation, using Latin names, and hopes the colonists will be flattered to have fish and aquatic creatures named for them. If you could see some of the creatures, I don't know how flattered you'd be.

"Zoologically, the area is very abundant and we see little of Ronald except when he emerges to eat. Even then, he and James sometimes manage to spoil meals for the rest of us with the discussions of dissection and internal organs of the various animals they have captured for study. They are attempting, as often as possible, to return the animals in perfect health to their original environment, but the biolab functions don't always seem to be able to mend their subjects, and they have lost some patients.

"Ecologically, there is almost a textape balance as compared to Earth records. There is a definite and obvious food chain ranging from small to large animals. We have observed some of the larger animals at a distance, but have made no attempts to capture them, fearing the stunning effect of the laser guns would not immobilize them for long enough. We have contented ourselves with photorecording and astonishment. None of them have taken any interest in us, fortunately, and Ronald has had, much to his disgust, to limit his studies to observation and classification in a most general sense.

"We anticipate moving within the next few days, and will decide the distance by the changing climate and terrain. We now realize our studies can only be cursory at this time and that there will have to be many expeditions of this type to give us a well-rounded knowledge of our planet. However, the rewards are enormous and we feel a great sense of accomplishment in our efforts.

"We have enjoyed the transmissions from the complex and are delighted to learn of the expected babies. Cilia and Kenneth, as always, have set an example for the rest of us. By the time we get home, you'll have a huge complex and we won't know anyone. We will attempt to transmit the reports of studies during the crossing to the next area, which we expect will take a number of days. It will help pass the time of traveling, which frustrates all of us because we'd like to study each thing we see, but must push on. Sarah observed something the other day which sums it up for all of us. She said our frustrations stem from the fact that we'd like to accomplish in two years what took the people of Earth ten thousand years. She's right, but as they weren't as well equipped as we are, we feel we should be able to do it. Our final satisfactions must stem from the fact that we are providing fodder for future scholars. We look forward to your next transmission. Blessing to everyone. Jeremy."

"End transmission," added the computer.

Congregation had been completely silent while they listened to Jeremy's report, though there had been smiles at some of his observations. His transmissions had become a part of the gathering to which everyone looked forward, even the toddlers who only vaguely understood the exploration.

There was a buzz of conversation after the transmission and Eve waited for it to still before she stood, raising her arms.

"We ask the Lord's blessing on the expedition and on all of us here." She lowered her arms. "If there is no further business in Congregation, we will close."

Morris stood, and Eve nodded in his direction, surprised. He hadn't mentioned in Council that he was intending to speak.

"Members of the colony, it is with great joy that I announce the marriage intention of Ellen Ashanti and me."

There was a hum of conversation and applause, but Eve was shocked.

It wasn't the match which distressed her, but the fact that Morris and Ellen, leaders of the community, had chosen to disregard the custom of bringing up their intentions to Eve as Chairman. They had to set the example for the rest of the colony and now they had put her in a bad position. If she acknowledged they hadn't been cooperative, it would make the Council look bad and if she didn't exert some pressure on them, they would think they were above the customs of the colony. If she were to deny or postpone their wedding now, there would be problems with the rest of the colonists, for Morris and Ellen were very popular and exerted a strong influence.

Her decision forced on her, she stood. "Let us ask the blessings of the Lord on their marriage. Now, if there is no further business, we will close."

"It's more than a courtesy, Morris, it's a custom, and our society is ruled by customs, not laws, so customs must be respected if we are to have a successful colony founded in freedom. You've put me in an uncomfortable position with your rash behavior and I'm telling you I don't approve."

Eve paced around her sitting room, angered by Morris's lack of contrition after his violations of courtesy. Ellen sat, her confusion enough evidence of contrition for Eve.

"Eve, I am an adult and a member of the governing body of this colony—"

"All the more reason for you, above all others, to comply with the customs of this colony."

"Don't interrupt, please. As I started to say, I am an adult and a Council member and feel as though Ellen and I can make choices about our lives without having to run to 'Mommy' for approval. You are Chairman of the Council, Eve Conner, but you are not God. You do not have the final word on everyone's life, to the contrary of what you think."

Eve laughed harshly. "This world is not run for your particular convenience, Morris, but for the convenience of all concerned. The point I am trying to make is that if we are all to live together on this planet in harmony, and that is my most fervent hope, we must live by certain common rules. Up to this point, the common rules of courtesy have dictated that marriage requests are first cleared with me, then in Congregation. The place to change those customs you find so offensive is in Council, not in public."

Morris looked at her steadily. "You are not the only adult here anymore. You do not have the right or the privilege to run our lives, and that is why I made the announcement without running to you. You speak of freedom but you deny it all the time. You're convinced you have the only rational mind and that the rest of us are simply tall children."

"Defiance is not particularly adult, Morris, and I do hold the final weapon. I can refuse to marry you, you know. Based, of course, on the premise that it isn't convenient at this time." She glared at him, knowing it was a hollow threat. As angry as she was at him, he was still her favorite and she felt that he and Ellen would make a good marriage. She simply had to impress on him the need to follow the customs they had established.

Ellen gasped at the thought that Eve might actually carry out her threat, but Morris waved her to silence. This was his battle with Eve and he knew the importance of, if not winning, at least achieving a draw. He was only trying to make her see she was becoming more and more tyrannical in some areas and she had to give them more freedom to really be adult members of the community. He knew some of her reactions to things came from her experience in the Project, for he had read the history of the training she had received and knew it was based on total control by the Directors of every waking thought and action of the potential colonists. He had to help her break down that rigidness of behavior and realize their colony would grow more effectively with an environment of nurturing freedom and cooperation by equals.

His voice was low. "Somehow I don't think you'll do that." His eyes captured hers and held them. "You and I both know how much you have to lose, not only with the others in the colony, but with yourself. You didn't like yourself very well when you blocked Cilia and Kenneth, and now if you do the same with us, your self-respect will diminish again." His voice became gentler, more persuasive. "You've told us all a thousand times that we are the best of the best. The products of genetically perfect-matched beings. Let us live up to our destiny and make you proud. Don't make us have to fight for what is ours."

Eve turned, knowing she would comply with his wishes, and put her palm against the door panel to her bedroom.

As the door slid aside, she turned toward them. "When is the wedding?"

"Whenever it is convenient for you to perform the ceremony."

She walked into her bedroom, the door sliding silently closed behind her. Morris watched the closed door for a moment, then took Ellen into his arms.

"She understands, believe me. It is as much my nature to be a rebel as it is hers to need to control me. We will someday arrive at a solution."

Mark appeared concerned as he came through the door to the sitting room. Eve seldom summoned anyone there, preferring to meet with visitors in more public, casual surroundings.

She was seated on the bench. He looked at her young, sleek body, set off by the clinging coverall, then was embarrassed at himself. Eve wasn't one of the women of the colony who could be considered as a potential mate. He chided himself. He would definitely have to marry soon because the pangs were getting bad. Audrey had kidded him about his "nesting impulse," and perhaps she was right.

"You wanted to talk to me?" he said, dismissing his personal life with his professional question.

"Mark, thank you for coming." Her smile was disarming. "Please join me here on the bench."

He sat down beside her, thrown off-balance by the role she had assumed. He was again aware of her femininity and her physical beauty, as if she were sending out some special strong signal.

"Mark, I've been giving a lot of thought lately to something and I'd like to discuss it with you. We are alien creatures here and, though our colony seems large to those of us who were here when it was terribly small, we are so few.

And we face so many unknown dangers." She turned to face him, her expression intense.

"I have a new sense of how large and diverse this planet is and what a tiny space we occupy. We must, above all else, protect the human race on this planet from as many dangers as we can, both internal and external. All these years later, and I still can feel the emotions of the night Richard was attacked by the leopard. And then in yesterday's report Jeremy talked about large animals they've observed. Mark, chronologically, I'm only fifty-six years old, yet I have suddenly developed a terrible sense of my own mortality."

He sensed a great emotional battle waging in her and kept his voice soothing. "Eve, that comes with the territory. You will probably live at least another three hundred years or more, depending upon the advances my associates and I are able to make in further refining the life-extending techniques. Your physicals check out very well, showing no deterioration at all as compared to the physical profile we have on you when you left Earth so long ago. I hardly think you have to worry about any problems from that quarter. What is really bothering you?"

Eve wandered around the room, touching various objects, obviously deep in thought. He waited patiently, wondering if he had offended her or overstepped his bounds. Finally, she turned to him, a look of pain on her face.

"I have to have your assurance that our conversation will remain private."

Mark nodded. "That's an old tradition of the medical profession and one which is stressed in the learning tapes very strongly. I won't violate your confidence."

She stood with her back to him and he wondered if she had changed her mind about talking to him. She didn't open up to anyone in the colony as a matter of practice and he knew she wasn't prone to changing her patterns.

Finally in a very small voice, she began. He settled back onto the bench, silently listening. "Back on Earth, when I was in training for the Project, there was a man I loved very much. Unfortunately, he belonged to another Project group and we were unable to marry. Since then I have not had any physical intimacy with a man and I am too well aware that the members of the colony wonder about that. Today, when I asked you to come here, I was entertaining vague thoughts of seducing you." He looked surprised, and she hurried to add, "Don't worry. Your reality precluded that fantasy. You see, I'm somehow trapped by the memory of the man I loved and can't imagine making love with any-one else, particularly the colonists, whom I've known since they were born. And yet, I'm very much aware such an atti-tude puts me in complete isolation from other people. I don't mean so much socially as physically and emotion-ally."

Mark tented his fingers, touching them to his nose while he thought and listened. She had paused and he felt she expected him to say something, so he answered, regretting instantly the lameness of what he said. "It's lonely to be the leader."

She turned to face him and he was afraid his inane com-ment had caused her to lose respect for him and would stop her flow of self-revelation.

"Was that intended to placate me?" Her tone was chilly.

"No, and I was sorry the minute I said it. You deserve either a better answer or silence, but not that. It's just that you seemed to expect something to be said and I didn't have any answers because everything you've said is all fairly obvious to everyone."

"You're right, it is. But you realize that for me to form an intimate association with anyone is to throw off the bal-ance of the colony. Or am I wrong?"

Mark wished he could tell her she was wrong, but he knew better. The emotional balance of the colony seemed to be based on Eve as the central figure, above the daily associations and intimacies of the average person. She was also correct about the difficulties of any one of the males in the colony adjusting to a changed role for her after she had functioned in loco parentis for them for so long. Even though his male ego had been touched by her rejection, he had found the emotion tempered with relief.

"You're not wrong, unfortunately. It's a role which you haven't chosen and that, too, is unfair. You know as well as I do there are factions here, even though they're not particularly strong or political. The colony has people of many different opinions and feelings. Any man you would choose would obviously become an ally and the people who didn't share his views on whatever subject would assume you were backing him. Your neutrality is extremely important. You're a good leader, probably at least partially because you keep yourself above the factions."

It interrupted her concentration to hear aloud that there were factions. She had assumed the changing currents of opinion she felt were not discussed but obviously there were things that weren't brought up to her. She was grateful for the knowledge, but it was another jolt for her: a realization that her colony was populated with thinking adults. Suddenly, she felt insecure, wondering how many other things had escaped her notice. She pushed the problem to the back of her mind, determined to explore it later.

"Mark, what I'm telling you is that I know it's impossible for me to marry because of the leadership situations we've discussed, but I would like very much to have someone who, in effect, belongs to me. We both know about the stored sperm in the biolab. I would like to conceive a child of my own and I think the only way in which I can do it is through the biolab."

Mark again tented his fingers, tapping his nose with the peak of the tip, thinking. Finally, he said, "There will be people who will assume you are trying to create a dynasty but I think your means of announcement of such a birth will strongly influence their opinion and you can turn it into a positive statement of yourself as a member of the colony and your own humanity. It will depend upon how you choose to present it and, more importantly, how you genuinely feel about it. If you feel others will think you're creating a dynasty, then you will project that and they will react accordingly. You've said it yourself. You're dealing with the best of the best; the smartest of the smartest. It's not easy to delude them and you mustn't delude yourself."

She sat next to him, looking intensely into his face. "I don't think I'm deluding myself. Having a child is contributing to the colony as well as fulfilling a personal need."

"And what about the child. Will you be able to let him grow up freely or will you create some kind of unrealistic dependency and damage the child? With us, you know, there was some of that need for dependency on your part and we were all aware of it. It wasn't strong, but you did let us know we were essentially your children and that you had certain expectations we had to live up to. With your own child could you be freer?"

Eve looked up at the ceiling, running the tip of her tongue over her lips. "I hope so. I will admit I want someone to call my own, but I hope I'm smart enough to be a good mother."

Mark smiled, patting her clasped hands. "I don't doubt you'd be a good mother. You have living proof around you of what a good mother you can be, for, as careful as you were to keep us from calling you 'Mother,' we all think of you in that way. I just wanted to be sure you had thought beyond your own needs. You couldn't smother the child with your frustrations. It wouldn't be fair. Not to the child and not to you, because any rejection then would be multiplied a thousandfold over what you're feeling now."

She nodded slowly, knowing he was right. "Is this your way of saying you don't approve?"

"It isn't my place to approve or disapprove of what you choose to do, but to consult with you, which is what I'm doing. You must make up your own mind."

She thought for a moment, then said, "There's something else I need to know. The man on Earth about whom I spoke and whom I wanted to marry was Morris Watson, the father of our Morris."

Mark's reaction was less than she had expected, a raised eyebrow conveying his lack of surprise. "We knew that. Morris told me long ago, so you must have told him at one time or another. Some of us, when we heard it, used to worry about you forming an association with Morris, romanticizing him into being his father. There was a general feeling of relief when he announced his marriage to Ellen."

Eve was again disturbed by his frank repetition of discussion among the people of the colony. What else had they talked about? She was now determined to find out, resenting the casual secrecy to which he referred as though everyone but she knew and it was common practice to keep things from her.

"I see. Well, that doesn't have to worry you anymore, does it?" She tried to keep the edge out of her voice, but it must have come through, for he looked at her sharply.

She smiled. "They are, after all, getting married with my wholehearted approval." She thought she saw his eyes reflect an instant of surprise but then it was gone and she decided she had imagined it. "At any rate, my curiosity is aroused. Our Morris was an exo-conceived child from the biolab, so there must have been sperm from his father stored in there. I am, I have confessed in all honesty, still deeply attached to his father, even though there is no hope of our ever meeting again, and could choose no better father for my child. If I decide to become pregnant from the stored gametes, I would like to know if Morris could be the father. Morris senior, I mean."

"And you would like me to check the tapes to see if that's possible?"

"Yes," she said, with relief at having told him. "If not, then I shall decide if I want to think about the possibility of having a child fathered by someone unknown or if I want to rethink the situation." She stood again, pacing the floor, then returned to stand in front him. "Is this all terribly neurotic?"

He smiled, reaching again for her hand, knowing the security his gesture would bring to her. "Eve, when will you learn you are allowed a few human frailties? Of course it's a little neurotic, but these are not normal circumstances and you are not an average woman living in a long-established society where I could tell you that the smartest thing you could do would be to take a lover. You are an exception within an exception and, as such, should have exceptional considerations afforded you. It is human and normal to need someone close to you. The only thing I would say, with respect to that, is that people can change their opinions, and perhaps choosing one of the men here would create problems for a time, but they would be solved eventually. Problems with the colonists, at any rate, would be solved, but I don't know if you or any of us could overcome the emotional problems of such an association. That, too, is a consideration. If you couldn't, then you would have generated more problems, potentially without solution."

"What you are saying is simply pushing me more and more toward my decision to have the child, you know."

He rose, still holding her hand. "Eve, you are free to make choices that are, as I said, exceptional. I would refuse any other woman in the colony the opportunity to even think about such a situation, but for you . . ."

Feeling a bit awkward, she put her arms around him and leaned for a moment against his chest. Slowly, he returned her hug. "Thank you for listening and for helping me make even a preliminary decision. It's not easy for me, you know."

"I know," he answered, wondering if he shouldn't have simply told her it was impossible. Now that he had opened the door, it wouldn't be possible to close it again.

"I'll gather that information for you and have the com-

puter put it in here on your screen. That way you can make
your decision in private. I'll help you with anything you
need."

He sat at the console in the biolab, watching the names
and genetic information about the stored sperm as it
marched across the screen in tidy little letters, knowing it
was simultaneously printing across Eve's viewing screen.
While he read, he reflected on her surprise that there were
dissenters and factions among the colony. So often she was
naive about the colony, treating them vaguely like children,
yet expecting more than adult responsibility from them.
She seemed to have some lack of basic understanding
about them as real human beings although no one should
have had more.

Obviously, he thought, she hadn't even been aware of the
level of gossip about Morris's possible role in her life, and
the discussions about that topic had been heated. There
was some distrust among the colony of Morris's forceful
nature and determined personality. Had he chosen to pursue Eve the way he had pursued Ellen, no one would have
been able to resist him, least of all Eve with her sentimen-
tal attachments to his Earth father.

It wasn't that he didn't trust Morris, for he respected the
man greatly for his abilities. It was just that there was something about him that seemed somehow devious, as though
the truth he told was enmeshed in half-truths and the listener
carried the responsibility of sorting out the two.

The computer letters continued to march across the
screen, impersonally cataloging the potential lives available for Eve's choosing. He read them with half his mind,
interested in the standards the Project Directors had used
in choosing future populations.

All were extremely intelligent, outstanding in their fields.
Every race was well represented, very democratic in its to-
talitarian way.

Suddenly the progression of characters on the screen

stopped. He checked to see if the printout had concluded, but the machine showed a "hold" light.

He leaned forward to read:

"Morris Edward Watson, 243-346-5543, United Europe, northern sector. Intelligence rated at 187; no genetic aberrations indicated; height, two meters, three centimeters; physiology, normal; hair, black; eyes, brown; complexion, dark. Chosen career: Project Group IV, astrophysicist; retrieval number 010-880-010."

Mark leaned back in his chair, apprehension building in him. The decision they had discussed in the abstract was no longer abstract.

The communication bell on his viewing screen didn't surprise him at all.

Chapter Eleven

RAMONA WIGGLED DOWN from Eve's lap, saying, "Going now," and went to join several of the exo toddlers who were playing in a far corner of the assembly hall. Since they had moved the nursery upstairs nearer the toddler's rooms, the size of the main room had increased enormously.

Morris's eyes wandered after the child and Eve saw, and resented again, the look of disgust on his face. They had argued about it at length more times than she cared to remember, from the moment her pregnancy was announced. He was obviously still vehement on the subject of her child, particularly when he discovered who the father was. He had given up talking to her about Ramona, preferring, she assumed, to wait and let her make her own mistakes.

Morris saw Ramona only as an "heir to the throne," in his words, and felt Eve had stepped beyond the "bounds of rationality" when she made the decision to have the baby. He couldn't understand her need to have the child as a purely personal situation and had made it very clear to Eve that he felt it was totally wrong.

Morris had been the only colonist who was open to her about his resentments and she had asked Mark if there were others. His answer had been less than satisfying to her, but he wouldn't elaborate and she didn't press the issue.

He had said, "There are always a number of views to every issue."

There had, also, been colonists who were vividly in favor of her pregnancy and she had finally decided to listen only to her own counsel. She adored Ramona, who returned the lavish affection in kind, and her raging pangs of loneliness had diminished rapidly after the child's birth.

Ramona was looking more and more like her father and like Morris as well, which she was sure was part of his resentment, for his own daughter looked exactly like Ellen. Harmony and Ramona had been born only a month apart and were close friends, even at their young age. They played together with the other endos of the community, and also mingled with the exos, but not for any length of time because of the maturity differences.

There were, however, always plenty of playmates for any child and Ramona seemed to be gregarious and well liked, which pleased Eve greatly. Harmony was the more retiring of the two, tending to follow Ramona wherever she went, playing the games Ramona wanted to play without complaint.

"As I was saying"—Morris's voice had an edge to it which quickly retrieved Eve from her attention to the child—"if we don't move quickly on the new community, we will become entrapped here. I don't oppose the expansion of this community again, but I really think we should assign a priority to the building of another location entirely. Then both communities could continue to grow and we wouldn't all be concentrated in one place."

"I agree with you, Morris, but the reality of the situation demands a certain amount of expansion here while the other community is being constructed. You have said yourself it will take four to six months to have it habitable by families and that will put us in just so much more overcrowding here."

Morris ran his hand through his hair. "Well, there will be ten or fifteen people working on the new community who won't be here during that time. The colony won't expand that much in six months, you know, even with the rash of new endos being born lately. If we focus any of our materials on expansion here, it will mean the new community will have to wait for the fabrication of their materials and that will delay the process even more. I really think we must begin on it now, and just put up with the crowding here for a little while longer."

Eve's eye wandered to Ramona for a moment, then back to Morris. "Have we even investigated a site for this new community? Water supply, hydrocarbon supply, climate—all have to be considered and studied."

"Joan has three locations which would be just fine, all within two hundred kilometers of here and all along the valley. Therefore, the hydrocarbon situation and the water supply will be similar to here, as certainly will be the climate. We're not, I know, ready to expand to the north where there is cold to contend with and we know the transportation of materials across the ocean will be most difficult until Fabrication has had time to build the big hover-transport that's still in the planning stages. It's not as though we're planning to go thousands of kilometers to start the new community."

"And what about choosing the colonists to live there? That, too, will be an arduous process."

"I should think"—his eyes held hers—"that such decisions will be made during the time we are in construction.

We will have to bring it up in Council and then in Congregation, and I'm sure there will be volunteers who will want to live in the new community and people who will prefer to stay here. We'll have all computer facilities, a biolab that produces new colonists, the necessary transportation to make travel easy between the new and old communities, and a food synthesizer. Decisions can be made about fabrication facilities and other more major installations as we go along. It's not that difficult."

"I'm not maintaining that it will be difficult, Morris, I am maintaining that we must plan carefully and if we rush into something and do it wrong, the entire colony will pay for our mistake, perhaps in a dangerous way. I am not opposed to another community, as I have said, but only to doing it too fast and upsetting the entire colony."

"And my point is that if we don't do it now, it will be more stressful because we will become hopelessly overcrowded. Are you sure your opposition doesn't come from a need to control?"

She bristled with anger. "Whenever you can't think of anything else to say, you accuse me of wanting to control the lives of the colonists. I'm getting tired of that argument, Morris, and would like to hear a lot less of it. You don't seem to be able to understand that my interest is in guidance, not in control."

He looked at her for a long moment, but didn't respond, so she continued. "I think we should take the interested members of the Council to check each of the three locations Joan has suggested and then we should make our decision after that. Then we will be able more accurately to suggest when and where the community should be built to the rest of the Council and to Congregation. Does that sound equitable to you?"

He nodded curtly, rising. "I'll make the arrangements for transportation and personnel. We can make each journey in one day's time, so we will have to devote three days to this. Is that equitable to you?" His sarcasm irritated her, but she didn't respond to it. She was determined to bridge the chasm between them before it became any wider.

"That should be fine, Morris. Is there anything you'd like me to do?"

He ignored her attempted courtesy. "I'm sure the demands of your office and your child are much too great to add any more to your work load now. I'll take care of everything and keep you apprised."

He wasn't wrong. She was faced with a number of decisions which had to be made besides the new community and all of them involved a great deal of thought and planning. Ramona, he would have been surprised to learn, took a rather low priority by comparison.

She was about to seek Mark to discuss the age arresting which had to be done shortly for the first group, when Ellen appeared with Harmony in tow. Ramona came running over to join them and she and Harmony returned to the group of children as Ellen sat down.

"Eve, I'm so glad to have found you alone for a moment." Ellen's smile was genuine and Eve felt her anger with Morris disappearing. Ellen always had a soothing effect on her.

"I don't get enough chance to talk to anyone anymore, Ellen, with all the activity going on around here. It seems as though I'm constantly involved in something."

"Well, I have two questions. First, Morris is worrying me. He seems to be constantly angry about something and he won't discuss it with me. Has he been troubled about something in Council?"

Eve explained the situation with the new community, and Ellen nodded. "I guess I suspected as much. He and Joan have been carefully going over maps and he's been meeting with Chen about fabrications. I'm supposed to be his assistant, but he's been carrying the whole weight of this on his own shoulders."

Eve saw the chance to build Morris's ego through Ellen, so she said, "Morris is deeply concerned about the future of the colony, for which I am most grateful, and he is carrying a huge responsibility right now. The establishment of a new community is no small task, and he is such a perfectionist that he wants to be sure everything is right. I'm sure he's not excluding you, but I know he's emphatic about wanting everything to be absolutely right, so he's doing it himself. He's a most valuable member of the Council and takes his responsibilities quite seriously. Don't worry about him, dear, he'll be fine once the construction is underway and he sees that everything is progressing smoothly."

Ellen looked relieved and Eve hoped she'd relay the information to Morris, which might help to span the gap between them.

"Thank you. I spend a lot of time with Harmony but sometimes I think he resents that."

"You know, there are times when I think he resents Ramona because she takes some of my attention away from colony business. He is dedicated and can't understand anything which keeps anyone else from being equally dedicated. In that way, he's much like his father. Morris was absolutely single-minded about some things and couldn't understand it when others didn't share his obsession."

"He seems to love Harmony, but both of us take a second role to the colony."

"Do you resent that?" Ellen looked startled at Eve's question.

"Yes, I guess I do, although I should have known it would be like that. Even when I was in labor with Harmony, he was anxious for her to be born so he could get back to reading the research tapes of the explorers."

Eve covered Ellen's hand with her own. "I think if you read some of the novels in the library tapes, you will discover that you are not very different from many women back on Earth who complained of the same thing. And many men, for that matter. I think there were times when my father resented my mother's involvement in the Project and that's why he studied philosophy and had his own interests. And then she'd resent his philosophy studies because they took time away from her, so it was a never-ending spiral. I don't remember them having discussions about much else, as a matter of fact."

Ellen smiled and shook her head. "The ties with Earth are still very strong, whether Morris likes to admit it or not, I guess."

Eve was a bit surprised to hear that ties with Earth were another of his dislikes, but she could understand it. He was fervently chauvinistic and considered the association with Earth to be a weakness in that patriotism. He was a mélange of strong emotions, she reflected.

"What was the other question you wanted to ask, Ellen?"

"I'm concerned about the age arresting process, frankly. I know it will take two days, and I want to be certain Harmony won't feel as though I've deserted her."

Eve smiled with understanding. "And that you won't be in danger."

Ellen's smile reflected her embarrassment. "You're right. I've only been in the biolab when I delivered Harmony and the whole machine frightened me. What's it like?"

"I assume you mean beyond the mechanics, which you've certainly read about. It's a nap, actually, and the only thing I found difficult when I went through it was that I had just lost two days and there were events I had missed. You don't feel anything physical except rested, and a renewed energy for months afterward. That comes from the cells in your body not having to constantly repair themselves, I guess, so the energy which is now taken up by that process can be directed elsewhere. It's actually a very lovely thing. Especially when you realize that it allows you to become almost immortal."

Eve saw Ellen studying her carefully, and was proud of herself and the admiration she saw in Ellen's eyes. She knew from experience with her mother that she would continue to look exactly as she did now for the rest of her life, even when the aging process finally started again when she was chronologically about three hundred years old.

"Ellen, it's not something to fear. I'll be here with Harmony and the other children of the group one mothers, so it won't be a big trial for anyone."

"Can Harmony be with Ramona during the time I'm gone?"

"Of course. We'll keep her so busy she won't even notice. I think it might be a good idea for you to prepare her so it won't be a shock. Just be sure you're not pregnant because you'd lose the baby. The age arresting would carry over to the child and stop its development."

"I'm not. I wanted to wait until after the process for that anyway and maybe after the new community is built, too. Morris seems too tired for anything lately, anyway." She shrugged. "If you know what I mean."

"Don't worry about it, dear. Once the new community is under construction, he'll have time to think about other things, and I know you will be one of them."

Mark was in the biolab with one of the older exo children who was crying unhappily and holding his arm.

Mark looked up from the printout screen and nodded to Eve, then said, "We have a little casualty here as a result of exploring the rocks."

Eve went to the child, putting her arm around his shoulders. "What happened, Christiano?"

Through his sniffling he explained that he had been climbing in the rocks at the base of the cliff and had slipped and fallen and that his arm hurt badly.

She comforted him, taking a cloth and wiping his face with cool water to remove the tracks of tears and some of the dirt.

"Mark will fix you up right away and you'll never notice that anything happened."

Christiano began crying again and she said, "What's wrong now?"

He sniffled loudly and she dabbed at his nose with the cloth. "He's going to take my arm away like Richard. I don't want him to take my arm away. Don't let him, Eve."

Mark looked up from the screen, startled, and Eve said, "That was a whole different thing, Christiano. Richard didn't break his arm, he was attacked by an animal and the only way to save his life was to replace his arm. That was a terrible emergency and not like what has happened to you. Let Mark tell you exactly what happens with the biolab so you'll know nothing is going to hurt you."

Patiently Mark explained. When the boy finally seemed to understand, Eve helped him lie down and Mark focused the machine over the break. Christiano watched intently during the whole process and they stood with him, reassuring him.

"Okay, Chris, you're all fixed. Wiggle your fingers for me."

Christiano moved his arm slowly, expecting the pain to be there, then broke into a happy grin when there was no pain and his fingers worked fine. Mark lifted him down from his table with an admonition to be more careful and the child raced out of the biolab, undoubtedly to regale his friends with the story of how brave he was.

Mark watched him go, then shook his head. "Richard's accident seems to have taken on a folklore nature. This isn't the first time it's come up from an injured child."

"Mark, when I was growing up the biggest threat we could use on each other was that a mutant would come down out of the mountains and steal us. We didn't even know what a mutant was, but we were sure we didn't want to meet one. Richard's false arm is an object of equal mystery, though I'm sure none of them could tell you which one it is. You just have to ignore it and dispel the story as much as possible. It isn't good to have the children fear the biolab, but there's no way we can stop them from scaring each other by talking about it. Every society needs a little folklore."

"Well, I don't like it very much."

"We have bigger things to think about right now. Like the age arresting procedure."

Mark indicated the console chairs and they both sat down. "I think the procedure is set up fairly clearly and I think with the first group there won't be as many problems if we take Kenneth, Ellen, and Morris alone first, then wait to do the other four. After that we can manage all eight from a particular year without difficulty."

"Experiment on the first three?"

Mark made a gesture of distaste. "I think experiment is a rather strong word. It's necessary for me to learn the process and if we do all seven of us at one time, then I won't have had the experience. Now, is that an experiment?"

"Not really, I suppose. I'll work with you so that when your group goes through, you'll have someone else with the proper experience."

"I'll have Elizabeth and about six other doctors who will train in the process with the first group, so that won't really be necessary. I don't want you to have to be trapped here for two days and be forced to let other things go that you should be attending to."

Eve was a bit sensitive about his dismissal, though she understood what he was saying. Another realization that her colony had specialists and she didn't have to oversee everything. She felt a wrench, even knowing that logically it was correct. She was forced to admit she liked to be involved with everything that went on and resented it when she wasn't needed.

"What schedule have you worked out?" She tried not to let her hurt show to Mark.

"I think we can begin with the first three at their earliest convenience. I don't know when they can take the two days off to complete the process, but if there is going to be a new community built, then it must be before that project is begun."

She nodded. The new community was on everyone's

mind since it had first been mentioned in Council. "We are planning to make three exploratory trips to look at possible locations and Morris is making those arrangements now, so he would have to be given fair notice. Also, Kenneth is deeply involved in something very new with the aliens and his schedule will have to be considered. Ellen is the least problem of the three, since she has only to worry about her work on the expansion team. I guess it can be brought up in Council and decided then."

Elizabeth came into the biolab with two medical students following close behind her. They were just beginning their studies of medicine and she had laughingly complained to Eve that she wasn't free of them unless she was sleeping. She was a patient teacher and had trained all of the colony's new doctors, providing an excellent education for them.

They greeted Eve as she left.

She took the elevator down to the lower complex which sprawled at the foot of the cliff. It not only contained the housing for the family groups but also a number of research teams. Off to one side was the fabrication building which manufactured all materials necessary for the colony except food.

Beyond the complex, out in the valley, was the farm project which had begun successfully producing local fruits and vegetables which could be eaten by the community members to supplement the food from the processor. She had tried some of them and they were remarkably good, though unfamiliar and unlike anything on Earth. The growing season was so long and the experiment so successful, some of the colonists were eating only foods from the farm.

Through the clear plasteel of the elevator walls she could see the familiar wisps of smoke far across the valley in the alien camp and felt the stability the smoke always represented to her.

She realized, on the slow ride down, she was looking forward to the exploratory trips to the possible new community locations, for she hadn't been out of the complex area since her nearly disastrous visit to the sea so many years before. Content with her duties, she hadn't really wanted to leave, but now that the opportunity presented itself, she found herself looking forward to it.

The lower complex was humming with activity as always and she stopped in each of the research labs to update herself on the projects. The explorers had brought back various animal specimens, both living and dead, from other parts of the planet and they had been experimenting with them.

Two other expeditions had added to the collection and the research facility for zoology was crammed with cages of various sizes. The noise was almost deafening as each animal reacted to the presence of a stranger. Ronald had a large staff working on the experiments and classifications, and had several times requested additional space.

He came to greet her, then brought her up to date on their discoveries and classifications. Much of what he told her was out of her realm of knowledge and she struggled to understand his excitement.

After the tour had finished, he said, "Do I get my new lab space? You can see we need it desperately."

"That's being discussed in Council. We are under a lot of pressure to build this new community and that seems to take precedence over expanding this one. Can you stand it another six months in these quarters?"

He shook his head. "Not unless we begin releasing the animals we've studied most thoroughly to make room for the new ones which will be coming with the latest expedition. Their reports have been filled with all sorts of exotic animal life that they've been finding in the jungle area. I can't tell you how much it will expand our horizons."

Eve nodded. "Ronald, I'll try to get some more space for you somehow, but I can't promise. Maybe you can use the transport's storage areas that aren't already in use."

He smiled sheepishly. "We already are. It started informally, but we depend upon that space as much as here for animals not currently in study. Botany has some space over there, too."

She laughed, shaking her head. "One step ahead of me."

He smiled. "If I weren't already married, I'd be thinking about it just to get more space to live in. Mary and I are waiting to have children until there will be more space to put them."

"Well, we'll make the decision about the new colony soon and then there will be an end in sight to the crowding."

"Eve, if you're going to make the assignments to the new community, Mary and I would like very much to remain here, as would most of our research staff. Trying to move this mess," he gestured with his hand, "would set us back months on our work."

The story was the same in the botany lab: overcrowding and pleas for more space from Richard. She looked, as they wandered around the lab, at his left arm. She was completely unable to tell that it was false, for it was so carefully constructed it exactly matched his natural arm, even to the matting of black, curly hair.

They stood in the door, talking.

"I tell you, it's incredible the subtle variations we find in plant life, even ten kilometers apart. From what I have been able to glean from Earth-made studies, they would have been enthralled with this planet. It's like opening a textbook. The ecological balance doesn't have any parallel in Earth's records."

"What is our community doing to the balance in this area?"

"That's another interesting thing. The balance is holding it's own even with all of us here. The plants seem to be able to grow quickly to replenish what we take and we don't seem to make a dent in the grasses, no matter how many feet trample over them. Have you seen the gardens?"

"Oh yes, they're beautiful. And the vegetables are delicious."

"The real beauty of them, Eve, is that we are now absolutely certain we could support the life of the colonists should the food processor fail. That is the most important product of our gardens: security."

"Richard, I will try to get more space for you as well as for Ronald. I'm well aware of how valuable your work is to our community. But, as I told you, it will have to wait until we have begun the new community. Will you be interested in going along on the research trips?"

He nodded vigorously. "Oh, most interested. Not so much for the new community, for I should like to stay here to continue my work, but for the balance of the plants and soils in the new area. I'm certain they will want to begin their own gardens and provision should be made for that when construction begins."

"Fine." She supposed Morris would probably be upset with her if he knew she had been laying the groundwork for his proposals to rush on the new construction. Now two members of the Council would be prepared to vote yes on immediate beginning.

Richard nodded. "I don't want to take too much time from my work, though. There's so much to do, and there are never enough hours in the day."

As she approached Kenneth and Cilia's quarters, she checked her chron and was relieved to see she was still on time for their appointment. She rapped quietly on the door and it slid to the side, revealing Kenneth and Cilia.

"What is this breakthrough? I'm so anxious to hear all about it," Eve said as she sat in the chair Kenneth was holding for her. Their quarters were unique. They had been building furniture from carved wood and woven grasses as a diversion, and their skills were developing very well.

"Eve, it's so exciting, but we wanted to share it with you before we brought it to the Council, for it could change the whole way of life of the community." Kenneth was as intense as she'd ever seen him, and Cilia sat, smiling widely.

Kenneth continued, "As you well know, we have spent the last five years working with the aliens in the village across the valley, and we have begun to be able to make ourselves understood fairly well in their language. The nasal gestures are impossible for us, but we have adapted one arm to cover those gestures, so we have a fairly broad understanding of their language and customs."

Eve nodded. She knew most of that information from their reports and presentations in Council.

"Well, we began questioning their needs and customs in an effort to learn what they would work or trade to get. We have found that cloth has become highly valued as a means of barter and a status symbol, so we capitalized on that to get what we wanted. Are you ready?"

Eve was completely mystified, but said, "Yes, but for what?"

Without answering, Cilia moved to the doorway to one of the back rooms, using a combination of gesture and a clicking-humming noise, said something. From the door of the back room one of the aliens emerged, carrying a tray of juices. It crossed the room, set the tray on a nearby table, then handed a glass to each of them, retrieved the tray and disappeared, as it had been trained to wait just outside the door until further instructions.

Eve held the glass in her hand, staring after the creature in complete astonishment. She had witnessed the impossible and was astounded by it. Cilia and Kenneth laughed with delight.

Finally, Kenneth said, "I see you're impressed by our trainee. She's been with us for about two weeks, learning simple household tasks. We're trying to teach her to understand our speech patterns, but I don't know if they can hear our language, since there are certain frequencies to which they seem to be completely deaf. But Cilia can ask her to do things in her own language, so it's not a problem for us. In order to apply it to the whole community, however, we will have to teach the aliens certain standard sounds of ours that everyone can learn. However, we want to present our lady to Richard because her people would make good farm and garden workers."

Eve was still speechless. She shook her head several times in wonder, which brought another laugh from Cilia and Kenneth. Finally, Eve said, "Do you really think you can train a whole group? You said at one time they didn't seem to retain much."

"That's another interesting thing we've discovered," Cilia interjected quickly. "They learn manual tasks very quickly. It's concepts and strangers who are infrequently seen that they have trouble retaining. She has been shown things here only once, twice at the most, and I haven't had to re-teach anything as long as it's simple. Not only that, but she will do it exactly the same way each time. You're sitting in the chair usually occupied by one of the children, so she served you. If you'd been sitting over there, she would have ignored you completely. It's something we have to work on, but it's a beginning."

Eve raised her glass. "I toast your accomplishment. It's really quite astonishing and you two have a great deal to be proud of. What I question is the rights of these people, aliens, creatures, whatever, to choose whether or not to do this. You're paying her with cloth?"

"Yes, for now. She goes over to the village when we go and she has told us others want to come back with us. Apparently she's rather a tribal celebrity and certainly with cloth as a barter, one of the wealthiest."

"I don't want to throw cold water on what you're doing, because it is truly spectacular, but I must speak in defense of the aliens as residents of Genesis. They are not to be forced to do anything against their will or that will in any way harm them. You are to pay them fairly for what they contribute and you must look out for their well-being at all times. Any abuses of these rules and we will be forced to cancel the project immediately."

Kenneth nodded. "We are completely in agreement and hoped it would be the position you'd take. If we have them trusting us, we can't have anyone turn them into slaves. They are a proud tribe and, for the planet, rather well evolved. We, too, desire to protect them, perhaps from their own greed for cloth."

Eve shook her head. "I hope we're not making a mistake. Have you looked beyond the effect on this one tribe? Do they communicate with the other settlements? If so, will we be faced with warring factions among them over cloth?"

Cilia nodded. "Valid questions and we don't know the answers to all of them. They don't seem to have any forms of communication with the other villages. In the five years we've been going over there, we haven't seen any unfamiliar faces."

"What about jealousies within the tribe between those you choose and those you don't?"

"We don't think jealousy is a very powerful emotion with these creatures. They seem to want things from us but not from each other. Any cloth we've given has been hung on the outside of the hut of the receiver and none of it has been stolen."

Eve considered for a moment, then said, "We're toying with their entire social structure, you know, and that's something you won't have an easy answer for. The Project Directors suggested we try to integrate with any local civilizations without damage to either group."

Kenneth and Cilia looked at each other, thoughtfully considering her words. Finally, Cilia said, "You're right, there is no answer to that. Nor is there an answer to the greater question of whether elevating their life-style and broadening their horizons is good or bad. Will they lose or gain from an association with us?"

Kenneth nodded gravely, then added, "And, in the greater

scheme of things, why do we assume that this is not exactly what is supposed to happen to their society at this time?"

Eve smiled and held up her hands. "Wait a minute. What started as a discussion about the right of humans to train other creatures to do their menial jobs has turned into a predestination debate, which is most interesting but doesn't accomplish anything." The creature/servant stood in the doorway, watching them with her little, stalked eyes. She seemed to understand the conversation centered around her, swiveling her eyes from one to the other as the talk ranged in a language most of which she couldn't absorb with her limited hearing.

She had no desire to let them know she could hear with her very sensitive mind. Not their language, which confused her with all its nuances and intricacies, but the pure emotion of the situation.

She stood, having no way to communicate with these creatures beyond her sign language which they seemed to be able to understand after much patient training. What they hadn't been able to grasp was the mind-speech which tied the tribe together so strongly, and she had little hope of their having ability to learn it quickly. They simply hadn't evolved far enough.

She wanted desperately to tell them that they offered her people a chance to regain some of their former life—before the wars which had murdered millions of their people and driven the rest into isolated primitive tribes who were afraid to leave their secure little villages to seek the life they had known. They had remained in the security of their primitive existence as generations passed, each one setting them more firmly into their ways. They mind-spoke to the nearby villages, but she had never seen anyone of her own kind outside her village.

She knew if they could only begin to work with the alien beings who had come in the great silver ship, they could teach themselves dignity again.

Eve felt an uncomfortable intensity from the creature in

the doorway, and again looked in her direction. The eyes swiveled to look directly at her, seemingly boring into her mind, and she pondered again the morality of using the time and abilities of another creature to free man of his tasks.

Kenneth's voice penetrated the silence. "We can stop the whole program now or we can begin to integrate the two cultures. It's really your decision, Eve, as Chairman of the Council."

Eve thought for a long moment, then surprised herself with her answer, curious about where her sudden change of mind had begun. "It is actually up to the creatures themselves. If they choose to work with us, they will continue to learn. You must promise me you will never force them into a situation which will in any way compromise their integrity."

Kenneth and Cilia both nodded, knowing Eve was totally serious about what she said, and the unspoken threat it contained.

In the doorway, the creature watched and knew. Her people would return to their rightful place on the planet.

Chapter Twelve

———◆———

THE COUNCIL MEETING had gone on for a long time, struggling with the difficult problems facing all of them now that the new colony was almost finished. Eve was tired and her back hurt from the uncomfortable chair in which she sat, but she used yoga to calm her nerves and relax her muscles.

The problems had started the day they began looking at potential sites. Joan had done her work carefully and her presentations of each site's advantages were planned and polished. She offered no subjective judgments, simply presenting the site, then retreating while the others wandered over the terrain and tried to imagine possible layouts for buildings and other necessary items like water and expansion space.

Richard VanDersant was vehement about not upsetting the ecological balance, no matter what area they chose. He was most negative about the possibility of putting a community at the edge of the forested lands about a hundred kilometers north of the complex. He said the weather would be cooler, demanding a different type of building construction. But more important, it would disrupt the ecological balance of the forest much more than it would the grassy plain.

Kenneth, speaking for the alien training program, objected equally strenuously to a site near the alien village. He was coldly contradicted by Morris remarking that Kenneth was doing as much or more harm with his training program than a nearby settlement of humans could hope to do. The ride back to the complex had been strained and Eve had wished Morris could be more patient with his fellow men.

The third site they had visited had elicited the fewest negative remarks, though no one had been particularly excited about the location, feeling it was almost too close to the original complex to be effective as an independent community. There was only a distance of about fifty kilometers between the two, and Morris felt the communities should be more widely spaced. Mark angrily contradicted him, citing the small towns of the frontiers on Earth that took security from proximity.

The debate in Council had been long and furious, with some people saying things they later regretted. Finally, in desperation and out of a desire for progress, Eve had insisted on a vote. The nearest location had won by a one vote majority.

The work had begun almost immediately, starting with the hauling of vast amounts of material, which produced its own set of frustrations and the breakdowns of much overworked equipment. Tempers both on and off site had raged as they struggled to meet a schedule no one had defined as critical but which had become an obsession.

Morris had taken control of the project in his capacity as head of Colonial Development. He drove men and machines mercilessly, generating resentments in every quarter. Eve had tried to quell this resentment, striving to maintain a balance in the colony.

The installation of the computer had contributed its own set of frustrations. It stubbornly refused to work until Chen had moved to the new community and spent almost a week tracing minute circuits until he located the problem: a tiny wire shorting out a main circuit. The repair had taken five minutes.

In the midst of all of it, the Council had been accepting applications for relocation. The new community was structured for an initial population of fifty and needed a cross section of skills, ages, and marital status. Some of the applications had been accepted instantly, while others were debated, sometimes heatedly. Finally, the selections had been made and approved, and the colonists who were departing had begun to get ready to go. Some made the whole process quite dramatic with repeated, tearful good-byes, starting almost the moment the choices were announced.

Morris had been approved to move to the new colony despite some reservations about his temper and dominating behavior. All agreed, however, that he would be good for the new community, providing strong direction should the sense of purpose begin to lag.

Mark had gone over to the new complex to start the reproductive function of the biolab, knowing there would be plenty of space for new babies and hoping to continue the highly accelerated growth rate of the colony in general.

But the complications continued. Morris was pushing for

an independent Council for the new community. Most of the Council members, some of whom would be in the new community, felt the two Councils should be represented in each other's government. Establishing a central Council for colonial decisions as opposed to community decisions was also favored.

Eve shifted in her chair, then finally stood, interrupting Mark in the middle of an angry rebuttal to something Morris had said.

"Just a moment, please. When we are faced with issues of this nature that seem insolvable, it might be a good idea to consult the suggestions of the Project Directors who, I'm sure, have many thoughts on this matter."

Morris glared at her. "Another tie to Mother Earth?"

Eve had had enough. Releasing her anger, she returned his glare and said, "Morris Watson, you have become disruptive and irritating to all of us here who are trying to accomplish something for the good of all the people. You are a bright man, but you must learn to temper your intelligence with respect for the opinions and ideas of those around you and those who came before you. You cannot eradicate our ties to Earth. It was the birthplace of our race and that race suffered many trials to achieve the level of evolution which we represent. Contrary to your opinion of yourself, you do not have all the answers to everything. I now ask for a democratic vote of the Council to determine the opinion on whether or not we should consult the tapes of the Project for their suggestions. Kindly vote now if you favor such a consultation."

She looked around the room as hands were tentatively raised in agreement.

"And now, kindly vote if you are opposed to such a consultation."

Again she counted the raised hands.

"It would seem, Mr. Watson, that your peers wish, in the majority, to consult with 'Mother Earth' in this matter. Olaf, will you please request the information?"

She watched Morris carefully. His anger was obvious as he sulked in his chair. At least, she thought, he didn't storm out.

Olaf returned shortly from the viewing screen. She nodded in his direction, recognizing him.

"Madame Chairman, Members of the Council, the Project Directors suggest autonomous local governments with a central governing body made up of members of the various local governments." He sat down immediately.

"Thank you. Discussion?"

Her anger was ebbing and she was a bit embarrassed by her outburst. Now she would have to work all the harder to regain the tentative truce she and Morris had been able to achieve.

Mark stood, and Eve nodded in his direction. "Madame Chairman, Members of the Council. I am in agreement with the Project Directors' suggested solution to this problem. It will facilitate strictly local decisions that shouldn't be of concern to the other community while still maintaining colony unity on an expanded basis."

Morris stood, and, reluctantly, she nodded in his direction. "Madame Chairman, Members of the Council. I would first like to extend my apologies for my outburst. The pressures of the new community have taken their toll on my temper and I regret I forced the Chairman to rebuke my lapse." Eve was startled at the display of maturity, but found herself distrusting his statement. He could be very persuasive when he felt things were not going as he wished.

He continued, not looking at Eve. "Actually, I must admit the Project solution is a logical one and certainly merits a try on our parts. We will have to feel our way in this and many other matters now that we are two separate cities instead of one colony and we should do so with consideration and cooperation. I wholeheartedly endorse the Project solution." He sat.

Eve waited for a moment, then said, "Are there any dissenting opinions?"

There was no response.

"Then we shall consider the government issue settled as the Project Directors suggested, with local Council elections to be held as soon as possible as well as colonial Council selections. Olaf, as head of Education, will you please work out a rough constitution or charter of such governments, defining various duties and so on, and submit it to Council at our next meeting?"

Olaf nodded eagerly, almost childlike in his obvious desire to please her. But, she reflected, if anyone could draft a constitution, it would be Olaf with his well-organized mind.

"Now, is there any other business before the Council?"

Richard VanDersant rose, and Eve quickly nodded in his direction. "Madame Chairman, Members of the Council, there is an issue which has been carefully avoided in Council for long enough, and, before we begin the expansion, I feel it must be discussed and resolved." The fingers of his right arm worked nervously. "The work done by Kenneth, Cilia, and their team of researchers is undeniably outstanding, and they have made exceptional progress with the training of the alien creatures."

Around the table, the members of the Council nodded their agreement.

"However, I think we must discuss the eventual purpose of this training and its potential effect upon not only their society but ours." He sat down.

Eve stood, fearing to open this avenue of thought, and said, "Discussion?"

It was a rule in Council that any point brought up must be given a fair hearing. She had to abide by the rules, even when she felt a discussion would bring no solution. She looked around the table. Kenneth was sitting abnormally upright in his chair, and she could see he was practicing yoga exercises to reduce his anxieties.

Morris rose, and Eve nodded in his direction. "Madame Chairman, Members of the Council, our people historically have an abhorrence of the practice of slavery in any form. I feel strongly the training of the aliens to perform the menial tasks of our society is, while certainly convenient, a form of exactly that disgusting practice and I am deeply opposed to it." Before anyone could interject he continued, "However, I am in favor of the integration of the two societies for the betterment of both. We have been negligent in our side of the bargain because we have been paying them off in gifts of cloth instead of contributing our vast knowledge to the betterment of their living conditions."

Kenneth stood and Eve nodded at him. "We who are involved in this training experiment wish in no way to put the creatures in a position of servitude or slavery. We had to begin our training program somewhere and it seemed to us, after careful study, that it would be most appropriate to start at a low level of comprehension and then work up. I, too, would favor suspension of the training before allowing those gentle creatures to be abused. Integration of the two societies cannot begin until we have a common language in which we can communicate and some common experience upon which to base our association. Such things take time. We have just begun to be able to communicate in the most rudimentary ways." He sat down, frustration on his face.

Mark stood, and again Eve nodded. "Madame Chairman, Members of the Council, I was asked to examine one of the creatures which Kenneth and Cilia have used in their training program. Physiologically, the difference between our two races goes a great deal deeper than simply surface details. Their minds have a much greater capacity than their society would indicate and their stamina is quite incredible. They have a digestive system which is completely different from ours, seeming to draw nutrients from air and soil, much as do plants. But don't make the mistake of assuming that they are plants, for their cellular tissue is surprisingly similar to ours. They have a circulatory system with a bloodlike substance and a system of glands I can only assume are related to our lymphatic system. I did not draw blood or lymphatic fluid from the creature I examined, as the sight of the needle produced extreme agitation. Their reproductive system also remains a mystery to me, as the biolab could not analyze it. Therefore, it must be substantially different from ours, perhaps related to the marsupials or the egg layers. Their young may be produced by some sort of cloning process. My point in this recitation is that these creatures will take time to integrate with our society and I am in favor of any system which allows them to become accustomed to us and us to them. They seem to be satisfied with cloth as a medium of exchange and too much technology forced upon them could serve to alienate them more than integrate them."

Jeremy stood and Eve nodded. "Madame Chairman, Members of the Council. In our explorations of the surface of the planet, we encountered a number of similar communities, all of them organized in much the same way as the one with which we are familiar. There was no attempt on our part to make contact and none on theirs, but there was also no aggression on either side. They seemed to know, somehow, in advance that we were coming and didn't seem surprised to find us at the edges of their villages. We have no idea what would have happened if we had ventured into the village. We didn't want to try it and inadvertently generate any aggression. However, in relation to the size of this planet, there seem to be very few of these creatures, so I feel integration, while desirable, isn't a necessity. We can, for many centuries to come, comfortably cohabit the same planet without need for deeper interaction. Should such interaction have a negative outcome, I would be categorically opposed to it."

Eve was surprised at how calmly the discussion had progressed, though she could feel the underlying tension of everyone there, particularly Richard and Kenneth.

Harrison, who normally had little to say in Council, stood and Eve nodded in his direction. "Madame Chairman, Members of the Council, I'm afraid my humanitarian interests are not as strongly developed as yours. My department deals not with humans, but with their needs. Consequently, I think I will be taking the most unpopular stance with my suggestion. These creatures are obviously a lower form of life than humans and, as such, deserve the normal considerations afforded to such lower forms of life. Our strongest mission here is to perpetuate and expand the human race, and it is from this viewpoint that I speak. There is an immense amount of developmental work to be done on the face of this planet. There are minerals to be discovered and used to our best advantage, petrocarbon wells to be drilled, forest resources to be tended and developed for exploitation. As this colony expands, the demands for manufactured goods will also expand, and we must have the manpower to develop all these avenues. We should take advantage of the alien creatures in order to better life for all of us. Perhaps they could be trained to assist in mining and drilling operations, in manufacturing and in forestry. They would integrate into the society we have here and they would also be evolving into the industrial age quickly."

Kenneth leapt to his feet, his face red with anger. "Harrison, that's exactly what we're trying to avoid here. We don't want to abuse these creatures or turn them into slaves, and what you're suggesting is exactly that. They are gentle creatures who deserve to be understood, not abused."

Harrison, still seated, turned his calm face toward Kenneth's angry one. "So you'd rather turn them into household servants or pets of some strange nature. Do you want to go to work on the drilling operations or digging the mines? Do any of us? Perhaps we could use the children who are growing up here to do the mining instead."

Morris interjected, "Harrison, our mining and drilling techniques were developed to preclude the suffering of previous methods."

Kenneth interrupted. "I would rather you used the children than to abuse the alien creatures in such a way. What you're suggesting is about one step from leg-irons and whips and I won't have it."

Harrison, rising to his feet again, responded. "Let's, for one minute, stop being such high and mighty defenders of the faith and face reality. There are going to be jobs on this planet none of us wants to do unless we absolutely have to. I'm not suggesting we don't pay the aliens whatever means of exchange they think is fair, but I am suggesting they could solve a lot of problems for us with respect to the manual labor which must be done. Kenneth had told us they learn repetitive things well and don't forget them once they're learned. Mark has made it clear they are smarter, or at least have the capacity to be smarter than we think they are. Who is to say they wouldn't want to learn these skills? They're at the same level of difficulty as delivering glasses and running a food processor unit. It's not exploitation, it's common sense."

Kenneth retorted, "I can't believe you're thinking in this way. You sound like the old capitalists in the nineteenth who used children as laborers in their factories because they didn't have to be paid or fed as much. It's disgusting to me."

Harrison shook his head. "You're listening with your heart, not your head. I'm not saying we should underpay these creatures or treat them badly. What I am suggesting is that you all have some grandiose humanitarian ideals about bringing these creatures up to our level and what I'm saying is that it's not necessary to be equals to coexist. If they do some of the more laborious and tedious jobs, it will free the rest of us to more intellectual pursuits, thereby developing the planet for all who live here. I'm not suggesting enslavement or anything of the sort."

Before Eve could rise to stop the argument and get the discussion back into civilized terms, Janet rose and began speaking. "I have listened to the two diametrically opposed sides of this issue and I agree with both. Kenneth wants to protect his charges from exploitation, yet is willing to let them be exploited to a degree to bring more comfort to all of us. Harrison doesn't particularly care about protecting them, but sees in the creatures the opportunity to expand our foothold here through developing the natural resources of this planet. His suggested exploitation is less esthetically pleasing than Kenneth's but equally valid. I personally have no desire to work in a mine or at a petrocarbon well, and I'm sure the rest of us, if we search our true thoughts, feel much the same way. We are discussing the same issue. Only the degree differs." She sat down, rigidly emphasizing her point with her body.

Joan stood. "Madame Chairman, Members of the Council, I think Janet's point is well taken. There is also one other alternative. We could return all aliens resident here to their villages and hope they will go back to their old way of life before we intruded our presence and ideas on their village."

Eve stood before anyone else did. "Fellow Council Members, this discussion is attempting to encompass too great a sphere, which is why we've been having so much disagreement. Let's try to break it down to basics. As I see it, the primary issue is whether we have the right to use the aliens for anything at all or whether Kenneth's experiments should be allowed to continue purely as a scientific study. Then, if we decide to use the aliens in any work function, how much work should we expect and of what type? Also, should we attempt to integrate the two cultures that are so vastly different? And finally, by what means should we pay them for their labor if it is decided to use them as a work force? Kindly address yourselves to one portion of the debate and not cloud the issue with everything at once."

The discussion continued, each member trying to address only one issue as she had suggested, but morality kept creeping back into their discussions, muddling the decision process until finally she again stood.

"Members of the Council, I should like to suggest we put each separate issue to a vote. Discussion?"

No one moved, so she said, "Then I assume each of you has made up his or her mind about his or her feelings on this matter. First, those in favor of Kenneth continuing his work with the creatures?"

Everyone voted in favor.

"Second, those in favor of using the creatures in work functions?"

The results were again unanimously in favor.

"Those in favor of limiting their work to light labor such as household work and gardening?"

Four hands were raised.

"Opposed?"

Six hands went up.

"Those in favor of expanding their work beyond light labor to include more physical labor in such jobs as mining and forestry?"

Six hands were again raised.

"Opposed?"

Four.

"The question of payment is too complex for a simple vote. I would like to propose the creation of an Alien Contol Committee to be headed by someone not on the Council who can remain impartial. Discussion?"

Kenneth rose, and Eve nodded. He seemed to have regained control of his temper, though disgruntled by the vote. "Madame Chairman, Members of the Council, I think that is an excellent suggestion and would like to propose Rebecca Hayes as the head of such a committee and would further suggest that she be afforded a seat on the Council."

There was a buzzing in the room, but no one else asked for recognition, so Eve stood. "Further discussion?"

There was no response.

"Then will all of you in favor of an Alien Control Committee please vote now?"

There were eight in favor.

"And will those in favor of Rebecca Hayes as its head please vote now."

Again eight.

"And will those in favor of granting her a seat on the Council please vote now, remembering that we need a majority of at least eight votes to place someone on the Council."

The same eight voted in favor, Morris and Janet again abstaining for unexpressed reasons.

"Thank you. The final business of this meeting, I believe, is in order. We must establish a date for the move to the new community. Morris, how close to ready are you?"

He stood. "Madame Chairman, Members of the Council, we are basically as ready as we can be for the first groups to move in." He continued, cataloging the work remaining. Eve listened with part of her mind, while she reflected on his attitude and competence, and the glaring difference between the two.

When he addressed the Council it was with a subtle sneer in his voice that made her feel as if they were somehow playing out a charade he found particularly childish and amusing. It angered her, but there seemed to be nothing she could do about it. Maybe by the time he was settled into the new colony, away from the central community, he would be less derisive, but she doubted it.

She thought about the new colony and again worried about it. Its existence would demand her traveling back and forth between the two locations to be sure things were running smoothly and that no factions were springing up in either place. Then she had a thought.

Daoud Rahman was assigned to the new colony. She could trust him to be her ears there. Daoud had been spending a lot of time with her and Ramona, sometimes almost acting as a father for Ramona. Ramona was deeply disappointed he was moving away, as well as her friend Harmony, but Eve had promised frequent visits in both directions, which had seemed to placate her to a degree.

Morris was concluding his list of jobs remaining, then said, "I would like to suggest the relocation take place in stages of ten people each week for five weeks. That way we will avoid the potential chaos of everyone moving in all at the same time and we will have the opportunity to finish the remaining work over a longer period rather than having to get everything all done while still trying to help fifty people get settled into new quarters and new routines."

Eve stood, saying, "It sounds like a valid suggestion. Discussion?"

There was none.

"Then will you please make up lists of colonists to move and on what date so they can begin making their plans?"

Morris nodded, returning to his seat.

"If there is no further business, this Council is in recess."

The chamber cleared quickly except for Kenneth, who joined her at the end of the table.

"Eve, do you want me to do anything to get Rebecca started?"

She had almost forgotten. "Not right now. Let's see if she takes the job first. I'll speak to her this afternoon. If she does accept, I'll expect her to work with you for a while, getting to know as much as she can about the alien culture and language. We don't want her to be ignorant of any facet of her job."

He thanked her and left. Her instincts told her Rebecca would be fair and just with the aliens. She would make a good administrator, but Eve right now was more concerned with talking to Daoud.

She used the viewing screen to signal his room, but there was no answer, so she went out into the main hall. Esther was sure she had seen Daoud with Ramona and several other children down near the transport, so she took the elevator to the lower complex and went outside.

It was a beautiful, balmy day, so typical of the weather in the valley, and she could hear the high giggles of children in the distance. She followed the sound to Daoud and about ten children of varying ages. He was telling them a preposterous story involving giants and skeletons. They were giggling and laughing at his characterizations and she stood to one side watching until he finished his recitation, then beckoned to him.

He sent the children back into the complex with orders to go for lunch, and they walked through the tall grasses away from the complex.

"You'll be very much missed by the children."

He smiled shyly. "I'll miss playing hookey from fabrication to become Hans Christian Anderson. As a matter of fact, I've stolen a lot of his material, but I don't think he'll ever find out."

She laughed, relaxing after the strenuous meeting. "There will be children at the new complex."

He shook his finger at her. "Yes, but not so many. I'll have to make up more stories so they don't get bored with the same ones all the time."

She looked at his impish grin. "I don't think it will be a problem for you, somehow."

They walked on silently for a few minutes, Eve trying to find a way to present her request.

Finally, when she was ready to abandon her idea, he said, "There is one thing I'm very worried about over there and it has nothing to do with tales for children."

Her response was a neutral, "What's that?"

"I would like to have you think about what I'm going to say outside of your official duties. As a person and a member of the new community, I'm concerned about Morris's abilities as a leader. He is far too inflexible in too many situations and I think he's going to hurt and offend a lot of people with his manner."

"I, too, have been concerned about that. I don't think he means ill, but I think he sometimes forgets how to treat people. You might do him and me a great service while you're there, if you're willing."

"What?"

She had a fleeting doubt, hoping he wouldn't choose to violate her confidence, then said, "I'd like you to keep me abreast of the mood of the people and Morris's relationships with everyone. Just so if there is a problem building, we can help him to correct it before it gets out of control."

They began walking back toward the complex, silence sitting uncomfortably between them.

Finally, he said, "I won't be an official spy. However, I will be glad to record some stories for the children here. If you listen carefully to them, you'll know what's going on. That's the best I can do."

She smiled at him. "I'll look forward to hearing your stories."

The first ten were ready to leave, and Eve was waiting for the elevator with Morris. Ever since his election as Chairman of the Council for the new community their relationship had become even more difficult, neither of them able to break down the barrier between them.

Eve had tried several times, but Morris had been unresponsive to her opening gambits, coldly informing her she need not worry about his abilities to conduct his job. She had finally given up trying to talk to him.

She suspected his resentments came from her having been elected overall Chairman of the Joint Council by an almost unanimous vote. Richard was Chairman of the original community's Council and he had been spending as much time as he could spare trying to learn about the job. Morris apparently resented his growing closeness with Eve, for they had several times exchanged heated words outside her chambers.

The elevator reached the floor of the valley and they emerged into the crowd assembled to say good-bye to the departing group. There were some tear-stained faces, among them Ramona's as she bade farewell to her friend Harmony.

Morris nodded a cursory good-bye to several people who spoke to him and boarded the hovercraft rapidly, starting the engines, then racing them unnecessarily, indicating his impatience with the delays.

The rest of the departing group said last-minute fare-wells and filtered into the craft slowly. Finally, Morris slid back one of the windows and called, "Let's get going or we'll never be there before dark. Come on!"

His impatience moved the rest of the crowd into the ho-vercraft. He sounded the warning bell to move the remain-ing people away, engaged the gears, and allowed the craft to move slowly forward, away from the mountains, headed south to the new community.

Eve felt a wrench as she watched the dusty trail they left hanging in the air, and regretfully acknowledged it was fear for the future of her colony.

Despite all her denials, it was still her colony.

Chapter Thirteen

———◆———

"THE JOINT MEETING of Councils will please come to order."

Eve stood behind the podium on the newly built plat-form in the Council chamber and watched as the members of the Central Council settled into their chairs.

Morris sat to her right and Richard to her left, as Chair-men of their respective Councils. The other members ranged along the long table stretching out from the po-dium.

"Members, please," she again called for order, and finally there was quiet.

We have a great deal of business to conduct today, and I must ask your indulgence. First, it is my joyful duty to wel-come all the newly elected members from each of the cities'

Councils and to congratulate you on your office. And, for those of you living down the valley, welcome back."

"One of our first orders of business today must be the naming of our respective cities. I'm aware this has been discussed in local Council meetings as well as in the various Congregations, but it is our task today to make it official. Morris, will you kindly present the names your Council has selected for your community?"

Morris rose. Eve was prepared now, as she hadn't been when he emerged from the transport. He had begun wearing the flowing white robe of his office. She was sure it was, in part, for psychological effect, both on her and on his own community, but wondered at his thinking. She made a mental note to question Daoud, who sat along the table as a member of Council, if Morris were affecting the robe all the time or if this was a special event. She hoped the latter was true.

"Madame Chairman, Fellow Chairman, Fellow Council Members, I was personally surprised and pleased at the amount of discussion the naming of our little community has provoked among her citizens. We have devoted a great deal of time, both in Council and in Congregation, to the selection of a proper name that expresses how we really feel about our community, and we have finally selected two choices with which the majority would be comfortable and happy.

"They are: Athena, for the ancient Earth goddess of wisdom, and Outward."

Eve could tell from his tone that his choice was the latter. Even without that clue in his voice, she knew the Earth-tied name would offend him.

She stood. "Discussion?"

Richard rose, his hand working in nervousness. He wore, in contrast to Morris, a standard coverall.

"Madame Chairman, Fellow Chairman, Council Members, first I'd also like to welcome you to our first meeting, and tell you how exciting it is for me to be a part of what we're doing." He smiled, somewhat shyly, and Eve reflected that botany would never intimidate him the way the robes of government did.

He cleared his throat and began again. "I'd like to propose that we from the original colony offer our two selections as well before any further discussion."

He looked at Eve who stood.

"Is that suggestion acceptable?"

Everyone along the table nodded, so she returned to her seat.

Richard said, "We, too, have had much discussion on the matter of naming our city, and have finally decided on two names. We've chosen—Eden, for this is where it all started, and Centralia." He sat down quickly.

Eve stood. "Discussion?"

The majority of the Council members, feeling their office, had a comment to make on their choice of name, though few commented on anything but their own city's concern. After the discussion had progressed to the point where everyone had had a chance to speak, Eve stood again. "I think it's time for us to vote on this matter and proceed to other business. First, let me make it clear that all members of Council will vote on both cities' names. Let us first deal with the original complex. Those in favor of the name Eden, kindly raise your hands."

She counted seventeen raised hands out of the twenty voting members.

"Then, I think we can assume that the original community will now be known as Eden."

There was applause from the Council members.

Eve allowed it to subside, then called for the vote on the second community.

"All those in favor of the name Athena, please raise your hands."

Ten members voted in favor. She grimaced. Unless some member chose to abstain, it would force her to vote.

"Those in favor of the name Outward, kindly vote now."

Again, ten hands.

"We have a tie vote. Is there any further discussion?"

For a moment, no one moved and she was about to speak when Morris rose. He had remained aloof from the previous discussion, for which she had been relieved. She nodded in his direction, then sat down, resigning herself to another of his anti-Earth outbursts.

"Fellow members of the Council, it is my opinion we must sever our ties with Earth. My personal feeling is that the choice of a name of a pagan Earth goddess would be denying our independence from that planet which our people left so long ago. I would encourage those of you who still think of our people as refugees to begin thinking of us as pioneers and treat this circumstance accordingly." He returned to his chair, crossing his arms and glaring.

Eve recognized Daoud, who stood. "Morris's point is well taken, but I feel he may have personalized the entire discussion. The people who suggested and supported the name Athena do not see it as a tie to a 'pagan goddess of Earth' but as a representation of the higher ideals of knowledge and wisdom that inspire all of us. Morris, Earth is part of our past and we cannot deny it."

Morris stared off into space as the discussion continued.

Finally, Eve again stopped the discussion and called for a vote, hoping to be able to move on. Again there was a deadlock.

Richard stood, and Eve nodded in his direction. "I think, according to the rules to which we subscribe, a secret vote is now called for."

Before Eve could call the secret vote, Morris stood.

"Madame Chairman, may I remind you the secret votes call for your participation as well."

She nodded as the members of the Council reached for their pocket terminals. The computer would record the vote without any indication from whom it originated.

Eve held her terminal for a moment, listening to the conflict ranging in her own mind. She truly preferred the name

Athena, but feared the choice would send Morris off into one of his rages. She sighed inwardly. He was obsessed with not being treated like one of her children, but sometimes he had to be humored to keep him from a childish tantrum. His responsibilities as leader had not tempered his headstrong personality, and she felt disappointment.

"If you are in favor of the name Athena, kindly press the 'A' key on your terminal. If you favor the name Outward, kindly press the 'B' key. Please vote now."

She hesitated for a moment, then, indulging Morris once more, pressed the 'B' key. The computer screen on her podium indicated:

A—ten votes

B—eleven votes

Morris looked at her, a smug smile on his face and she almost regretted her decision, because she realized he viewed her act of conciliation as weakness.

The Council continued in session, hearing progress reports from each community, then from each department. No one lingered too long over a report and the meeting came to a conclusion.

When they emerged from the Council chamber, Richard announced the naming decisions to Eden, while Morris sent a message to Outward. The central hall filled with the people of Eden, anxious to talk with friends who had been gone for as long as two months. The room rang with greetings and laughter. Daoud waited until Eve had finished talking with a group from Outward, then walked with her away from the center of the activity.

"Well?"

"Yes, and you?"

He laughed. "You are sometimes the most evasive woman in the world. You know what I meant."

"Yes," she said with a smile, "I did. And I also know from speaking with Chen about your intended modifications to the transports to extend their life and potentially to make them able to fly over long distances."

He laughed again. "You don't miss much, do you? We've been studying the prerocket flight machines in the tapes and they sound as though they would be very practical for our situation, not only for the obvious transportation between the two cities, but also for the explorers. Presently the hovercraft can attain a flying height of about fifteen meters, which is helpful, but if we were to add a propeller of some sort, the machine could support itself in the air without using the ground-directed air stream. We found pictures and designs of a craft they called a helicopter, which had a bladelike propeller on the top, and, according to the specs, could hover as well as fly. We think it would really expand our horizons."

"... were the primary instruments of the war. The airplane and its allied machines could swoop low to the ground, affording accurate placement of bombs and greater destruction capability. The transport rocket made the airplane obsolete for human and cargo transfer, thus the airplane was outlawed."

The professor studied them all, sitting in their tidy rows. "Someday, on your future planets, you will decide the airplane is a more important means of transportation than the hovercraft; speed is more important than safety; and thus will begin the eventual destruction of your civilization. In my opinion."

Morris waited until most of the class had left, then approached the professor hesitantly. He was a fierce man who disapproved of the Project, but had agreed to teach its members after publicly announcing he hoped to give them a dose of common sense in the midst of all the dreaming.

Eve waited beside Morris, knowing what he was getting himself into and wishing he'd reconsider.

"Excuse me, sir, but I'd like to ask a question."

The professor looked up from his notes, irritation on his face.

"Yes, I'm sure you would."

Morris was undeterred. "Sir, you hold so little hope for mankind to be able to succeed on other planets. Why is it you think we will fail to progress? Why condemn the airplane, for *example, as a symbol of failure instead of realizing it can be a tool for successful colonization?"*

The professor stood slowly, tapping his long fingers on the shiny surface of the table. "Mr. Watson, my views on mankind and his failures are hardly a secret. I have been most vocal in the classroom and the press concerning my perpetual despair for the state of our species. The airplane simply represents the technical ability to approach one's enemy from above his head and rain death upon him. Yes, of course there are many practical applications for such a machine, but eventually someone will come along who will decide it can be used to dominate, and that, my dear man, is the end of that. As historically every technical advance has eventually been used as a tool for one or another form of domination by the members of our race. We are not, by our nature, a very peaceful species and I hardly think converting everyone's atoms into energy and back again will make them any less stupid about their relationships with their fellow man. We've had more than two million years to learn peace, and all we've been able to achieve is the invention of larger clubs with which to cudgel greater numbers of the enemy at one time. Not much progress, Mr. Watson."

Without another word, he turned and left the room, leaving Morris with a scowl on his face.

"Eve, he's wrong. He's got to be wrong."

"Eve?" Daoud's voice intruded on her. "Are you all right?"

"Yes, I'm sorry. You sent my mind back to another conversation about flying craft. It's not terribly important."

Daoud studied her for a moment, then finally said, "Rarely is anything you think about unimportant. The other piece of business I assume you want to discuss is our friend, the Chairman of Outward."

"Before you begin, let's be sure we understand one very important thing. Morris is sometimes a bit of a problem, but he is truly our friend. He's trying to wear leadership comfortably, but it's still resting heavily on his shoulders.

Before he was in a position of complete responsibility he thought it would be easy. Now that he must make the decisions, I sense it has become a task."

Daoud raised his eyebrow. "Eve, you haven't been living at Outward. There are a number of people there who regret their choice of Chairman. He intervenes constantly in the work of everyone, directing and demanding what he doesn't understand. He's even forbidden me to tell stories to the children. Can you get him to relax a bit?"

She shook her head. "I was concerned about that. His reports to the Joint Council have indicated it, but I had hoped it would settle down on its own accord as he grew into his role and the community became adjusted to their new environment."

"Is that why you haven't come for a visit?"

She nodded. "I was afraid a visit from me would appear to be an attempt to intervene in his authority, so I've let it pass. Daoud, I'm still adjusting to my new role as overall Chairman. It has necessitated my withdrawing from some of the daily events here, as well. I mustn't interfere with Richard or Morris unless the appropriate Councils ask."

Daoud shook his head. "No one on our Council would dare propose such a request. Morris's temper seems to have gotten more volatile and such a suggestion would be treated as treasonous by him. There must be something you can do."

They stood in silence, looking out across the valley. The extended community of Eden glimmered in the sun, melting in the distance into the sea of grasses. Across the valley, the smoke from the alien village fires rose, then spread away in the breeze. Eve felt a remote sense of doom.

"Daoud, we've lost our innocence here. When I was alone, and then when most everyone else was a child, it was easy to go to one another and point out mistakes or praise a success. Now we must all relate to each other as adults and adults all have different views of life. Morris has chosen his way of approaching the position of responsibility he carries and I can't interfere with that unless he begins to be destructive. You, the members of the Council of Outward, must be the controlling force. If you, as a group, see his direction is no longer constructive, then, despite his rages, you must ask for intervention or hold another election. You have gone beyond the phase of running to me to solve your problems."

She returned her gaze to the valley. She could feel him breathing beside her, but the comfortable ease was gone between them. She knew she had destroyed it, having to choose her official role over her personal relationships.

She and Mark had discussed the disadvantages of friendships and alliances, and now a vivid demonstration had occurred, stressing her isolation again. She was glad for Ramona.

She felt him leave, but stood on the ledge for a long time, watching the sun moving in the pale green sky, listening to the noises in the complex behind her and feeling completely empty.

Ramona came dashing out the door with Harmony close behind, and they each grabbed one of her hands to drag her back into the complex in time for Congregation.

"Mom, is it all right if Harmony stays with us for a few days, please?"

Eve stood looking at her child, feeling fear for her future, but managed a smile. "Of course she can stay with us. Have you asked Morris?"

The two little girls looked at each other, then back at her. "We thought you might ask him. That way he'll know it's all right."

"You two! I'll ask him for you, since we have to talk anyway, but you'd better start learning to stand on your own four feet pretty soon."

Morris was withdrawn from the others in the room, sitting with his robes gathered around him, watching the activity. She joined him on the bench without invitation.

"How are things going over at Outward? I've read your reports, of course, but I'd like to hear your personal view."

"I'm sure you would; now that you've had a chance to talk to all your spies, you're going to give me a chance to present my side. Just checking up on the kids again."

She sighed. "It would be so much easier if you would be pleasant. I'm not out to usurp your power or undermine your authority. I am, both as Chairman and as your friend, concerned about the community you head and would like to hear your analysis of how everything is going. Can we talk or must I make it an order?"

"Oh, certainly we can talk." His tone was laden with sarcasm. "You needn't issue any orders, Madame Chairman. Everything is moving along as well as can be expected in a new community still finding its way. We're all adjusting to jobs and scheduling and mechanical tricks of the associated machinery involved. I foresee a great future for Outward and other communities like it. Anything else?"

"Yes. What about personalities? Is everyone getting along with everyone else comfortably?"

"Of course. Remember, we're all adults now and we've been raised by you. How could we not get along?"

She knew any further questioning would simply produce more sarcasm from him, so she changed the subject abruptly.

"Harmony and Ramona would like to spend a few days together. Would it be all right if Harmony stayed here?"

He leaned close to her. "I don't think so. My daughter has her lessons and her duties and she must learn early that no one has special privileges in Outward simply by virtue of their relatives. Excuse me."

Eve felt tears stinging her eyes.

PART IV

Chapter Fourteen

———◆———

RAMONA'S PERSONAL SERVANT padded silently into her room, laying out the fresh coverall she would need when she emerged from the sonar cleaner. Out of the wall safe she selected a string of the shiny stones Ramona liked to wear around her neck and in her hair.

Ramona emerged from the small room, singing. Seeing the servant, she smiled and said in the common speech, "Good morning. Are you well?"

The servant nodded rapidly, replying, "Very well. And you, madame?"

Ramona slipped into her coverall, then sat in front of the mirror, arranging her hair. She had tried to teach the alien creature the skill, but the complicated styles Ramona liked eluded her dexterity. The servant stood behind her, waiting with the jewels. They were a by-product of the mining operation and one of the chemists had said they were close to an Earth gem called a diamond. He had cut along the crystal planes to make the stones sparkle. They amused her so she wore them.

She heard the thumping of one of the aircraft as it hovered to land down in the valley and grabbed the jewels from the servant, winding them around her throat as she hurried through the halls of the complex and out onto the ledge.

This was the flight from New Rome, the colony being built across the sea on the other large land mass of the planet. She had been eagerly awaiting the return of the first fabrication crew, but not because of the work that they had been doing. Warren Mead had been gone for three months with the first crew and she had missed him terribly. Before he left neither of them had been ready to make a marriage commitment, even though they had kept constant company for the previous eight years.

Ramona, frivolous and clownish on the surface, was dedicated to her job of assisting Eve with the various demands of the Chairmanship and she moved, without portfolio, freely among the other communities: Gateway to the north in the forested lands, and Atlantis, perched on its hill in the midst of the tropical jungle to the southwest, over the mountains. Atlantis was her favorite despite the summer heat which became almost unbearable. It was surrounded with lush green growth filled with beautiful birds and animals. The area was rich with hydrocarbon sources and the fabricators had found a way to concentrate the hydrocarbons to supply the rest of the communities, if necessary.

Outward, on the other hand, was her least favorite spot to visit. Everyone there was so serious, including Harmony, who had become a surgical technician working with the aliens. She was immersed in her research and they had grown further apart when she had married the man she assisted in the lab, a studious exo with no sense of fun at all. It had been almost two years since she and Harmony had really talked, and that last time had convinced her they now had little in common.

She hurried down the stairs and in the direction of the landing pad in the middle of the complex. Eden had grown since her childhood with buildings springing up seemingly overnight, stretching out along the edge of the mountains in both directions as well as out into the valley.

She hopped onto the back of a passing hovercraft, momentarily upsetting its balance and getting a dirty look from the driver until he realized who it was.

"Hi, Ramona. Where are you going?"

"To the landing pad. And be quick about it," she teased.

"Then you'd better hold on." He gunned the engine and the craft leapt up the street, horn hooting to warn people emerging from side streets.

They arrived just as the passengers began to emerge. She jumped off, throwing a "Thanks, John" over her shoulder as she ran, whooping, to meet Warren.

He was the last to emerge from the helicopter, standing in the doorway, looking nonchalant, unresponsive to her waving, yelling greeting.

He waited until she was leaping up and down, then made an elaborate show of recognizing her and waving, as though they'd only seen each other the day before. As soon as he passed through the exit port, she leapt into his arms, covering his face with kisses while some of the crew on the craft watched, laughing.

Warren finally disengaged her grasp. "Ramona, my love, you're hardly behaving in a dignified way. You obviously haven't been to Outward lately."

She looked up at him, mischief in her eyes, then threw her arms around him again. "You'll never get away again, Warren Mead. Not for more than ten minutes. I can't stand these long separations."

"Ramona, you know I have to go back to New Rome."

"This time I'm coming with you. I'll go as the emissary and be there in an official capacity. You'll never get rid of me again."

"And what makes you think I'd want to?"

They walked along the street toward his dwelling rooms. The expansion had cured the previous crowding so every person reaching maturity had his or her own generous space for living.

"It's nice to be home. New Rome is a little like Outward. It's very sterile and cold in design. All the streets and paths will be straight lines and the buildings are all almost the same. You have to put numbers on them so people will know where they are."

Ramona nodded. She would have expected as much since Morris had designed the city, as he had Outward, and straight lines and look-alike buildings were his style.

Atlantis had been partly her city and it reflected her style: free spirited and happy, its streets flowing curves; its buildings individualistic as its people, a very lively environment.

"The magic touch of Morris creating another sterile environment for serious people. Oh, I suppose there must be some serious people, but everyone around him seems to have completely lost the ability to laugh. Mother is threatening to send me off to Outward again on some sort of mission or another, but I'm trying to postpone it. I get so somber when I'm there I can't stand myself." She leaned toward him conspiratorially. "Did you know that no one there, I mean no one, laughs when they make love?"

He stopped abruptly, looking at her quizzically. "Is that on the basis of rumor, or have you been terribly busy since I left?"

"What do you think? Don't you trust me?"

He put his arm around her waist and hoisted her, like a bundle of fabrication rods, over his shoulder. She shrieked and pounded on his back, but he only laughed and continued down the street singing a song and patting the tempo on her slim backside, producing little yelps in time to the music.

She finally resigned herself to being carried and continued the conversation as best she could. "Tell me, umpf, don't bounce, what else is going on in New Rome? Umpf. Warren, umpf, don't jar so on your heels. Unh."

"Well, Ramona, if you didn't have to be carried everywhere, it wouldn't be so hard to talk to you. Good morning."

Ramona heard the snicker from the two passing teenagers.

"Let's see, what else is going on in New Rome.... Well, there's a lot of building and very few appealing women and there was lots of rain while I was there and the food synthesizer has only two settings and I'm very tired of steak and chicken and I haven't made love for three months and two days and"—he shifted her weight, looking at his chron—"seven hours, and so you know what you're going to be doing for the rest of the day When we get back to my dwelling, you'd better ring Mama and tell her you're in conference. Speaking of Mama, how is she?"

"If you don't put me down, I won't call her."

He set her on her feet immediately.

"Thank you. She's fine. I think she's happier now than she's been for a long time, probably because Morris is keeping to his own business and not causing problems in Council. I think he has something up his sleeve because it's not like him to be courteous and quiet in Council. The meetings have been almost boring."

"The one I feel sorry for is Ellen. She's been married to him for over thirty years and if he's like he is in public, can you imagine what he's like in the privacy of their own home?"

"Warren, there are about six hundred things I'd rather talk about than Morris Watson. And at least one I'd rather do."

He touched the palm lock at his door and it slid to the side. As he dropped his carry-bag and wandered around the house, refamiliarizing himself with it, she tapped the number of her mother's private quarters on the viewing screen.

Eve's face appeared, smiling when she saw Ramona.

"Hello, dear. How's Warren?"

"I'm fine, Eve," he called from the background. "You?"

"Fine, Warren. Welcome home. I'll expect to hear all about New Rome at your earliest convenience, but I'm sure the two of you have details to discuss."

"Mother, please. I sometimes wish you were just a bit less understanding. Half the fun is sneaking around."

Eve laughed. "Have a nice time, dear. I'll see you both later." Her face, so much like Ramona's, disappeared from the screen.

Warren sat on the wide bench in the living room, pulling her down beside him.

"I have a question for you, Ramona, and, for once, I'd like a straight answer with no jokes."

She put on a somber face.

"Ramona, I really think it's time we got married. We've been going together for a long time and I have the feeling that if I don't push you, you'll end up like your mother— alone with only a job to fill her life."

Ramona twirled the hair on his arm. "Mother does what she does for good reasons. She feels her isolation from personal alliances is germane to her effectiveness as Chairman."

"Are you suggesting she will be opposed to our marriage on that basis?"

"No, of course not. I'm simply saying mother is not going to be wildly in favor of my marrying anyone, though she approves of you. I've wanted to marry you for years, but haven't dared broach the subject to her. She sees us in some goddesslike pristine role, you know, no temptations of the flesh and all that. Her greatest fear is that someone will try to corrupt either of us for their own devices."

"And she thinks that of me after all this time?"

"No, she thinks that of everyone. I guess we can ask her."

He cradled her in his arms, resting her head against his

chest. "We can marry without her permission, you know. She doesn't have to approve."

She shook her head, hearing his heart beating as she moved. "We can, technically. But I can't do that to her. You can't imagine how many times she's reminded me I'm all she has, how important I am to the community image and so on ad nauseam. It's a touchy problem, but we can solve it. It's a matter, with her, of how you approach it. And I think I have the solution."

He raised his eyebrows over her head, but she heard only the questioning "hum?" that rumbled in his chest.

"Well, Morris has requested a transfer to New Rome, and she's considering it. I think she really just wants him far enough away so he stops being such an irritant to her. However, Morris also has requested the transfer of some of his aides and techs so there will be some big gaps in personnel at Outward. I'm not wild about living there, but if we both request to be stationed there, she'll probably suggest we get married, knowing how strict that community's standards are about people doing what I sure hope you're thinking about doing right now."

He chuckled, sending another rumble into her, then said, "You've been planning this."

"Yes, I have. I thought it was about time we got around to making some decisions."

"Ramona, you are a conniving woman. You are also a very sexy woman, and I've missed that."

She felt his urgency in the tensions of his muscles and turned against him. As they slid down on the bench, she heard him say again, "Tomorrow. We'll ask her tomorrow."

Ramona's murmured answer was lost in the catch of her breath.

Eve's long robe swished across the smooth plasteel as she paced the floor of the conference room, thinking.

The complex was so much quieter now that most of the people had moved to the city below and the nursery relocated into the general education building. She was virtually alone in the complex again, and was sometimes amused by the idea that it had taken her almost fifty years to regain her solitude.

There were still a few staff members living in expanded apartments on the floors above, and they would pass in the halls, speak, but respect the sanctity of everyone's privacy. Today the quiet was unsettling because she could hear the little noises of the community, distracting in their ambiguity. She finally lowered herself into the classic lotus position on the floor, sliding into a trance to increase her concentration.

Morris's face hovered before her mind's eye, blending with his father's almost forgotten one, then drifting into itself again. He wanted New Rome so badly, pressuring her in and out of Council in his condescending way. She was badly torn, wanting to deny him the post for some indefinable reason, yet knowing that, in his rigid and uncompromising fashion, he had become a fine administrator.

He had learned, over the years, a way in which to build loyalties in his staff which were sometimes almost unreasonable, somehow coercing them to produce far beyond the expectations of normalcy. They would deny him nothing, follow him anywhere, and put everything aside for one of his projects. Yet, they hated him and never tired of complaining about his gruffness and lack of tact. They were impressed with his ability to get things done, as was she.

Eve pondered his obsession with New Rome. There were obvious reasons why he wanted the post—he had designed the city, chosen the location, and supervised the construction details to the tiniest fabrication clip. He had done the same for Outward and it was a functional city, if relatively beautiless.

New Rome, from the videos she had seen, was much the same in concept, with straight, even structures, each similar to the next, and clean lines with no embellishments to soften the impact of the plasteel against the gentle landscape of the rolling foothills in which it was built.

Her mind wandered away from Morris to the planet herself. Genesis had been very good to her people, sparing them the hostile storms and earthquakes with which Earth had punished her populations. Genesis provided uncomplicated shelter, seemingly endless resources, a moderate climate, and many usable hydrocarbons. She smiled, wishing again she could somehow bring the Project Directors here to see that at least one of their dreams had come true.

That brought her wandering thoughts back to New Rome. It would be a Project Director's delight, practical and efficient. Morris would delight them, too. So why couldn't she freely assign him to New Rome? She searched back into her mind, seeking the answer to her reluctance. It wasn't the external Morris who worried her in the post, but the secret man nobody knew. She realized, almost with a physical start, that she feared him. There was something in that secret man she found dark and threatening, though she couldn't focus or define it. A subtle threat, perhaps, deeper than his derision and condescension which many had felt. It was as though he carried a dark burden somewhere inside his head that he concealed from everyone around him. It was that burden she had to consider when thinking about New Rome.

She rose from the lotus and again paced the room.

But, really, she thought, what difference does it make if it's Outward or New Rome? The only difference between the two is distance, and if he is thinking of something outside the bounds of acceptable behavior, if that is his secret self, he could do it virtually right under her nose at Outward.

There was something else, she had to admit, that had nothing to do with capabilities or reason, and that was her own failing. She felt, by granting him the transfer to New Rome, she was once more giving in to his demands, allowing him anything he professed to want without seeming to put up any kind of a battle. There had been comments before over one or another instance, and she was certain this decision would produce similar reactions. Well, she had weathered such storms before and would be able to cite his excellent work in Outward in defense of her decision. After all, New Rome was the first city on a new continent and it would be important to have strong leadership there to guide its growth.

Suddenly she smiled, relief flooding through her. She would nominate each of the city Chairmen for the post and allow the decision to be made in Council. That way, if Morris were chosen, it would be the choice of the people, not the choice of the Chairman. If Morris were approved for the transfer, she would have to be sure to maintain her sources of information, just as she had in Outward.

She reached for the small silver bell Warren had made for her from the vein he had discovered in one of the exploratory mineral mines. Fabrication in minerals for personal items had become a hobby for some of the colonists and Warren made effective use of the laser equipment which was supposed to be used in construction. He had made not only the bell but the chain and badge of office she wore so proudly.

The gentle tinkle of the bell brought her alien maid gliding into the room.

"Madame?"

Eve heard the strange voice in her head as though there were a speaker hidden somewhere in her skull. The telepathic communication between them had begun many years before, in an eerily accidental way, when she suddenly realized the maid, Aiegna, was not only arriving almost before she was called but also was capable of planting thoughts and concepts in Eve's mind.

"Aiegna, how many of your people will be going to New Rome? What have you heard?"

"Madame, the lines are crowded with gossip among all my people."

Sometimes Eve would become frustrated with Aiegna's evasiveness but she had to respect the customs of her people and they were slow to tell the whole story. Eve had learned that the more evasive Aiegna was, the more she could learn with patience.

"As they are with my people. New Rome has caused much excitement."

"Many of my people are there now, working with the fabrications. They speak of great size of the city."

Eve felt a sense of alarm rising in her. New Rome was not supposed to be a large city until it was established with an initial, small colony.

Aiegna felt her concern. *"Apparently the construction people wanted to accomplish more than the originally intended plans so less construction would be necessary later. They had a lot of extra fabrication materials."*

"Who ordered those materials and where did they come from?" Eve felt her anger rising.

Aiegna's eye stalks swiveled toward Eve. She had seen her mistress angry before and feared the outbursts.

"They came from every city. My people say there were too many people able to order materials and there was a lot of duplication."

She tried to tell Eve what was necessary without feeding her anger.

"Aiegna, will some of our friends who are there now continue to live in New Rome when the colonists arrive?"

"Yes, Madame, many of our friends will stay. We will continue to receive information."

"Thank you, Aiegna, that will be all."

Aiegna moved from the room quietly. Eve often wondered just how many of her thoughts were not private at all because Aiegna had such a strong talent for "hearing." She also wondered if others had discovered the telepathy. Kenneth and Cilia had never mentioned it in any of their reports, though many things they considered to be remarkable advances could well be attributed to the ability of the aliens to listen to their thoughts.

The aliens gossiped constantly among themselves, able to pinpoint a particular individual even thousands of kilometers away, but they seemed only to enjoy making comments on the failings of their human employers rather than discussing more serious matters. Eve had found that an asset. Their "friends" had provided more than one piece of useful gossip, though Eve also wondered how much Aiegna neglected to tell her that might be important, not through negligence but through a lack of understanding of the complexities of the human condition.

The Council chamber buzzed with reunions until Eve entered and stepped to the head of the long table around which they sat.

The meeting progressed smoothly, with reports from each of the cities as well as business, such as material allocations for new structures as well as for New Rome. When the subject of New Rome arose, Eve waited for all reports to be finished, then stood.

"I understand that there have been some instances of ordering too much material for New Rome, gathering it from various fabrication plants. Can we please, at our next meeting, have a total accounting of all fabrications for New Rome?"

Chen rose immediately. "Madame Chairman, that matter has come to my attention as well, and I have compiled the information. Apparently there was a major miscalculation on the part of the original estimators and too much has been shipped. Morris suggested we make use of the extra material by constructing additional structures as long as the manpower was at the location."

"And has that been approved by the Fabrication Department?" She was pushing Chen, but was angry with him for not discussing it with her.

He lowered his eyes. "I approved it."

The silence hung in the room. Finally Eve said, "I see."

Chen watched her from the corner of his eye. She knew he was merely dealing with pragmatic considerations and was not aware of the power play to which he had contributed.

Finally, she said, "If you have approved it, then it must be for good reason. It is unfortunate such an error could occur, but you have found a practical solution."

She could feel the ebb of tension, except from Morris who watched her intently knowing the next order of business before the Council.

"With reference to New Rome, several highly competent administrators have spoken to me of their desire to work there."

Morris's eyes narrowed in response to the unexpected news of competition and she felt a sense of victory, which made her almost uncomfortable with herself.

"I feel each of them is well qualified to handle the demands and responsibilities of the circumstance there and that this is a decision which must be made in Council, not only by me."

There was nodding approval around the table.

"I have added to the list some I feel would also be more than competent in the role of administrator and temporary chairman there."

Again Morris reacted to the word "temporary" as she had expected he would. He was anticipating an appointed Chairmanship and she was obviously making it more difficult for him to achieve that goal.

"Anyone nominated is, of course, free to decline if it would cause inconvenience to make the move. We are all aware this is a very special circumstance. The individuals I would like to submit for consideration are: Morris Watson,

Joan Crane, Michael Bellanova, Jeremy Wilson, Richard VanDersant, and Frank Howsman."

Various Council members sought recognition to speak to the qualifications of one or another of the candidates and each received glowing reports on their capabilities. None declined the nomination.

Finally, when everyone who wished to speak had done so, Eve rose and said, "I think it would be most appropriate to vote using the computer."

She reread the list as the Council members voted.

The first vote was a tie among Morris, Michael, and Joan, and further discussion followed.

Eve again called for a secret ballot and the members voted among the three. Morris and Joan tied again and there was an expectant pause.

"Both Joan and Morris are more than qualified to serve in the temporary Chairmanship of New Rome and it is certainly a difficult choice for all of us to make. I would like to call for another vote between Joan and Morris."

The vote was taken and again the Council members were evenly split.

Morris rose. "Madame Chairman, in the event of a deadlock, it is custom that the Chairman of Council shall break that vote. Let us hear your decision."

He challenged her with his attitude.

"Morris, I think we should call another vote in which all members of Council participate. Anyone is free to change his or her vote and that way it does not become my decision, though I shall vote along with the rest of the members.

She knew what she had to do. Much as she worried about Morris, she knew he was by far the more capable of the two to launch the new community. Looking down the table, she saw the same feeling reflected in Joan's face. She tried to apologize to Joan using speech without voice, but there

was no change in the younger woman's expression and Eve
knew she hadn't heard her message.

The vote was a majority of one for Morris.

As he left the Council chamber, without speaking to her,
he turned in the doorway and looked at her across the long
table, his expression smug.

PART V

Chapter Fifteen

———◆———

RAMONA WATCHED EVE walk through the Council chamber, greeting various members and making her strong presence felt in the room, and marveled. Her mother had gathered a stately aura about her over the past years that lent power to her beyond that of her position.

It occurred to Ramona it had been a long time since she had heard her mother laugh in public, though in private, with her grandchildren around her, she laughed delightedly and was her old self. Her public image was one of dignity and aloofness, but tempered with a radiant warmth drawing people to her.

Ramona had even felt it, this need to be subservient in Eve's presence, and had seen it thousands of times. Powerful people, leaders of their communities, would diminish themselves physically in Eve's presence, speaking in low, respectful tones, eager for her approval.

Ramona's eyes wandered around the room. Council West was a large organization, but still only half of the world's governing body. When the representatives of Morris's Council East (she involuntarily wrinkled her nose at the thought) joined them for a general meeting, the room was crowded nearly beyond its capacity.

Eve, however, insisted on using the original Council chamber at Eden, rather than moving to a larger site, even down in the valley. Ramona knew it was a power logic on her mother's part, for the original complex was now Eve's private domain and she wanted to remind the Council members with each meeting that they had to make the effort to come to her.

The Council chamber occupied the entire upper floor above Eve's quarters. Fabrication had taken out the room partitions then installed a long, U-shaped table in the center of the space with an observation gallery for visitors. The gallery was frequently filled with citizens who were free to comment on subjects under discussion and often did.

Warren had encouraged Ramona to delve into the computer tapes on government structures of Earth after she had been elected Chairman of Outward, and, after study, she heartily approved of Eve's style of governing. Eve had blended republicanism, democracy, and communism with her own personal form of benign dictatorship and it worked.

The rapidly growing population was generally happy and certainly productive beyond most expectations. They had been able to accomplish a great deal in the forty years since Outward had begun the colonial expansion. Ramona knew it was Eve's steady guidance and push for growth in the new cities which had helped them achieve so much. She still exerted control over initial governments of the new cities, often appointing temporary Chairmen who she knew would serve their new cities well, and usually her appointments were elected to the office in open elections after the cities had become established.

Eve had just returned from a trip to New Rome and was

attending the Council West meeting to report on the developments of colonies in Council East. Ramona could feel a tension in her mother she was sure none of the others knew was there. Obviously there had been another dispute with Morris. It would be unmentioned in the meeting, but Ramona knew she would hear the details later. Her own visits there had been disquieting in a subtle way.

Morris's Council East Chairmanship had been a coup for him, and he wasn't loathe to use the power at his disposal. Eastern Region was not a very happy place to live, making her more uncomfortable than Outward ever did when Morris had been there. Regimentation of the population was obvious, but there seemed to be no chafing against the bonds. Somehow Morris had been able to convince the people of his region that he knew what was right for them and they responded with almost a fanatic loyalty to him. She had once engaged a childhood friend from Morris's region in conversation about the structure of the society there and had been surprised at the coldnesss with which her questions were received. He had almost a magical power over his people and it made her uncomfortable.

Ramona stepped to the raised podium at the head of the Council table and the members settled into their chairs. She opened the meeting, then gave the podium to Eve.

"My friends, it's good to be home." Eve's quiet voice carried throughout the room, filling every corner with sound. Ramona knew it was a microphone and speaker system that Eve had installed for just this effect, but it still intimidated her.

"The growth in the Eastern Region is totally astonishing to me, even after seeing the videos and reading the reports from their Council, and I wish that all of you could venture to that distant land to see it for yourselves."

There was a quiet buzz of interest in the room, not an audible word, but more of a general hum.

"New Rome is a busy, populous city which has grown enormously since my last visit, including the addition of a large stadium for sport and public events where Morris and his Council hold their public meetings. A large reception in that facility afforded me the opportunity to greet and speak with almost everyone in New Rome and all are well.

"Outside the city itself, the Eastern Council has set aside some lands for farming experiments and they have produced highly nutritious mutations of common plants which merit the attention of all of our farming workers. I have brought samples of the fruits and vegetables with me and, if there is interest, Eastern Council will send a consultant." She looked in the direction of Antonio Nessman who nodded in agreement.

Antonio was in charge of a large farming complex north of Eden which supplied much food to the nearby communities and he was always interested in new products and ideas, though not very creative in his own domain.

"I also traveled, while there, to New Athens, across the central mountain range. New Athens has been styled to duplicate the old Earth city of Athens during the peak of the Greek period in their history and it is truly an outstanding accomplishment of the fabrication departments. The population is still very small there, for they are attempting to create a specific society, gathering intellectuals and artists as did ancient Athens. It is a noble experiment."

Now Ramona knew the source of the conflict with Morris. For all his practicality, he was attempting to create a virtually nonproductive city and she knew Eve would find that offensive in a world needing to continue to grow and develop. There was so much work to be done by the great minds to better the human condition on Genesis that sequestering them in an isolated community would seem absurd to her mother.

"I also visited the city of Etheria while there and found a number of very interesting projects going on with development of fabrication techniques for various machines which will expand our abilities to travel, produce, and live...."

Ramona, sitting to her mother's right at the head of the

long table, allowed her attention to wander to the faces at the meeting. There was great interest in Eve's report, for most of the Council members were unable to travel due to their work demands. She had been to New Rome entirely too many times for her own taste and had visited the great stadium. She saw it as a representation of Morris's ego, a place where he could gather a large mass of people together to impress them with his powerful personality.

And now New Athens, which was simply another ego expression for Morris—his own corps of thinkers who didn't have to function in society. Certainly an arrogant expression of his ideas. Not ideals, however, she reflected, for Morris seemed to her to be consumed with power as his only ideal.

She looked down at her hands, wondering what their common father had really been like. She was sure Eve had created a personal mythology to cover his faults, not intentionally so much as wishfully, giving him an unreal saintliness. Eve had told her both she and Morris resembled their father physically, but Ramona could see little in common between the two of them. Morris's face had a harshness and angularity she found unpleasant at times, strong at others.

She did have to admit she had ambivalent feelings about him. There was much to respect in the man: his intelligence, his instincts about people, and his determination all impressed her, even when she didn't agree with the methods by which he operated. But there was one big flaw that always tempered her respect. Morris was completely selfish. He wanted everything, but only for his personal power and satisfaction, then secondarily for the people he ruled, and that was abhorrent to her.

Warren was less tolerant. He hated Morris with an undying passion and would often make remarks to Ramona and even to Eve about his ambitions and maneuvering. She had given up trying to make him understand the better side of her half-brother's nature, resigning herself to silence in the face of a diatribe.

In the corner of her mind, she heard Eve's report on her visit concluding and drew her attention back to the meeting at hand. There was some discussion and questioning, then Eve retired leaving Ramona to run the balance of the Council West meeting.

Eve retreated to her quarters, not wishing to seem as though she were interfering with the course of the business of Council West. Ramona could more than handle any problems that might arise, and she respected her daughter's subtle requests to intervene only if asked.

Ramona delighted her, as did Warren and their lovely children. She realized she could hardly call them children anymore. Gene, the eldest, was now concluding his first tour of duty in the mining district in the far south, below the jungles, where they had been mining diamonds and other precious stones. They were not only useful for adornment, but also for concentrating the laser beams used in so much of the mining and drilling operations, as well as fabrication. Most of the stones closely resembled those on Earth for which they were named, but there were several interesting colored crystals which mineralogists were studying to determine their uses.

Lucy, the second of their children, was studying medicine with Elizabeth at the University complex in Eden and would graduate soon. She was a brilliant, successful student and had her mother's sense of humor, her father's handsome looks, and her grandmother's determination. She was, Eve had to admit, her favorite of all the children.

Alan, now fourteen, intended to follow in his father's profession of fabrication and was constantly building little cities from small pieces of plasteel. Alan was tall and serious with a spill of dark curls that reminded her so much of his grandfather. She often wished Morris could see these remote progeny of theirs.

Christine, the baby, was eleven and a whimsical child who took great fascination with clothing and jewelry and had demonstrated more than once she had a wonderful sense of design with creations made from the stones Gene brought home. Ramona allowed her to study art with a private teacher in Outward in addition to her usual academics, and she was learning to paint very well. Eve had several of her pictures on the walls of her quarters and they pleased her greatly.

Aiegna came sliding silently into the room, unbidden, which was most unusual. She was sending out strong messages of agitation and Eve felt her tensions.

"Aiegna, what's the matter?"

"Madame, I disturb you with distress."

The telepathic speech, unlike the language of the aliens, was formal and filled with subtle nuances. Eve had finally come to understand the meaning of her first encounter with the alien culture so long ago. What had appeared to be confusion then forgetfulness was actually the limitations of their complex language in discussion of her presence. Aiegna had told her that at one time she had become the object of great folklore and that her tribe had gained in status for their proximity to the strange creature.

"You must not feel stress, Aiegna. You know we can solve problems best by being calm. Tell me your distress."

"Madame, words have reached me from far away that mean danger to all of us. I must tell you about my people for you to understand my distress, and it is a long tale."

Eve indicated the bench at her side. She was worried, for Aiegna had never before asked for such attention from her, though they had been together for many years and Aiegna had grown old by the standards of her tribe. Eve was often secretly concerned about losing her companion, but Aiegna had assured her there was another ready to take her place.

"Madame, many generations ago we, too, lived in cities as do your tribe and we had machines of our own invention to do work for us as your machines do. We covered the planet with ourselves, using the minerals you now discover, as well as the others you think are of no value.

"We had a great leader, Mndema, who had purified our people and brought us to The Understanding, but there were members of our population who could not see his ways and they sought the ending of Mndema. They, too, had a strong leader whose name is still so evil that for any of us to think or say it now is cause for the immediate ending by members of the tribes. He is called the Blue Figure in common talk and now there are few who know his true name.

"The Blue Figure took his people into the mountains to a secret place in what you now call the Eastern Region and they began to live in a world below, burrowing into the ground, making secret evil.

"Mndema warned us against him, but since that was before the speech without voice, he knew only because the holy stones told him the Blue Figure was making evil.

"Strange things began to happen. People would go away and never return, leaving not a trace; structures began to crumble and break without explanation; our machines started malfunctioning; tribe members became very ill and died with no reason. We became frightened of something mysterious and beyond explaining, and Mndema, who grew very old, told us the Blue Figure was causing this decay. A meeting was held, and the decision was made to stop the evil of the Blue Figure and his followers, so we sent a scouting group into the mountains to seek his hiding place.

"Suddenly the Blue Figure came from nowhere with a weapon of great power which turned everything it struck to powder. After he powdered the exploratory group, he rode down from the mountains, killing everything in his path, including buildings and machines, anything that had to do with Mndema. Our people hid in fear, but nothing could protect us.

"Finally, the Blue Figure came to the place where Mndema lived. So much of the planet had been destroyed and so many people killed that there were few left. Mndema went to face the Blue Figure, holding the holy stones in his hands and calling to the powers to destroy the evil one.

"They met on the plain below here, the power radiating from

around them, and Mndema called for the Blue Figure to re-
pent his evil ways and discover the ways of the true power. The
Blue Figure laughed at him, teasing him with the weapon of
destruction, powdering things around him.

"Mndema did not back away or show fear, moving ever
closer to the Blue Figure and his weapon, until they stood face
to face across the weapon.

"Mndema reached out his hands to the Blue Figure, as
though in friendship, but the evil one knew he would die if he
touched the holy one, so he backed away. Mndema kept calling
to the powers to help him, and again reached for the Blue
Figure. This time, the Blue Figure called on his own evil
forces and grabbed the hands of Mndema, trying to take the
stones. There was a flash, then a great rumbling as the earth
below their feet opened and they were drawn down, still locked
in combat. The earth closed behind them and they disappeared forever.

"We who were left behind, my ancestors, fled from the valley
and lived in small groups, not wanting to risk the chance of
the great evil again. The machines were forbidden. We learned
to speak without voice and to live from the land, and our
planet grew peaceful and beautiful.

"It was many generations ago, and we had begun to forget
when one day your machine came from the sky and we
watched you as you built this place with the false materials
and rode in your machine and came to our village, and the
warnings again came from the old holy ones who have remembered the story for the young buds.

"We watched you bringing your young ones and making
your city grow, but you didn't seem to bring harm to us. Kenneth and Cilia came offering friendship with their minds,
though they did some strange things we didn't understand, we
knew what they intended and we agreed to cooperate. But we
watched and listened carefully, trying to understand your language and customs, until we finally knew that you did not
mean evil to yourselves or to us.

"None of the others have been allowed to hear speech with-

*out voice as you have, and they will not be allowed, for you
are the only one we trust with our secret.*

*"Now I will tell you what I have heard. Master Morris has
begun research on some kind of evil machine. My people have
been told to stay away from the place where the work goes on,
but they can hear the ideas of Master Morris and it's frightening all of them. He is the only one who knows what the work
is about, with three or four of his advisors, but the people who
are working on it think it is to be used for fabrication. He
keeps it a secret beyond whispering."*

Eve was overcome with the information Aiegna had presented, not only about Morris but also about the secret
weapons project. The implications were overwhelming.

*"Aiegna, where is the place that Morris is doing this re-
search and work? Are you certain it is a weapon and not some
new device as the others think?"*

*"Too many of my people feel it is some instrument of de-
struction for us to be incorrect. The place is near what you
call New Athens."*

So, that was the purpose of New Athens, she thought.

*"Aiegna, I know I must stop him now, but I will not betray
the speech without voice. You must tell your people I will protect all of us."*

Aiegna rose from the bench, bowing to Eve and gliding
from the room.

Eve could hear the sound of conversations above, signal-
ing the end of the Council meeting and debated who, in
addition to Ramona, should know. Finally, she decided on
Richard VanDersant, for his loyalty was beyond question
and his mind was clever. Besides, as Chairman of Eden, he
was a powerful member of Council.

She moved into the common room, catching Ramona's
eye, then found Richard in a small group of laughing visitors from Gateway and Atlantis. She joined them with a
smile, listening superficially while she pondered the question of Morris's traitorous behavior. Finally, she was able to

move Richard away from the group and they joined Ramona.

"I would like the three of us to take a walk together into the fields beyond Eden. There is something of great importance we must discuss in complete privacy."

Eve was afraid they might be overheard, and stepped to the elevator, talking brightly about the special farming experiment Richard's team was starting. They followed her, participating in the conversation. When they reached the edge of town, appearing as though they were going to the experimental fields to anyone who might have been watching, Eve stepped between them and told them the information she had received without naming her source. Ramona's mouth was set in a firm line of disapproval and Richard shook his head sadly as she spoke.

As Eve finished, he burst out, "We must somehow stop him. Are you certain your information is correct? We would not do well to be wrong about something this serious."

Eve nodded. "My sources are above reproach. He is apparently using his intellectual community to hide his real purpose from all of us. I have no idea of his intentions, but it is something we must stop for all time or risk war among our people."

Ramona's eyes flashed with her anger. "That son of a machine! I think we should recycle his hydrocarbons and be done with it."

Eve took her daughter's arm. "No, never. The taking of a life on a planet with only two human deaths in seventy years is not correct. However, there is an island in the middle of the vast sea to the west. I think he and his comrades should be provided with a food synthesizer and shelter there. The greatest punishment for Morris would be the removal of his power. But it must be done quickly and with as little uproar as possible, for we do not want any misplaced loyalties among his followers in Eastern Region. And, the weapons project must be destroyed. We must also find out if there are others who are instrumental in his plans, and send them with him to exile. Then their survival is in their own hands."

Richard, scuffing his feet through the long grasses, worked the fingers of his right hand. Finally, he said, "I agree with the exile idea, though we must be sure he cannot escape nor communicate with anyone off the island for he does have a loyal group of people who might try to rescue him. How strange it is to speak of exile with respect to someone who has been my friend for many years. I am overcome with sadness."

Eve nodded her agreement. "Morris has always been the voice of dissent, and that is a very healthy function. He has taken his ambition too far beyond his common sense, and we cannot allow that sort of disruption in our society."

Ramona, looking at the horizon with her jaw clamped tightly, said, "You two are so busy feeling sorry for a man who doesn't, obviously, respect the customs of our society. One does not build a secret weapon without intending to use it. We have all grown up believing that war is the worst of man's conditions, yet, among us, is one who plots what can only be war and you two are busy understanding him. How much do you think that would mean to him? He'd scoff at it as weakness, just as he does at everything we do in love. Exile won't be successful."

Eve's anger rose. "What do you want to do, Ramona? Begin a war to stop a war? Kill innocent citizens for the failings of one or two? March in with an army of laser-equipped men and announce that we are here to stop him from his evil ways? And then what happens? He suddenly has a holy cause and the world goes to war. No, that is not the answer. The answer is through a change in government in the East and the removal of Morris."

Ramona turned to her. "Mother, do you really think that we can simply hold elections and vote him out of power?"

Eve shook her head. "No, but I think if we create the illusion that he has died accidentally, then the democratic process will follow in logical order. I don't want to kill him, but make it look as though he has died. There will be appropriate mourning for him, but it will quell his power rather than increase it."

Richard smiled. "Brilliant. But what about his co-conspirators? We can't have a rash of convenient accidents."

Eve shook her head, the plan gelling in her mind. "Not all accidents are related to machinery. We should be able to remove Morris and perhaps one other that way, and certainly even our sophisticated medicine can't cure all diseases. The weapons project is so secret that I'm reasonably certain some of the people working on it don't even know what they're really working on. It would be easy enough to convert it to a peaceful use without everyone being aware. But this must all be accomplished quickly."

They had reached the experimental farm and the workers were within hearing distance. Richard explained the experiment as though it had been the topic of their conversation on the walk out, and Eve and Ramona duly admired the work being done.

As soon as they felt it was reasonable, they returned to the complex. By the time Ramona's shuttle to Outward was ready to depart, they had made a tentative plan of action and had assembled a list of trusted friends who could fill the gaps of the people who would be removed.

Richard stayed with Eve, completing the plans and they sat late into the night, both of them sad at the need to do what they had decided, but determined to save their world from a destructive war.

Richard's visit to New Rome was much heralded, and Morris entertained him lavishly at a dinner party with various dignitaries of Eastern Council in attendance. They talked at length about the intellectual community at New Athens and the promise it held for the future of man's development on Genesis. Morris was expansive, an ancient potentate in his court, and Richard realized Morris's secret was taking control of him. It strengthened his resolve.

Richard observed each of Morris's advisors, questioning

in his mind their involvement in the project. Finally, he felt he knew which ones were conspirators and was surprised it was only three in addition to Morris. He grudgingly had to admit Morris had great skill at organization, for his Council seemed in accord about everything. He listened carefully, wanting not to be wrong about any of them.

Finally, when he was sure, he asked about a possible visit to New Athens. Harold Armitage, Chairman of New Athens and certainly one of the conspirators in Richard's view, agreed willingly and Morris offered to go along, to Richard's relief. He didn't want to be obvious. Morris suggested several other possible attendees, including the other two Richard felt might be part of the situation. One nonsuspect declined due to research pressures, and another felt there wouldn't be enough room in the shuttle, so he too declined. That meant there would be the four conspirators—Morris, Harold, Edward Jahlman, and Darren Adams—as well as Richard and, regrettably, Anita Lester, on the trip.

Richard decided to try to eliminate Anita from the trip to save her from the fate he knew awaited the others, and, uncomfortably, became vaguely insulting to her, implying that a rumor had reached Eden that she was attempting to take over Ellen's position with Morris, if not legally.

Anita listened to him incredulously, certain Richard had become ill or deranged, for he had never spoken to her any way but kindly before.

Finally, as the evening was coming to a close, Anita, who was far too well-bred to make public Richard's implications, pleaded forgotten appointments and declined to go along. Richard breathed an inward sigh.

Morris installed Richard in the guest chamber with a friendly farewell, reminding him that they would be leaving early for New Athens, and that we would be awakened in plenty of time.

Richard knew he was being watched, somehow, so prepared for sleep normally. He was wearing a device that would allow the hovercraft to be located by the kidnappers who waited between New Rome and New Athens to whisk the conspirators off to their exile. Richard felt the tension of fear, hoping nothing would go awry and that there would be no violence. He lay awake long, finally sleeping fitfully just before dawn.

The chime on his viewing screen rang gently to wake him and he got up groggily, aches of sleeplessness in every muscle, but alert for the distasteful job to be done. They boarded Morris's private hovercraft which he insisted on piloting. Richard had been afraid there would be aides or a pilot, but Morris liked to demonstrate his skills and they left New Rome early.

The craft, skimming over the landscape, ran smoothly past forests and peaceful lakes, and Richard was lost in the beauty of the landscape. Many times he remarked about some interesting feature that bore investigation, and Morris would stop while Richard recorded it on his portable video machine.

As they moved through a narrow valley, Richard again asked that they might stop for a moment while he filmed something of interest. By that time, the others had grown bored with getting out of the craft as he filmed and they waited aboard while he moved some distance away to film a plant and take a specimen.

Behind him, he heard the whoosh of the great airship descending in the valley and looked around in time to see the men in the hovercraft looking up in surprise. He ran toward the hovercraft, meeting the crew of six from the airship. He pulled the canister of anesthetic from his tunic as he ran, felling Harold into unconsciousness as he tried to run into the woods.

Morris was climbing from the pilot's seat when Richard rounded the hovercraft. The men from the airship were retrieving the other two who had fled, and they faced each other alone.

Richard hesitated on the trigger of the spray canister for a moment, and Morris froze, staring at him.

"So, Richard, you have ambition beyond mine. You won't survive, for you lack the ability to put everything else aside. I would have won, you know, and that weak woman will bring you all down."

Richard pulled the trigger and Morris crumpled before him, deeply unconscious, as he would stay until they had reached the island of his exile.

Richard, badly shaken, helped the crew get the sleeping men aboard the airship, then watched as it lifted away, leaving him alone in the wilderness. He knew there would soon be people looking for them, as they had recently passed a checkpoint on the road, and, when they didn't appear at the next one, there would be concern.

He lifted the engine cover on the hovercraft, adding the device he carried in another tunic pocket and setting the timer. Warren had guaranteed it would explode the power pack of the craft, and the fire would be so intense no bodies, or lack of them, would ever be found. He placed the canister of anesthetic on the seat, then moved quickly away from the empty craft, returning to his filming of the plants in the area and bracing himself for the explosion he knew would follow.

Even though he was prepared, the force of it threw him to the ground, and he had trouble regaining his breath. With the video recorder running, he rolled over slowly, filming the blaze, then got up as though to move toward it. He was intensely aware the filmed evidence would be the only verification of his story, and he had to make the film look like the reaction of a man in complete panic. Jogging, he got as close as he could to the intensely burning craft, then backed away as the heat became overwhelming.

Warren had been right. In a matter of minutes, the craft was a tangle of melting plasteel that began collapsing into a sticky mass. The whole sight sickened him, as though there had still been people aboard, because he knew now it was possible for these reliable little machines to take lives. He watched it burn until the flames died, then began walking briskly along the road toward the last checkpoint, his video recorder swinging beside him.

As he walked, he reflected on the fate awaiting Morris, Harold, Edward, and Darren. He had studied the maps of the island to which they were going and though it wasn't small or savage, it was totally isolated. Eve had provided a food synthesizer, enough plasteel to build a shelter for six, and a playback-only unit with a huge supply of books and textapes. She had been adamant about the books, declaring that she, better than anyone, knew the meaning of isolation and exile.

They would never be found except by a very strange accident and he wondered how they would react. The aircraft which carried them would leave them, still unconscious, so when they awoke, they would be alone in exile.

Ramona had held out for a trial, insisting that, no matter how she felt about it personally, it was unfair to exile on assumption. Finally, Eve and Richard and Warren had been able to convince her a trial would have the same effect on the population as an attack would have had, and she had capitulated.

Richard had known Morris, with his mechanical skills, would attempt to convert the playback unit to a transmitter, so he and Warren had carefully adjusted it to be tamper-proof. The food synthesizer could be converted to produce cloth, but never plasteel, so they didn't have to be concerned about eventual construction of a craft in which the exiles could escape.

In the distance, he saw the plume of dust that showed a hovercraft's approach and he quickly added more dirt to his clothes and skin, preparing himself for the role he would have to play.

He stood beside the road, watching the approaching

craft, tears making slick tracks through the dust on his face. The tears were real, but it wasn't until much later he realized he was mourning, not the loss of Morris, but the end of the innocence of Genesis. From then on, his world would never be paradise again, and he knew that was the worst death of all.

PART VI

Chapter Sixteen

———◆———

RAMONA'S FACE on the screen was a welcome sight and Eve smiled warmly at her.

"Ramona! What a nice surprise. Am I a great-great-grandmother yet?"

Ramona laughed. "Mother, when will you stop keeping track? In a way, you're a great-great-grandmother many times over, and you know it. If you're asking if Jessica's baby has arrived, the answer is still no. I don't know what that child is waiting for, but Lucy reminds me Jessica herself was a late baby, so we're being patient. Warren and the children and grandchildren are all fine. I just wanted to see how you are and if you're still planning to visit before we leave for the far south expedition."

"I don't know if I'm going to be able to visit. You know how many pressing matters there are here in Eden and I can't seem to find the time to get everything done."

Ramona's smile faded. "Mother, you're becoming more and more of a recluse, and I would like it if you'd stop making excuses and get out again. Not only for personal reasons but also because the people need to see more of you."

Eve scowled. Her watchers had told her of pockets of unrest among the populations and rumors she had died sprung up frequently. Ramona was correct that the people didn't see her very often, but she hated to leave her secure complex for the insecurities of the streets.

"Ramona, I know this line is clear, so I feel free to speak. There are even Ruffians in the streets of Eden now, and the guards are not able to control some of them.

"I fear you and Warren traveling even though it is to the far south where there is less trouble. And I fear to leave the complex for I am told of plots and counterplots and only feel safe here." She shook her head sadly, and Ramona felt a wave of concern for her mother. Eve's sparkle seemed to have dimmed in the face of the civil problems.

"Mother, you mustn't personalize these incidents. There is something foundationally wrong in our society, but you are not supposed to carry that weight on your shoulders alone. It's all of us who must combat it."

Again Eve shook her head. "A rumor has reached me that is just one more example of the undermining of our society." She paused, seeming to consider her words carefully. "You recall that when I arrived here, I alone had survived the hardships of the time-jump of our colony of one hundred." She sighed again. "The most current rumor in Eden is that I had an active role in the deaths of the others on the ship; that I had intended to establish a dictatorship here."

"Mother, why are you worrying about such nonsense?"

"To you and me, Ramona, it's nonsense. But to some of the younger ones, the ones who have come along since we were all one family...." Her voice trailed off, pain showing in her face.

"Mother, do you truly believe any member of this society could believe such a thing of you?"

Eve laughed bitterly. "Fifty years ago, no. Now, with the Ruffians running wild in the streets of Eden, with people frightened of each other, with inexplicable acts of destruction . . . yes, I do."

Ramona wasn't surprised. Outward was having its own set of problems with the gangs of unknown people who roamed the streets, attacking unsuspecting citizens. Their motives were mixed, often taking jewelry or other possessions, but as often only tormenting their captive, physically and mentally.

"I can't completely guarantee your safety, but certainly you could take some of the complex guard with you and use your high security hovercraft. Also, if you make it a public event, perhaps the citizens will respond. Mother, I think you must overcome your fears and venture out. You are too dearly loved by the people for anyone to harm you."

Eve shook her head, her hand idly fingering the chain holding her medallion of office.

"No one of us, Ramona, is that greatly loved. The Ruffians respect nothing and no one, and my physical presence might tempt them to do something rash. I have, however, been contemplating a video visit with the people to let them know what steps we are taking to prevent the spread of the Ruffians."

"Have you arrived at a new program since we last spoke?"

Eve shook her head. "No, nothing more than we were doing before. When they can be caught or identified, the Ruffians are taken into custody and submitted for the retraining process. Marta seems to be having more success than before with the new drugs that have been developed. The problem is, since they wear masks, no one can name them for sure and they must be caught in the act, which is almost impossible. They have an uncanny knowledge of where the guards are, and none of the watchers seem to be able to get identification with any certainty. We are contemplating a curfew in Eden to see if that will control the nighttime attacks on homes, and we are recommending the installation of more sensitive palm locks. Nothing seems to help."

Ramona said, "I have heard they are organized and have a leader, but there is no more information than that. No one even seems to know what it is they want except to disrupt society. It seems to have no purpose. But it has become more intense here and in Atlantis. Gateway appears to have the least problem, but even they are suffering. What does Richard report from the East?"

"I spoke with him yesterday at length, and they are experiencing similar problems, but more of the attacks there have been directed against fabrication centers and communication facilities than against people. The crime level in New Rome is up over one hundred percent from last year, and many people are applying for transfers. There must be a leader, for everything does seem to have some organization to it. I am assigning extra guards from among the tribal ranks. They refuse to be violent, but can hold someone until the armed guards come to aid. It seems some sort of an answer."

Ramona shook her head. "It's not enough. We must seek out the leader and find out what it is the Ruffians want, if there is something they want. All I know is five years ago we had only one antisocial act in Outward in a year. Now we have several a day and the number increases all the time. But, Mother, you must stop being intimidated, for that's what they want. Come, stay with us for a few days and maybe it will inspire Jessica. During the time you're here, we can discuss the Ruffian problem at length and work out a way to combat it. Please."

Eve smiled at her daughter's plea. "Ramona, you know I can never refuse you anything you really want. It would be good to see the whole family again before it gets too large. Oh, Ramona, is Ellen still living in Outward?"

After Morris's lavish state funeral, Ellen had faded physically and emotionally, and eventually had requested to be transferred back to Outward to her old quarters, feeling that New Rome carried too many remembrances of him. She lived alone in their apartments, seeing no one and withdrawing from even her own children. Harmony had been with her mother for a time, but, when her own family demanded her return, went back to New Athens where she still lived.

"I checked on her the other day. She wouldn't come to the screen to talk, but her servant said she is well. Nothing has changed. She went into mourning almost forty years ago, and she still hasn't come out. We've all tried, including Harmony, but nothing seems to bring her back to us. Harmony says she just sits, staring out the window or at the video. She rarely talks to anyone."

"I'll try to see her while I'm there. It's been at least ten years since my last visit to her and that's much too long, I fear. There are so many small things that I neglect."

"When will you arrive?"

"You'll be advised as we approach the city. I think it's best."

She shut down the screen, then summoned her personal maid, Aiegna's bud, Wndanga. It had been many years since Aiegna's death, but Eve still missed her quiet presence.

Her bud was not like her mother in many ways, more stern and less willing to tell Eve what news the winds carried. She had begun to be more free until the trouble started with the Ruffians, but now they had reached almost an impasse again and Eve had had to find other information sources.

"*Wndanga, we will travel this week to Outward to visit Ramona and her family. I must make security arrangements as well as travel provisions. Will you kindly summon both Lawrence of the guards and Ztuzza of your people for a conference.*"

Wndanga nodded her compliance, gliding from the room. Aiegna had recommended her without reservation and Eve felt trusting of her most of the time. There were simply moments when she doubted the creature had any loyalties to anyone but her own tribe.

Lawrence and Ztuzza arrived together, the human wearing his decorated tunic and laser weapon, the alien in his ribbon of office.

Ztuzza was a tribal chieftain and high priest of his people, and chief among her watchers, acute and sensitive, as well as discriminating, in his choice of what was information and what was rumor. He had become a trusted advisor and guard; but refused, as did all his people, to carry a weapon. His perceptiveness was more of a weapon than a laser, so she allowed it, bowing to his wishes.

Lawrence was chief of the city guards, a rugged, ruddy man of great height and girth, whose presence alone was more of a deterrent than his gun, with which he was most adept.

They sat in the great hall, long since deserted of Congregation and other gatherings. Eve used the room for private meetings and socializing after Genesis Council meetings.

"With your permission, Lawrence, I shall use the common speech in deference to Ztuzza." The alien creatures had cooperated in the creation of a language which encompassed both their and human speeches. It had become a matter of courtesy to use the common speech when addressing a mixed group, even though the majority of the aliens understood human speech well.

"Of course."

"The three of us, with our infinite sources of information and intelligence, have been unable to discover very much about the Ruffians and their mysterious leader. They are getting more and more out of control. I have spoken to Richard and Marcellus and Joan and Ramona, and they all complain of problems similar to ours. We must find a solution to this trouble, for it is taking energy away from our real purposes and creating fear among the population. Have either of you any thoughts on this matter?"

Common speech, with its formality of expression, often sounded more serious than her normal tongue, but Eve was adept at it.

Lawrence nodded. "With your permission, Madame. The crux of the matter is we are too lenient with those who are caught. The drugs being administered have an effect, it's true, but for every one who is returned to his place, three others appear. It is as though they are constantly recruiting new members. None of the captured ones will talk about a leader or where they are gathering their instructions for the acts they commit. They speak of boredom, lack of amusements, lessening in work available, and other inconsequentials. They speak around the truth, for there need not be boredom or a lack of work, even here in Eden where there is not as much work as in other places. I think we must become stronger with them, not allowing them to frighten the citizens who go about their business by custom."

"Lawrence, you are perceptive, certainly, but you are not always sensitive. We will not commit violence on any member of society in Genesis, no matter what he has done to others. Violence is not our way of life. You use the laser weapons to stun, but never to kill and we will not use any greater force to extract information, no matter how important it is. There are other ways."

Ztuzza swiveled his eye stalks to her, then said in his raspy, lisping voice, "Yes, there are other ways to gather information, but even those ways have been unsuccessful for us. We must try a new approach, and in that I agree with Lawrence. Not with violence, but with isolation. There is a mining village in the north which is no longer in use. It could be used to isolate all the Ruffians from the region and I am certain the Eastern Region must have a similar area."

Eve shook her head. "Everyone in this society has a pro-

ductive function, Ztuzza, and to eliminate any of the manpower we have is to disrupt the social order more than the
Ruffians do. Each one who has been caught has had a job of
importance to the society in which we live. We are not
dealing with some type of street trash or criminals, but
with people who are part of what we are."

Lawrence looked at her, then at Ztuzza. "With all due
respect, Madame, what do you suggest, since nothing we've
tried has worked?"

"A number of years ago, Mark developed a medication
intended to broaden the awareness of the user. He anticipated it could potentially increase the thinking power of us
all. Unfortunately, it had a strange side effect we found incompatible with the normal privacy of our people, but I
think that side effect may be just what we're seeking. In
large dosage, it produces hallucinations, but when administered in smaller doses, causes the taker to speak everything that is on his mind. Perhaps this is our next step.
We'll have to ask Mark. Do either of you object?"

Lawrence, smiling, shook his head emphatically, but
Ztuzza pondered longer, then said, "I should like to see one
usage of this medication on the next of the Ruffians we
capture. Then I shall make my decision. We must not in-
vade the privacy of anyone, and if one reveals everything
on one's mind, then perhaps it would accomplish only
that."

Lawrence agreed quickly to his suggestion, so Eve asked
that he prepare the situation with Mark.

"There is another matter related to the Ruffians. We must
increase our patrols and I am considering a curfew to expose fewer people to their activities."

Both nodded their agreement to her suggestions, and
Ztuzza added that he had staff members available for the
extra patrols.

"I shall travel to Outward during the coming week, and
will need security during that trip. Lawrence, will you
make whatever arrangements you feel are appropriate?"

He nodded, then asked to be excused to meet with Mark. She waited until he left the room, then switched to speech without voice with Ztuzza.

"Why are we unable to hear, Ztuzza? How are we being blocked from knowledge about this mysterious leader?"

His intensity translated to loudness in her head.

"Madame, my greatest failing is that I cannot give answers to such questions. My people and your watchers are listening and watching and interpreting, but only the faintest rumors come to us, none of them true. We only recently learned of this leader, but know nothing of his name or place."

"How is the blocking accomplished?"

"If there are none of my people in the area to hear the thoughts, you humans can hide your minds from us. Your people do not focus their thoughts as mine do, so there is little transmission. We continue to search. There are search groups in the mountains and throughout the valley here, in addition to similar groups in the Eastern Region. We will find something soon. Until then, do not venture out alone."

He stood, bowing as he left, and she watched him glide from the room, his long arms almost dragging on the floor.

Eve went to the door of the complex leading out to her ledge.

The sun hung low on the horizon, a haze of dust and smoke mitigating its strength. Below her, the city of Eden stretched away, skirting the rocks and spreading out over the grasses of the valley. The transport had long ago been disassembled to make room for a large fabrication area and she watched a loaded transport threading its way to the building, carrying minerals for conversion. People hurried through the streets, but she could see no signs of masked Ruffians anywhere. They kept to the night, waiting in the shadows of the city and she felt great frustration at being unable to identify them or locate this mysterious leader.

There had been factions before. After Morris's funeral there had been certain of his followers who had declared themselves to be no longer of the society and they had attempted to build a city in the north of the Eastern Region. Soon, however, they began to filter back into New Rome, telling stories of starvation and disease. The rebellious people were soon reintegrated into the society.

But this time it was different and she didn't understand it. Nothing had changed particularly, since expansion had begun. There were still plenty of jobs to be done, no one was without food, lodging, clothing, or amusements and there was no illness. Yet, this unrest seemed to draw support from everywhere.

She looked across the valley, seeking what she knew was no longer there, and found herself longing for the simpler life when that plume of smoke from the alien village was her company and her security, when her world could be encompassed behind her in the complex. Now the population was well over fifteen thousand people in the Western Region alone, and growing constantly. Hundred of endos and exos were added each year, facilities growing with them. New, nonproductive jobs were as important as those more traditional. Now there were touring companies of actors reviving old Earth plays as well as presenting the works of Genesis's young writers. There were video entertainments being produced in quantity for the home viewer and social organizations had blossomed with games and organized sports.

Yet, with more to do and to see, there was more unrest. Lawrence had estimated there were probably only a hundred Ruffians in Eden, a city of over four thousand people, but they were able to disrupt the lives of everyone, replacing comfortable security with suspicious tensions.

The sunset wind moaned gently in the crack above the complex and she listened to the familiar sound with her soul, questioning herself. What she had done with the colony had been instinctive and personal; choices she made on the basis of common sense, but now she felt as though there must have been something terribly wrong, something she must have forgotten to do. Why, otherwise, would her people not respect themselves and each other as she hoped she had taught and demonstrated?

The rays of the setting sun made a halo over the distant hills and the lights in the streets below began to glow: another of Lawrence's attempts to control the Ruffians. Eve slid to a sitting position. Only now was she able to understand her grandfather's condemnation of the very process he had invented. She was, chronologically, almost one hundred and fifty years old, but there was no physical evidence of her age. Her skin was taut and blemish free, without wrinkles to betray her years. Her hair, always healthy, was long and shiny and cascaded down her back, her figure was trim without effort.

But there was an emotional accumulation she wished weren't there and that was the curse of the ageless, for she now had to live with whatever mistakes she had made, unlike the pioneers of Earth who could create and leave in due time, allowing others to evolve changes. There was no resigning from her job, no retirement possible, for she was not only the General Chairman of Genesis, but also a leadership figure of stature. She was allowed no human failings and, more and more, expected by the average person to perform some sort of miracle. She no longer knew the names of everyone in the society, no longer knew their dreams, and hopes, and desires, no longer could walk freely among them. Now she had to listen to the gossip, rumors, and secret information gathered by her watchers—the trusted few who were able to gain her ear past her advisors who were so protective.

She watched Eden below her as lights came on in dwellings and people went about the business of living. She longed to be one of them, free to do what she wanted without the pressure of public opinions surrounding her every action. She realized the deep loneliness of her first two years, so long ago, had never left, but only been lost in the business of building a world. Now that the world was becoming something less than she had remembered or dreamed or wanted, she was again isolated, trapped by her own failures, real or imagined.

It had been a long time since she had been able to conjure up Morris's face, feel his presence. Perhaps it was the reality of his two children, one so good and one so lost, that pushed him into the ethereal place he inhabited. His son, so long in exile, possibly dead or mad, would anger and delight him, for Morris had carried that kind of ambition, but directed it toward his career rather than himself. He would have understood Eve's need to eliminate that force from the lives of her people, to maintain peace above all else. Or would he have seen her decision to eliminate him as just another power maneuver, as not allowing life to take its natural course?

"Heaven or Hell, Eve? What would you create if you could? How do you make those decisions? How do you know the answers?"

"Morris, how could it be that we could, with all the information and technology that will be available and being as aware of previous mistakes as we are, make too many wrong choices?"

He had laughed bitterly, and she had felt his laugh deep inside her, piercing her dreams. "You believe in only the good of mankind, don't you? With all you know of the evil, you believe only the good."

He held her tenderly against him, his warmth encompassing her.

"I hope you never lose that. And more, I hope no one ever pulls it away from you with a dose of reality."

The conversation, now more than a hundred years distant, rang in her ears so clearly she looked to see if somehow he had appeared.

This was the dose of reality about which he had spoken. Had she failed or was it simply a function of the natural order of things? Was mankind incapable of living in peace and harmony with himself? She smiled, ironically, reflecting that she was certainly not the first to ask such questions and would probably not be the last.

The sun had slid behind the hills and Home, her brightest star, appeared in the sky. The memories flooded her of her first years on the planet, and she remembered her cry of defiance against the strange place which had seemed so overwhelming. Now there was little of it that hadn't been explored or at least charted, and the careful exploration continued as her people spread themselves out over its surface.

"Well, gentlemen of the Project, what now? Violence? Truth drugs? Murder, perhaps?" None of them fit with her idealized picture or goals, and she shuddered at the thought of all the possibilities, all negatives to her.

Yet there was the pervasive negative of the Ruffians, the nameless, faceless wreakers of havoc on the society.

The air began to chill with the advancing night as the last of the sun's green glow disappeared from the hills and the breezes increased. She drew her robes around her, retreating into herself, watching Eden below. She could see the lanterns of patrols moving down several streets at the edge of the city and wondered who they would discover behind the masks of the Ruffians this time.

She sat for a long time, watching the life below her, outlined by the lights of the dwellings as they changed and flowed like a living creature moving through the night. While she sat, she searched through her memories seeking the answer to her circumstance. Finally, when most of the city below was quiet, she returned to her chambers, lying sleepless, staring into the dark.

"My dear friends, and fellow colonists of Genesis, welcome to my home here in Eden."

Eve sat, wearing her robes and medallion of office, in her official Council chamber seat, speaking to the video camera and assorted technicians who filled the room, but trying to conjure up the faces of the people of her planet.

"One of the great regrets I have is that I am no longer available to each of you all the time; that I no longer can stop for a conversation to share your thoughts.

"It is my intention to alter that. I will be visiting each of our cities in the future and will want to meet and talk with each of you. Please, when I do arrive, take the time to stop by and visit. It's time we all got in touch with each other again.

"My purpose in speaking with you tonight is, however, beyond the simple announcement of my impending visits. We all face a problem together which must be solved together. We are confronted with a secret society seemingly bent on disruption of the peace we work so hard to maintain. They make no demands on us, yet extract a price of fear. We must find a way to control their random acts and become again a free and peaceful people working together to build our world.

"Tonight, after much discussion in Council and deliberations among the various city administrators, and Chairmen, we have come to the following decision: In each city, curfews will be imposed from sunset to sunrise except for those with official passes. Anyone in the streets beyond those limits will be taken into custody and extensively questioned. If there is anyone who has information about these destructive members of our society, your revelations will be held in the most strict confidence. We will appreciate your stepping forward to help your fellow members of our communities and to help protect all of us against these outrages.

"I regret any inconvenience you will suffer due to these curfews but promise that soon we will be back to normal. I shall look forward to seeing each of you in person as I visit your cities. Blessings to each of you. And good night."

In the darkened central room of his dwelling, the unknown leader of the Ruffians watched her image fade from the screen, then laughed long and deeply.

Chapter Seventeen

———◆———

EVE WAS TIRED of shaking hands, idle conversations, kissing babies, and talking to city officials, but she was totally satisfied with the results of the tour and felt as though she had accomplished at least a bridge between her people and herself, and a feeling of greater knowledge about the prevailing opinions and attitudes in her world.

The Ruffians' activities hadn't subsided in her absence, but they had moved their action to the period of dusk and dawn.

Lawrence had met her in Outward where she was spending a few days before returning to Eden. He was filled with agitation because the experiments with the truth drug were not working as they had hoped. There seemed to be some deep-seated block, even to that, and the Ruffians they had captured continued with the theme of boredom and lack of work.

"Lawrence, I'm at a loss to explain any of it. They're putting us in a position of being tyrannical by ever tightening the precautions against them, and soon they'll begin condemning us for what they have created. They've given you nothing?"

He shook his head. "Nothing. Except one thing that's very important. Each one of them, when they're captured, give exactly the same speech, word for word. It begins with a comment about boredom, speaks of lack of amusement, and complains of low interest jobs. We've taped the ones lately, and even the vocal inflections and speech patterns are the same. Mark and I think the block is induced by hypnosis, and the drug is unable to penetrate it. Mark is trying to find a means to rehypnotize them, but it seems there has been a posthypnotic suggestion about that, too. I think we can only assume that whoever is programming these people is programming their acts of vandalism along with the speech. Also, once they've been caught, they seem not to be involved in the Ruffian activities at all anymore, so it means there are constantly new members."

Eve paced, thinking. Hypnosis was such an ancient technique and, after the Zombie armies of the Arab Wars, hypnosis had been outlawed on Earth. She tried to remember whether or not there was reference to it in the computapes.

"Lawrence, we must find a way to control this somehow. How are they getting recruits in the first place? You can't just walk up to someone on the street and hypnotize him. The circumstances must be controlled. It takes time."

He nodded again. "It also takes more than one person to do the hypnosis. It's happening simultaneously in several cities. What about if some of our security men become decoys?"

"You mean in case people are being taken from the streets?" Lawrence nodded.

"It won't work. Security staff people are all known. If we only knew what they wanted. What about the curfews?"

Lawrence shrugged. "People are good about it sometimes and other times, particularly before leisure days, they either forget or ignore the cufew. The warning notices don't seem to mean much."

"Then make it stricter. Stop giving warning notices and begin issuing leisure day penalties. Make second offenses more strongly punishable. We must stop these Ruffians at any cost."

Lawrence nodded, almost bowing, and left the room.

Eve spent the days enjoying the company of her daughter, her grandchildren, her great-grandchildren, and her newest great-great-granddaughter. She felt a sense of continuity in her family and looked at them proudly as they flowed around her.

In the quiet times, she, Ramona, and Warren would talk at length about the future of Genesis and its growing population. Ramona and Warren had strong ideas about control of resources and reservation of lands, of which Eve approved, and ideas about the creation of a monetary unit, of which she disapproved. Their arguments were heated, but constructive, and Eve promised to try to implement some of the changes they suggested, at least with reference to conservation and resources planning. Money was another subject entirely, and she refused to budge.

"Look, Warren, no one is taking any particular advantage of the free access system we have. No one is hoarding or using more than their share of anything. Why go through all the bother to create something which has been a problem throughout the history of mankind?"

"Yes, but what about the people who choose not to make their regular work something which is for everyone? What about the artists? What about the stone-setters and jewelers?"

"They take from the general stores, don't they?"

"Yes, but their works belong only to one family or person. That's not fair. Their works should be available to anyone, not just their friends, and that involves some medium of exchange."

Eve shook her head. "Warren, if they are paid money for their work, then they would have to purchase somehow from the general supply areas and suddenly we'd be in chaos. It's simply not worth the necessary paperwork."

Ramona leaned toward Warren, putting her hand on his arm affectionately. "Darling, I think we'd better wait with this project until Mother gets rid of her Ruffians. Then maybe we can bring it up again."

Warren nodded. "You're right, of course." He smiled warmly at Eve. "But don't get too confident that you've heard the end of this. It'll come up again."

Eve laughed. "I wouldn't doubt it for a minute, knowing you. At least we've agreed on some of your ideas."

But in the privacy of her sleeping chamber, she again wondered if she were blocking the normal changes through which the planet would grow and develop. Would money provide the kinds of incentives needed to spur people to do the less desirable, but equally necessary, jobs? Would it provide the impetus for additional expansion into areas rich in resources, but far less comfortable to live in?

She watched the gently moving lights on the ceiling as the moon shone through the clouds above. It came back to living too long. The body stays young, but the mind cannot forget the past and it piles up like unrecycled hydrocarbons, she thought restlessly. The vast piles of the past had been closing in on her increasingly, with memories of Earth vivid against the pale tapestry of now.

She was anxious, she realized, as the hovercraft sped toward Eden, to be back in her complex, alone within her territory to think and reason. Somewhere, deep in her mind, lurked the answer to the Ruffians, if she could only draw it to the fore, but it evaded her and angered her.

The complex was quiet and she wandered through the chambers, feeling comfortable in her familiar surroundings. Wndanga had prepared her favorite foods for dinner and she ate in solitude, reviewing some recent letter tapes and reports on the Ruffians. Somehow, here in her own place, they seemed less threatening and ominous than they had as she traveled, and she again sighed with relief at being home.

As she stood, finished with dinner and ready to retire early, the laser weapon Lawrence insisted she keep with her against any possible Ruffian attacks on her, slid from its holster sling and clanged to the floor. She picked it up in disgust, first setting it on the table and beginning to walk out, then reconsidering and going back to retrieve it. She doubted there would be any threat, but didn't want Lawrence to be upset if he dropped in.

Wndanga had adjusted the lights in her sleeping chamber and had selected an old Earth video from the library for her relaxation. Eve sighed comfortably as she lowered herself onto the sleeping mat.

The room was dark when she awoke and she wasn't sure why she had risen from the deep sleep. She lay silently, listening, and then she heard the quiet breathing in the shadows across the room. She lay motionless, feigning sleep, while fear pounded in her head. There was someone watching her in the dark, invading her territory, and she could feel the strong vibrations as she came to alertness, a jumble of hatred and power, and suddenly she knew.

"Morris."

Her voice sounded loud in the stillness of the complex. She heard his sharp intake of breath.

"How long have you been back among us?"

The silence between them was filled with his powerful vibrations and she shuddered against the hatred that crossed the room.

"You are, then, the missing piece in the puzzle of the Ruffians, aren't you? You'll never understand why I did what I did so very long ago, will you? You're here for revenge."

Again the silence was filled with hate. Finally he spoke and she felt chills from his voice.

"Not revenge, for I am beyond that. I am here to assume my rightful place. The one I should have had when you took fate into your own hands. You're old now, Eve, and this world has left you behind. You couldn't stop my Ruffians, so how would you fare against an army under my special control? This has all been a demonstration for you. To show you you can't stop the progress of the world. It must grow beyond you or die."

"The government of this planet is by all people. I've been voted into office."

His laugh was harsh. "Voted. And if it didn't come out as you wanted, you could always adjust the computer to your own ends. Oh no, Eve, you've outlived your time, yet you still cling to the people, making a "good-will tour" to reassure them, when you don't even know what the threat is.

Lawrence finally had to tell you about hypnosis or you never would have thought of it. You're a creature from another world. You are the alien here. You alone. The time has come for this planet to be ruled by one of her own."

The lights came up slowly in the room as he adjusted the panel. She studied him across the room. He had grown a beard, but hadn't changed in any other way, and she remembered him as a child, his eyes challenging and questioning the world around him, and felt a wrenching pain.

"What do you intend to do?"

He laughed harshly again. "I certainly wouldn't want to go against all your teachings. All your lies. 'Man never killed unless he was insane; war was the exception, not the rule; killing is unnatural.' Certainly you don't think I'd take your life. No, I have something else much more interesting planned. You won't disappear from view as you did to me, you will become more visible. The people will find themselves with a strong, innovative leader who will give them the kind of world they deserve. You see, Eve, hypnosis is a very powerful weapon."

She felt the fear rising in her again and tried to keep control of it. She could pretend to be hypnotized, but still remain conscious, then somehow overpower him.

She felt her desperation arising from her lack of knowledge about hypnosis, and cursed the laziness which had prevented her from reading the information in the computer as she had intended.

Morris caught her eyes with his and began moving toward her. His look seemed to penetrate into her being and she felt herself captivated. She closed her eyes.

His voice seemed far away. "It doesn't matter if you look at me or not. I've had forty years to perfect this technique and willing subjects to try it on. You can't avoid the hypnosis, just as the people in their homes, following your curfew, had no resistance. They never knew they were being programmed. You may as well relax."

She was lulled by his voice and felt a vague ambivalence

about his demands. At least someone else would have to make the decisions now.

His liquid, soothing voice continued. "You thought exile was the final solution to our conflicts. A living death—the ultimate revenge on me. Do you think that's not a dictatorship? You are a conniving, dominating woman, and it's time now to change that course of events. I have come back to help you. It took many years for me to make enough corrections in the food processor so it would produce a material that would float. I spent many days drifting back to the main body of land. I suffered to get back here—I starved, almost drowned in a storm, and had no water to drink for the last three days, but I came back."

Eve listened to his voice, feeling her will to resist sliding away as he talked. He certainly had suffered to rejoin the society. Maybe it was his rightful place.

"I have walked almost across this continent, eating plants in the forest, frightened and cold most of the time. I'm sure you haven't begun to see what I've seen on this planet. You're part of the past and now it's time for the future to take over. I have a grand plan for our people and you will be the instrument of that plan. You will still be loved and revered, but things will change. Slowly at first, so people don't get upset, but steadily and constantly they will come to their rightful conclusion and this world will advance and grow, and I shall be the guiding force."

Strangely, almost physically, she felt a slithering sensation in her mind as he forced his will upon her. It suddenly didn't seem to be so important who ran Genesis or to what ends. The only thing that was important was power. In a small corner of her mind, the objections rang loudly, but they were being forced back further and further.

From far away, she heard the speech without voice of Wndanga approaching, calling to her with urgency. She felt herself straining to hear her words as though listening to sounds in another room. The voice kept repeating, "No! Don't listen!" and she tried to focus on it.

In the distance, she heard the door slide to the side, then she felt the probe releasing from her mind and the objections came flooding in clearly. Her vision focused and she could see Wndanga in the door, her eye stalks aiming at Morris, a laser weapon in one of her ungainly hands.

Wndanga continued to stare at him. Then Eve heard her, in speech without voice, speaking to Morris.

"You have no right to the speech without voice. That is the property and the domain of my people and you have no right to use it for evil."

"You creatures have no rights. You are not human, you're slaves to the humans here and you have no claim to anything. I have my plans for you creatures, too. Now give me the weapon."

Wndanga stood her ground, her eyes still intense upon him.

"It is you who will bend to my will, for I have grown up with the techniques of speech without voice and you are yet beginning. There is much you have to learn."

Morris's face distorted with pain and he grabbed his head with both hands, doubling over and screaming.

"That is but a taste of the power you will never have."

As he began to straighten, his complexion pale and looking ill, she again forced the mind pressure on him and he again doubled. Eve, receptive as she was, felt twinges of the intense pain he was feeling and winced.

Wndanga turned one of her eye stalks to Eve as Morris writhed on the floor.

"Madame, you may never understand this or anything about my people, but you must allow me to do what I need to do for my own kind. None but you must know of the speech without voice and this one has discovered it for himself. He is already dead in the records and I shall, in my own way, complete the task. You will have no memory."

*   *   *

Eve awoke, sweating and clammy in the still of the complex. There was still a terrible dream rambling through her sensory memories and she felt drawn and pained. Her head ached and she got up slowly, calling to Wndanga.

Her dreams had something vague to do with Morris and Wndanga, but she couldn't recapture them somehow. Nothing would come clearly through the headache she felt. Her call had produced no response and she dressed slowly and moved into the main hall, irritation with the maid filling her.

She heard the hiss of Wndanga's footsteps coming from the elevator. That explained why she hadn't come when she was called. Eve closed her eyes, squinting them in an effort to clear her head. When she opened them, Wndanga stood before her, holding a container in her hands. The physical image brought back a fleeting memory of her dream, but it was gone before she could capture it.

"You are ill this morning, Madame? You do not seem well."

"Thank you. It's not really important. I think I've had a strange dream, though I can't seem to recall it."

There was something subtly different about Wndanga, but Eve couldn't be sure in her present state of mind whether it was her imagination or reality.

"What are you carrying?"

Wndanga smiled with her eyes. That indefinable something was there again, and it made Eve uncomfortable, but she couldn't find the reason why.

"This came on the morning flight from New Rome for you. Master Richard has sent these from his farming project."

In the container were bright spheres of orange.

Eve bent to smell them and it was a rich, bright odor that matched the color in intensity.

Inside the container was a note in Richard's broad scrawl.

"Despite the problems, we have managed to create something of Earth on Genesis and, as the only true Earth citizen, you have been chosen to have the first of the crop. From what the computer analysis tells us, they are a perfect duplication of a fruit grown on Earth, though only you would know. Do these seem like the oranges you remember?"

EPILOGUE

Epilogue

"...you know there is a special reason we have chosen this day over the others. Today is the three thousandth anniversary of the arrival on this planet of Mother Eve, our sainted founder from whose loins has sprung the greatest race ever known.

"Now you, the hopes and dreams of our people, are venturing out into the stars beyond, seeking to carry the finest of our race across the stars to a new life and new hopes.

"With you go our prayers and our blessings. You will know not to make the mistakes we have made. You will, we pray, be able to conquer your new homes with love and planning, preventing things before they overcome you as they did us."

Aleta Eve sat in the vast stadium, among the others in the Pioneer Chosen, and tried desperately to control the fear which gripped her at the words of the Chairman. He seemed somehow to know everything and make it believable. His people had that special gift, but no one seemed to be able to figure out what it was.

The legends said Mother Eve had been a party to their knowledge, but who knew if she'd even existed. Three thousand years ago, the technology was so primitive no records had survived with any surety except for a few personal tape records which were badly fragmented and the silver chain of office their Chairman wore. He claimed it had belonged to Mother Eve, but who knew?

In one day it wouldn't really matter. The Chosen Pioneers would rise to the huge ships and launch themselves into the stars, leaving this ruined place behind in search of a new home.

Not everyone could go, but if they found something promising, then the ship would return for more to come to the new place and they could grow and build again.

"...carry with you our love and belief in the purpose of your voyages. May the spirit of Mother Eve travel with you, guiding and protecting you from all harm."

Aleta Eve swiveled her eye stalks to the vast gray-green sky over the stadium and wondered.

Reading—
For The
Fun Of It

Ask a teacher to define the most important skill for success and inevitably she will reply, "the ability to read."

But millions of young people never acquire that skill for the simple reason that they've never discovered the pleasures books bring.

That's why there's RIF—Reading is Fundamental. The nation's largest reading motivation program, RIF works with community groups to get youngsters into books and reading. RIF makes it possible for young people to have books that interest them, books they can choose and keep. And RIF involves young people in activities that make them want to read—**for the fun of it.**

The more children read, the more they learn, and the more they **want** to learn.

There are children in your community—maybe in your own home—who need RIF. For more information, write to:

RIF
Dept. BK-3
Box 23444
Washington, D.C.
20026

Founded in 1966, RIF is a national, nonprofit organization with local projects run by volunteers in every state of the union.

OUTPASSAGE

JANET MORRIS & CHRIS MORRIS

It could have been the ultimate in blind dates, but before Dennis Cox and Paige Barnett can cement their mutual attraction for each other, they are shanghaied to a backwater planet where a fermenting rebellion threatens IST's mining interests as well as the planet's existence. Drawn together in their mutual desire for truth and justice, Dennis and Paige battle the unknown in an epic adventure complete with New Age space war, politics, and spirituality.

ISBN: 0-517-00832-7 $3.50

AN INTERSTELLAR EXPERIENCE

ON SALE NOW!